Here Comes the Body

Maria DiRico

𝓀

KENSINGTON BOOKS
KENSINGTON PUBLISHING CORP.
www.kensingtonbooks.com

KENSINGTON BOOKS are published by

Kensington Publishing Corp.
119 West 40th Street
New York, NY 10018

First Printing: March 2020
ISBN-13: 978-1-4967-2534-9
ISBN-10: 1-4967-2534-4

ISBN-13: 978-1-4967-2537-0 (eBook)
ISBN-10: 1-4967-2537-9 (eBook)

10 9 8 7 6 5 4 3 2 1

Printed in the United States of America

MURDER AT THE CATERING HALL

She found the anniversary couple posing for photos in the outdoor gazebo where they'd renewed their vows. The photographer finished taking pictures of the couple and Mia was herding everyone back to the Marina Ballroom when her headset buzzed. It was Cody.

"We have a situation, ma'am."

The tone of his voice alarmed her. "What's going on?"

"No one jumped out of the cake."

"Did you look inside to make sure someone was there?"

"Affirmative. I had one of the waiters double-check before we wheeled the cake out. Something must be wrong with the lady inside it."

"I'm on my way."

She hurried out of the Marina Ballroom into the foyer and was about to start up the stairs when an attractive woman in a trench coat burst through the Belle View front doors. "Sorry I'm late," she gasped, out of breath.

Mia stared at her. "Who are you?"

The woman opened her coat, revealing a sequined bikini. "Park Lexington. I'm working the bachelor party."

"You're the stripper? Then who's in the—"

Mia's stomach clenched. She raced up the stairs and burst into the Bay Ballroom.

Cody helped her climb to the top of the cake. She threw open the lid and peered inside. A woman lay crumpled on the bottom. Mia prayed she was unconscious, but the blood pooling under the knife sticking out of Angie's chest told a different story . . .

<u>BOOK YOUR PLACE ON OUR WEBSITE AND MAKE THE READING CONNECTION!</u>

We've created a customized website just for our very special readers, where you can get the inside scoop on everything that's going on with Zebra, Pinnacle and Kensington books.

When you come online, you'll have the exciting opportunity to:

• View covers of upcoming books
• Read sample chapters
• Learn about our future publishing schedule (listed by publication month and author)
• Find out when your favorite authors will be visiting a city near you
• Search for and order backlist books from our online catalog
• Check out author bios and background information
• Send e-mail to your favorite authors
• Meet the Kensington staff online
• Join us in weekly chats with authors, readers and other guests
• Get writing guidelines
• AND MUCH MORE!

**Visit our website at
http://www.kensingtonbooks.com**

ACKNOWLEDGMENTS

I'm grateful to my terrific agent, Doug Grad, who found the perfect home for the Catering Hall Mysteries, as well as the perfect editor, John Scognamilio. *Mille grazie* to both of you! I couldn't write this series without the priceless help of Kristen Sagona, senior event planner at Pickwick Gardens Conference Center in Burbank, California. Kristen, thank you for your infinite patience with all my questions and your boundless enthusiasm for this series. And thanks to your wonderful staff as well.

A shout-out to my fabulous partners in crime (writing) at chicksonthecase.com: Lisa Q. Mathews, Mariella Krause, Kellye Garrett, Leslie Karst, Vickie Fee, Cynthia Kuhn, Becky Clark, and Kathy Valenti. A special thank-you to Leslie for a great beta read of this book, as well as to friend and fellow mystery author Nancy Cole Silverman for her insightful notes. Thanks to Sisters in Crime (especially SinCLA), the Guppies, and my pals at SoCalMWA for the inspiration and camaraderie. Kimberly and George Taweel, thank you for letting your beautiful Sphinxy inspire Mia's kitty, Doorstop. And as always, I'm eternally grateful to my husband, Jer, and daughter, Eliza, for their support and the sacrifices they make for my mystery writing career.

A heartfelt thank-you to my late cousins Ralphy and Pauly for the great events they supervised at Astoria Manor and Grand Bay Marina, and to all my Italian relatives for the endless engagement parties, weddings, birthdays, Sweet Sixteens, and yes, even funeral luncheons. I will never forget the wonderful times I got to share with you. *Ti amo tutti.*

And finally, I never could have written this book had I not been lucky enough to cater-waiter for Martha Stewart when she was just launching her meteoric career. If you have an early edition of her first book, *Entertaining,* you'll find me standing next to her on page 29. Martha, you inspired me then . . . and you inspire me now.

Chapter One

At 6:45 A.M., Mia Carina woke up to Frank Sinatra singing "New York, New York" from the alarm on her phone, a happy reminder that she was in Queens, not Florida, and no longer a "person of interest" in her adulterous husband's disappearance.

Mia had only been back in Astoria a few days. She could have left the Sunshine State months earlier. But she'd chosen to hold her head high, despite the cloud over it, and retain her position as general manager for the Palm Beach branch of Korri Designs, a go-to destination for the uber-wealthy seeking ridiculously expensive leather goods. Luckily, a little notoriety had proved a good thing sales-wise. Between her status as a person of interest in a salacious murder investigation and the whispered rumor that her father was a well-known mafioso—which happened to be true—Mia sold enough overpriced accessories to pay for a first-class ticket out of town when she gave notice.

She yawned, stretched, and snuggled up to Doorstop, the sleek ginger Abyssinian cat sharing her pillow. Then she threw off the covers. Doorstop responded with an annoyed meow. "Sorry, bud," the thirty-one-year-old-most-likely-a-widow said, grinning at the smoky blob of orange fur burying its head under the covers. "Mama's got to get to work."

Mia rolled off the blow-up mattress currently serving as her bed and scrambled to her feet. She noticed the birdcage on top of a still-to-be-emptied box and got a pang of sadness. Formerly the home of her pet parakeet, Pizzazz, the cage stood empty of its resident. As she was leaving her Palm Beach apartment, she had been jostled by a crowd of local reporters eager to make their bones by getting a departing comment from her. The cage door flew open and Pizzazz, confused and scared, flew off. Mia delayed her flight home and plastered the neighborhood with flyers promising a hefty reward for the bird's return, but so far no one had reported a sighting.

She padded through the empty second floor of her grandmother's two-family house into the bathroom for a shower, then pulled clothing out of her suitcase: a black pencil skirt and fitted jacket she paired with a silk turquoise top that brought out the blue in her eyes. Mia had learned from her boss at Korri that her crystalline orbs, wavy dark brunette hair, and pale skin made her a "Winter." Cool, bright colors flattered Mia. She'd also learned never to dress better than the customers, something she kept in mind while putting together an outfit for her first day of work at Belle View Banquet Manor, a party venue surrendered to her father, Ravello Carina, by a gambler who couldn't pay his debts.

Mia filled Doorstop's food and water bowls, grabbed her purse, then headed downstairs, a pair of black high heels in one hand. Elisabetta Carina, Mia's beloved grandmother, stood waiting in the home's small vestibule. Mia kissed Elisabetta on both cheeks as Hero, her grandmother's chubby terrier mix, barked protectively. "*Hero, stai zitto,*" Elisabetta scolded in her native tongue, which she still preferred to English despite decades in America. Hero responded with an annoyed grumble.

"At least he likes Doorstop. He'll get used to me." Mia bent down to pet the mutt, who gave her a haughty glance, then succumbed to the affection.

"I made you breakfast. Fried eggs and sausage," Elisabetta said. The eighty-three-year-old was not one to let a clogged artery or two get in the way of her favorite fatty foods, much to her cardiologist's chagrin.

"*Grazie,* but I don't have time. I want to get to Belle View early. Suss out the place."

"*Va bene,* I'll put it in a container. You can have it tomorrow." While the thought of day-old, reheated fried eggs might be anathema to the average human, Mia took it in stride. For the Carinas, wasting food was sacrilege.

Elisabetta zipped up the jacket of her velour track suit, her daily uniform. Today's outfit was burgundy with navy trim. "I'm going on a power walk with the Army."

Mia couldn't help smiling. The "Army" was a posse of Italian and Greek grandmothers who'd lived on the block for fifty, sixty, even seventy years, and "power walk" was a euphemism for gossipy stroll.

"I'll see if anyone's giving away furniture," Elisabetta continued as she did a few half-hearted stretches to ostensibly warm up. "Maybe someone's decided to turn their second bedroom into a sewing room." "Sewing room" was another neighborhood euphemism. It meant an ancient, dusty sewing machine squashed between boxes of half-broken Christmas ornaments and polyester clothes from the seventies that were "too nice to give away."

"That would be great."

Elisabetta hugged her granddaughter. "I'm so glad you're back. *Ti amo.* I love you, *bella bambina.*"

"I love you too, Nonna. *Ci vediamo stasera.* See you tonight."

Elisabetta left to meet up with her senior crew. Mia opened the Pick-You-Up rideshare app on her phone and tapped in a request, then put on her heels and stepped outside. Easter had just passed, but the tidy front yards of the brick two-family homes were still awash in pastel decorations and strings of lights shaped like rabbits, eggs, lambs, and chicks. No holiday went uncelebrated or undecorated on 46th Place. Competition to outspend and one-up each other turned the sweet little old ladies of the neighborhood into bloodthirsty competitors. Mia's own grandmother was the worst offender. When Mia was little, Elisabetta even roped her into undercover spy work. While Elisabetta delivered batches of her famous pizzelle cookies to unsuspecting neighbors, her granddaughter would plead a need to use the bathroom, but instead sneak a peek at any decorations laid out in a spare room, later reporting as many details as she could remember to her eager *nonna,* who'd then make sure to top them.

A moving van at the far end of the block caught Mia's eye. Gentrification was starting to rear its upscale head in the neighborhood. She was furious when Elisabetta told her that real estate agents were intimidating elderly locals by implying they were losing their wits, then offering flyers for assisted living facilities along with their business cards. The block was an oasis of tradition and neighborliness—holiday decoration battles excepted—and Mia would fight to keep it that way.

A silver, older-model Prius pulled up in front of the Carina home. Mia shook her head but marched down the stairs and got into the back seat of the car. "First the airport, now here? You can't be the only Pick-U-Up car in the area."

The driver, Jamie Boldano, shrugged and smiled. "Let's just call it luck." Jamie, whose father, Donny, was Ravello's boss, had the misfortune of being the sole intellectual in a family of mobster goombahs. Determined to forge his own path, he'd embarked on a teaching career, but was now earning a master's degree in family therapy and ridesharing to pay the bills. Mia and Jamie had grown up together and even briefly dated in high school. Mia wasn't the only Carina who wished she'd married Jamie instead of adulterer Adam Grosso. But Jamie, struggling to find himself, hadn't asked. And now Mia, burned by her marital disaster, had more interest in cold fried eggs than in another relationship.

Jamie followed local streets until he merged onto Grand Central Parkway. As they drove past LaGuardia Airport, Mia flashed on when she and husband Adam made their move to Palm Beach. Theirs was a whirlwind relationship that began during Mia's celebration of her twenty-seventh birthday with some girlfriends at Mingles, an aptly named Astoria hangout. Her friends were impressed when a 750 liter of Dom Perignon champagne was delivered to their table, "courtesy of the gentleman at the bar." Mia was more impressed by the "gentleman at the bar," who had the tawny blond looks of a Northern Italian and introduced himself as "your future husband, Adam Grosso."

At the end of the evening, Adam had helped a drunk Mia into a taxi, then jumped in with her. A hookup turned into a torrid romance, which turned into an impulsive wedding a month later during a weekend getaway in Vegas. Adam revealed to Mia that when they met, he was only supposed to be in town for a week before moving to Florida to begin work as a manager at Tutta Pasta, a popular Palm Beach restaurant. He'd extended his stay for a few weeks just to be with her. She rewarded him with her hand in marriage and relocation to the Sunshine State, much to her brokenhearted family's chagrin.

Basta, Mia said to herself. *Enough focusing on four years of my life I'll never get back. Like the saying goes, that was then, this is now. And now I'm in a car with Jamie. Smart, kind and cute Ja—No! Stop! Basta!* She pulled out her tablet and tried to focus.

"So," Jamie said, "looking forward to today?"

"Yes, in a big way." Mia hesitated. "But I'm nervous. I've never done anything like this. Neither has my dad. It has to work out. I don't want him going back to his old job. No offense to your dad or anything."

"No worries, I get it. If it makes you feel better, I hear Ravello's doing a great job running the place. Nothing seems to throw him, which is important when you're dealing with the biggest events in people's lives. Weddings, anniversaries, birthdays— they're all emotionally high-octane events that can cause as much stress as pleasure."

"I think that's your psych degree talking."

Jamie blushed. The fact that Mia found this trait of

his attractive made her blush as well. "We're here," Jamie said as he drove through a parking lot and pulled up in front of a nondescript building from the mid-1960s.

Mia released a breath, and the unexpected sexual tension she felt dissipated. She looked out the window at her new work home. Belle View Banquet Manor was perched on a small outcropping of land squeezed between Flushing Bay and the parking lot that served its marina. Belle View's glass-paned architecture was designed to take advantage of the views—some scenic, some not so much. The catering venue was also adjacent to the landing pattern for LaGuardia.

"Nice location," Jamie said. "You know, it has the same name as the mental ward in Manhattan."

"Yeah, we're not gonna lead with that on the website." Mia shoved her tablet back in her purse. "Thanks, Jamie."

"See you later."

"You might. Or you might not."

"Odds favor the former." Jamie shot her a slightly devilish grin and drove off. The son of Donny Boldano might claim independence from his mobbed-up family, but that didn't mean he wouldn't occasionally take a page from their dicey book.

Mia inhaled and exhaled a few times to quell her nerves. *I can do this,* she told herself. Still feeling insecure, she said it out loud, yelling at the parked cars surrounding her, "I can do this!"

"Go for it!" someone yelled back. Mia hadn't noticed a deliveryman sitting in the driver's seat of a UPS van, checking his phone. Embarrassed, she returned the thumbs-up he flashed her. Then she adjusted her skirt, pulled open one of Belle View's heavy glass doors, and entered the grand foyer.

A massive crystal chandelier dangled over the space, which with its white walls and tiled floor, was otherwise unremarkable, even bordering on dingy. The baseboards were scuffed; a faded triptych of a wedding from decades ago decorated one wall; a gilded plaster statue of Cupid did a valiant job of hiding a water stain. Mia felt deflated. She'd pictured a more grandiose venue, like the legendary Leonard's of Great Neck, with its ornate ballrooms and twenty-foot chandelier presiding over a two-story grand foyer. Then Mia looked past Belle View's far less impressive foyer into a large banquet room. A wall of windows framed the view of Flushing Bay, where boats bobbed serenely at the World's Fair Marina's docks. Her spirits rose again. Despite the hints of shabbiness, Belle View enjoyed a lovely location, much nicer than the flashier party palaces in the area. *I can work with this,* she thought.

Mia was about to go look for her father when she was startled by a large rumble. Two decorative urns filled with ferns began to vibrate. Her heart raced. "What the—"

"Don't worry, sweetheart, that's just a 737 coming in for a landing."

Mia turned and saw Ravello Carina standing at the entry to a hallway. Ravello threw open his arms. "*Bambina.*"

"Dad."

She ran to her father and disappeared into the large man's bear hug. Ravello Carina was built like an ancient growth oak tree, majestically tall and broad of trunk. Mia knew his imposing presence was the main reason Donny Boldano anointed him head of the Boldano family's illegal gambling enterprise; it deterred participants from welching on their debts. Still, Ravello wasn't a fan of confrontation. He'd eagerly segued from intimidation to the challenge of running Belle View as a legit business, much to his daughter's relief.

Ravello released Mia. "You look good. You feel good?" He said this with a Queens accent thick as a slice of hand-cut hard salami.

Mia nodded. "I like this place, Dad. It has a lot of potential."

"I think so, too. The room you were looking at is the Marina Ballroom. The Bay Ballroom is upstairs. Place needs work but it's got good bones. You almost forget LaGuardia's there." Ravello pointed west, where the 737 that had landed could be seen lumbering down the runway toward the terminal. "I'll give you the royal tour in a little. First, coffee."

Mia followed her father up a glass-paneled circular staircase with a steel railing. They reached the landing and Ravello threw open the doors of the Bay Ballroom, revealing a banquet table laden with breakfast treats. A banner above it read WELCOME, MIA.

"Surprise!"

The greeting was bellowed by a small group of unfamiliar faces except for one. Ravello had hired Cammie Dianopolis, a neighbor who lived around the corner from Elisabetta, to help him coordinate events, with the proviso—put in place by Cammie—that her duties would lessen once his daughter came on board. Cammie ran up to Mia and gave her a hug that rivaled Ravello's in strength. "You're here. I'm so happy. Now I can coast."

"Thanks so much for helping out my dad. I'm excited about working with you."

"But you working harder, right?"

"Right." Mia extricated herself from the woman's grip and subtly massaged a bruised rib while Cammie checked out her reflection in a nearby mirror, patting a few stray hairs from her fluffy frosted 'do back in place. She'd found her style in 1988 and stuck with it, to the point of ordering her favorite lavender eye shadow from a website that specialized in locating discontinued makeup.

Ravello put his arm around Mia's shoulder. "Let me introduce you to the rest of the staff."

He was about to do exactly that when the door to the room flung open. A slim woman with stringy black hair appeared, clad in a mini dress that looked like it was made from bright red ace bandages. She was pretty but in a hard way. She pointed a finger attached to a tattoo-sleeved arm at Ravello. "You," she said, her tone angry and accusing.

"Me what?" Ravello seemed flummoxed by the intruder.

"You know what." The woman pulled a cell phone out of her tiny purse and held it up to him.

Mia moved closer to her father. "Dad, what's going on?" Ravello responded with a confused shrug.

The woman waved the phone in the air. "Our date. Through Meet Your Match dot com. What'd you think, it was a freebie? Angie here doesn't do freebies." She pointed a long, red-lacquered nail at herself. "You owe me."

Mia was incredulous. She knew her father had barely dated since his marriage to her mother had been annulled five years earlier. But she couldn't imagine him resorting to a paid escort.

"Sweetie, I don't know what she's talking about," Ravello said. He looked embarrassed. "I swear on a bible, I've never seen her before in my life."

"Liar." The woman spit out the word. She took a step toward Ravello, who remained frozen in place. "Either give me my fee or I'll make big trouble. I know who you are."

"Oh please," Mia scoffed. "Everyone knows who he is. If that's your biggest threat, you need better material."

The woman, still holding the phone, waved her arms in the air dramatically. "I want my—"

A giantess wearing a chef toque stepped out of the group. "Okay, we've had enough of the crazy, sister."

"That's Guadalupe Cruz, our chef," Cammie, who'd been watching the odd scene with fascination, whispered to Mia. "She was an army cook in Iraq."

Guadalupe approached the interloper, then took all of a second to grab the woman and hold her under one arm like a football. She strode out of the room, her charge kicking and screaming a stream of profanities. "As you were," the chef called to the others as she disappeared down the stairs.

There was a moment of stunned silence. Then Cammie pointed to the buffet. "Let's eat before the bagels get stale."

A murmur of agreement was followed by a rush to grab a plate. Ravello started to follow, but Mia pulled him back. "Hold up, Dad. What *was* that?"

The mobster gave a helpless shrug. "Mia, believe me, I have no idea. There are nut jobs all over this city. I guess one found her way to Belle View.

This Belle View, not the one in Manhattan. Where she obviously belongs. Because she needs mental help." There was a loud buzzing overhead. "Sounds like a turboprop. Must be the 9:10 from Syracuse on its final approach."

Ravello detached himself from Mia and joined the others at the buffet. She frowned as she watched him pour a cup of coffee and chat with the others. She knew her father well. He was telling the truth when he said he didn't know the woman. But he was also hiding something.

And it was never good when a Carina hid something.

Chapter Two

Mia tried to corner her father and press him for more information about the mysterious Angie, but Ravello avoided his daughter, segueing into a conversation with a different employee every time she approached him. She finally gave up and concentrated on meeting her new co-workers, who were a rainbow coalition of a few full-time but mostly part-time cooks, waiters, and support staff. They raved about Ravello with genuine fondness, which made her happy. Even Evans, the odd, monosyllabic sous chef, put two words together to form a compliment: "He's cool."

After half an hour of snacking and making small talk, Cammie pulled Mia aside. "Let's go to your office and go over the day. I want to hand over a couple of clients to you and leave early. I booked a mani-pedi at Spa Castle in College Point."

Mia followed Cammie down the stairs into a warren of small offices tucked into the less scenic side of the hall facing the west side of the parking lot. They stopped in front of a door sporting a nameplate that read MIA CARINA: ASSISTANT GENERAL MANAGER. Mia fought back the urge to burst into happy tears.

"I have a title," she said, her tone colored with emotion. "I have an office. I never had one before."

"Trust me, the thrill wears off," Cammie said. "Especially after your first pain-in-the-tushy client."

Cammie opened the door and the women entered the office. With its ancient metal desk, battered file cabinet, and large corkboard missing chunks of cork, it had all the charm of a supply closet, which Mia assumed it once was. But it was hers, and she loved it for that. The tiny room was where she would start her new career, her new life, and put the misery of Florida behind her.

A bright spot was the large flower arrangement taking up half the desk and scenting the room with lilies. Mia pulled out the card and smiled as she read it. "Aw, it's from my dad."

"He probably put it together himself."

"Really? He does that now?" Mia examined the bouquet, trying to imagine her father's meaty fingers arranging the delicate baby's breath, tiger lilies, and iris. "He hasn't mentioned it."

"You know that Bermuda cruise he went on? He took some class on napkin folding and floral display. The teacher lives in Manhattan and he still goes to her for classes. Private classes, if you know what I mean." Cammie followed this surprising statement with a wink.

"Dad's got a girlfriend?" Mia digested this second unexpected development.

"I don't know if they're up to anything, but when he talks about her, he gets all red and shy and can't look you in the eye."

Maggie thought of the intruder Guadalupe had carried out of the upstairs ballroom. "So that woman

Angie who said he owed her for a date. She really was a scam artist."

"Totally. Now, fire up the computer to make sure it's working."

"Okay." Mia sat on the office chair and immediately toppled over. Cammie glanced down as Mia picked herself up off the floor. "Oh, that's missing a wheel. We'll roll in my chair."

"Don't you need it?"

"I thought I'd take an early lunch."

"We just had breakfast."

Cammie wagged a finger at Mia. "What's my word of the day?"

"Coasting," the women said together.

"Anyhoo," Cammie said, "your clients should be here in ten. His bachelor party's Saturday, they're getting married three weeks from Saturday. They wanna lock stuff down. Their file is labeled '*archiko gamo*.'"

"What does that mean?"

"Starter marriage. Let's get you that chair."

Cammie and Mia wheeled out the broken office chair and wheeled in Cammie's. "You're all set," Cammie said. She headed out the door. "Oh, and a little tip," she threw over her shoulder as she left. "Always make sure the mother of the groom is happy or you'll regret it."

"Wait, what?"

"Bye-yee." With that, Cammie was gone for her day of coasting.

Mia hurried to make her office somewhat presentable before her first clients. She opened a desk drawer to look for a pen and saw a small rectangular box. On top was a sticky note with a heart and her father's signature. She opened the box—it was filled with business cards. Her very first. *I have the best dad in the world,* she thought fondly, *despite his occasional jail stint.* She placed the box on the desk, then turned on her computer, which slowly wheezed to life.

She barely had time to glance at the file for the John Grazio and Alice Paluski nuptials when a young couple appeared in her doorway. The girl cast a wary glance around the office. "Are you our new event planner?"

"Yes, hi, I'm Mia Carina. I'll be taking over for Cammie. I'm so happy to be working with you. Come on in."

The couple introduced themselves, stepped into Mia's office, and stood there. She realized there was no place for them to sit. "Be right back." She raced into Cammie's office, grabbed two metal chairs, and dragged them into her office. "Sorry about that."

"No worries, happy to wait for you." John, the groom-to-be, said this with a suggestive smirk. Alice, his bride-to-be, rolled her eyes. They were in their mid-twenties, if that. He had slicked-back brown hair and the build of a weightlifter. She wore the uniform of the animal technician she was, scrubs covered with cartoons of cheerful puppies and kittens. The animals' happy expressions contrasted with the sour one on Alice's face.

"Okay, so let's start with the wedding," Mia said, adopting a tone that she hoped combined a business-like attitude with a touch of warmth and enthusiasm. She scanned the open file on her computer. "I see all the vendors are confirmed. All we need is the final decision on the size and flavors of your wedding cake."

"Just make it bigger and better than my sister's," Alice said.

"Oh," Mia said, thrown. "I'll have to look that up. Did she get married here?"

"Yes." Alice's sour expression grew more sour, if such a thing was possible.

"Lemme bring you up to speed." John leaned in toward Mia, who instinctively leaned back. "Alice and Annamaria are twins. And they hate each other."

"She's always holding it over my head that she's younger than me but got married first," Alice grumped.

"You're twins," Mia said. "How much younger can she be?"

"A whole friggin' minute. Which she never lets me forget. She always does better than me. She even got the prettier name. Who's named Alice anymore? All I want is for my wedding to be better than hers. A bigger cake, a bigger band, a bigger horse-drawn carriage. I want it bigger and better in every. Single. Way."

Mia's skin began to tingle. It was the tingle she got when a customer with a black platinum card walked into Korri Designs. The tingle of a potential up-sell. She made a show of scanning the couple's file. "I'll look up your sister's wedding and confirm that every one of your choices is 'bigger and better.' But I can tell you right now that you won't be able to get a bigger horse-drawn carriage than the one you ordered. What do you think about arriving by boat?"

"By boat?" A gleam appeared in Alice's eyes.

"Think about it." Mia gave her voice a hypnotic edge as she painted a picture for the future bride she had hooked on a line. "Roaring up to Belle View on a powerboat. One of those beautiful vintage wooden models. Your veil floating behind you in the breeze as every guest stares at you in wonder, awed and inspired by your majestic arrival."

A sly smile replaced the sour look on Alice's face. "I love that. Go for it."

"Great." Mia shelved the seduction and returned to business. "I'll price out some options and get back to you with them. Now, John, do you want to talk about your bachelor party?" She framed the question in a way that gave Alice the option of leaving, which she didn't take. Mia got the impression she kept her fiancé on a short leash—with a choke collar.

"I can't believe it's only two days away," the groom-to-be enthused. "Did you get the oysters? I want all sexy food like oysters."

"They've been ordered." Mia checked the file. "We haven't received your party favors yet."

"Condoms with the party date on them," John said with pride. "It was my idea." This engendered another eye roll from Alice. His brow creased with worry. "They're gonna get here on time, right?"

"They'll be here. If worse comes to worst, I'll make the company overnight them and pay for shipping."

"That's a girl. And the cake, that's all set? The one the stripper jumps out of?"

Mia perused the computer screen. "All set. There's a note here to confirm the . . . entertainment."

"As long as someone hot jumps out. I don't care who it is. Hey, if she can't make it, feel free to jump out yourself."

John laughed, then let out a yelp of pain as Alice elbowed him and said, "That's sexual harassment, idiot."

"No it ain't. It's flirting. What, is that against the

law now? What kind of world do we live in where a guy can't say something nice to a girl?"

It was John's turn to look sour. Alice once again rolled her eyes. She was doing this so much Mia feared she'd detach her retina. "Everything is in great shape," Mia said, trying to defuse the tension and bring the awkward appointment to an end. "If you have any questions or concerns, call me anytime day or night." She extricated two of her new business cards, then stood up and handed the "happy" couple each a card. "Get ready for the most exciting night of your lives."

John pumped a fist in the air. "Saturday night, baby."

This earned him another elbow in the ribs from Alice. "She's talking about the wedding, not your stupid bachelor party."

"I'm sure both events will be unforgettable," Mia said in as neutral a tone as she could muster up.

The betrothed couple departed, arguing their way out the door. Spent, Mia closed her eyes and fell into her office chair, which rolled backward a few feet. *Jamie's right,* she thought. *The biggest events in people's lives can be the most stressful—on* me. She opened her eyes and inhaled the rejuvenating scent of Ravello's flowers. This led to an idea. Could her father have dipped a toe in the dating waters prior to falling for his floral arrangement teacher?

She left her office and went in search of Ravello's, which she found at the end of the hallway. It was lunchtime, which could only mean one thing— Ravello was having the pasta of the day at Roberto's Trattoria. It was the one aspect of the mobster's life where he was obsessive-compulsive. As predicted, his office was empty. Mia stepped behind his desk and opened the Internet browser connection on his computer. Knowing her somewhat-Luddite of a father, she assumed he never cleared his search history, which proved to be true. She scrolled down until she finally saw it: a search for Meet Your Match, which Ravello's poor typing skills had misspelled as Meeet Your Match. "Oh boy," she muttered.

Mia closed the browser and returned to her office. She needed to talk to someone about the situation, and she knew exactly who: her older brother, Positano "Posi" Carina. Mia sat down at her desk and tapped out an address on her keyboard. A website for the Triborough Correctional Facility appeared on her monitor. She dialed the number on the screen from the landline on her desk, then pressed through a series of numbers until she finally reached a human being. "Yes, hi. I was wondering what your visiting hours are today. I need to talk to an inmate."

Chapter Three

Mia sat across from her brother at a beat-up table in the correctional facility visiting room. A guard leaned against a wall, checking his cell phone. Triborough was a minimum-security facility whose mission was to transition offenders to life outside the big house. Mia had been greeted at the entry like a long-lost friend. It wasn't her family's first stint in the place.

Posi's prison grays did nothing to detract from his model-handsome looks. But he was glum today. "You got nothing? Not one bite?"

"Sorry." Mia had done her brother a favor and shared his mug shot on social media with the hashtag, #anotherhotconvict. Posi had hoped to become a viral sensation, like a convict before him who'd parlayed his good looks into a post-prison modeling career and billionaire heiress girlfriend. So far, that hadn't happened for Posi.

"I don't get it," he said. "I figured I could glom on to all the people who were following you because of the Adam disappearing thing, and you being a suspect. I guess your fifteen minutes is up."

Mia fought to maintain patience with her self-involved sibling. "My 'fifteen minutes' was fifteen minutes I never wanted and I'm glad it's over. Sorry it ended before you could 'glom on' to it. Can we talk about Dad?"

"Yeah, sure. What's going on?" Mia filled Posi in on what had happened at Belle View. "Whoa. This is bad."

"I know."

"Dad's making flower arrangements? Is he wearing lipstick and dresses, too? If the Family finds out, he's a dead man."

Mia gave an exasperated sigh. "Can we focus on what's important here? The girl who wanted money from Dad? Guadalupe got rid of her, but I have a really strong feeling she'll be back. And Dad did visit that Meet Your Match website."

"Hmmm . . ." Posi stared out a barred window, his gaze thoughtful.

"Stop looking at your reflection in the window."

"Sorry, they don't have mirrors in here."

"I feel bad for Dad," Mia said. "He's obviously ready to date again. But he was so nervous going to that website, he didn't even spell it right."

This got Posi's attention. "Wait, what? How did he spell it?"

"With an extra *e. M-e-e-e-t.*"

Posi ran a hand through his dark, wavy hair. "Oh, man. I think I know what happened. There are these hackers in Eastern Europe and what they do is create websites that are only one letter off from legit sites, but take you to a whole other, darker place. Meet Your Match is a real popular dating site. So, what do these guys do? Create a site that people accidentally get to when they make an obvious typing error. They don't even know they're on the wrong site sometimes, like with this. Guys like Dad think they're making dates with interested ladies. Instead, they're booking working girls. Usually the scammers throw in a little identity or credit card theft. It's kind of genius. Wish I was better with computers."

Mia frowned at her brother. "I'm glad you're not. We've got enough trouble with you stealing all those sports cars. Will you stop already?"

"Hey, with the stupid tariffs, people in China can't afford those cars. I'm like a Robin Hood. I take from the rich and give to the not-as-rich. Well, not so much give as sell. But for a very fair price."

Mia shook her head. Still, she couldn't help smiling at her brother's insouciant attitude. "Whatever. We miss you."

"'We' being you and Dad," Posi said, his tone acerbic. "Heard from Mom lately?"

"Hah," Mia said, matching her brother's attitude. "'Heard from Mom?' Funny stuff."

The siblings' mother, Gia formerly-Carina-now-Gabanetti, had moved to Rome with her second husband, Angelo Gabanetti, who'd been deported as soon as he completed a two-year jail sentence for selling forged passports and driver's licenses. Vibrant and beautiful, Gia was also what psychology student Jamie Boldano called a "clinical narcissist." Whether it was conscious or unconscious, Gia managed to switch the focus of any situation back to herself. She dreamed of being an actress, despite the fact the only dramas she ever appeared in were the ones she created at family events. Between their father's demanding schedule working for Donny Boldano and their mother's self-involvement, Mia and Posi had learned to rely on each other at an early age, hence their close relationship.

"Any word on when you'll be out?" Mia asked her brother.

"Mickey's working on it," Posi said, referencing Mickey Bauer, the defense attorney the Carinas kept on a retainer. "In the meantime, share my mug shot again, and keep sharing until it goes viral. Love ya, sis."

Rather than risk Jamie Boldano showing up for the third time in less than twenty-four hours, Mia hailed a cab instead of summoning a rideshare. The conversation with Posi had helped her parse out the mixed message her father was sending. She thought Ravello told the truth when he said he didn't know the belligerent woman who showed up at Belle View. But he was also doing his best to cover up the fact he'd gone to an illegal website. Ravello, who'd done time at Triborough himself, had met his parole requirements, so he wasn't in danger of violating them. Mia assumed he was simply too embarrassed to admit the truth to his daughter.

The cab dropped her at home, and she made her way up the stoop stairs. She was greeted at the front door by Elisabetta. It was only seven P.M. but her grandmother had already changed from the track suit into pajamas. Her hair, still dyed brown despite her status as an octogenarian, was in pink curlers. "I found you furniture," she said.

"That's wonderful, Nonna, thank you. Where? How much?"

Elisabetta pointed down the street to where the moving van had been earlier. "It's free. Rose Caniglia is moving to assisted living. Her kids and grandkids don't want her stuff and she'd rather see it go to a good home than sell it to some dealer."

Mia's excitement dimmed a bit. She'd been in Rose's home many times and understood her family's reluctance to inherit the matriarch's gilded, ornately carved, basically hideous furniture. Still, the price was right, as in free.

"I told her you'd be by as soon as you got home," Elisabetta said. "The movers finish up tomorrow. Go. She's waiting. I'll have dinner for you when you're done. Eggplant parmigiana."

Mia headed down the block to Rose's. She rang the doorbell, which sang out a tarantella tune. There was a pause as the senior checked her out through the peephole, then the sound of multiple locks being unlocked. A few minutes later, the door opened. Senior citizen Rose Caniglia, skin weathered and height shrunken below its original 4'11", greeted Mia with a hug and a cheek pinch that hurt. "Look at you, such a beauty." Rose tugged the bouffant wig that had been knocked askew by her hearty embrace back in place. "Come in, come in. You want espresso?"

"Thanks, but I'm good. Nonna's holding dinner for me."

"She's some cook, that one. Okay, let me show you what I'm giving away."

Rose and Mia navigated a maze of boxes as the older woman pointed out Mia's future furnishings. The living room set was every bit as ugly as Mia remembered it and included a sofa, coffee table, end tables, plus two chairs upholstered in the same bright crushed red velvet as the sofa. All seating surfaces were encased in plastic, much like at Nonna's home, which brought back memories of painfully peeling damp thighs off the couch during a hot summer day. The plastic would go, but Mia didn't dare tell Rose that in case it killed the deal. Plastic-covered cushions were a sacred part of the décor in every home on 46th Place.

They moved on to the dining room and then the bedroom. All the furniture was a match to the living room pieces. Rose's decorating style was nothing if not consistent. Mia imagined there was quite a celebration at the gaudy furnishings store where Rose shopped when she cleaned out their inventory.

"You can have it all," the senior said, gesturing to the room with an expansive sweep of her hands. "I don't need it where I'm going. The place is already furnished."

"Thank you so much, Rose. You have to let me pay you something for this."

Rose gave her head a vehement shake. "Absolutely not. I'm just happy to find everything a good home. And with someone from your generation who appreciates quality."

Mia managed a weak smile. "Right. So, Nonna said you're moving to assisted living."

"Yeah, a place on the Island. Here."

Rose handed Mia a glossy brochure with a flyer attached to it. Mia was less interested in the brochure, which extolled the virtues of the Ocean Shores Adult Living Community, than the flyer, which trumpeted the sales record of Astoria's "Number One Real Estate Agent," a woman named Felicity Stewart Forbes. In case anyone missed the ad copy, a photo showed Felicity, a fortysomething blonde with a Botoxed upper lip and forehead, striking a cutesy pose with her index finger in the air to indicate she was numero uno. So this was the woman turning 46th Place from geriatric to gentrified. Mia took an instant dislike to her.

She handed the brochure back to Rose, who turned a page. "It's in Syosset, so it's not really near a shore. But it's got what they call amenities, if you're around long enough to use them. I didn't want to go at first. But Felicity here made a very good point when she said I wasn't gonna get sharper as time went on."

Mia fumed at the real estate agent's manipulations. "That's ridiculous. You're sharp as a tack, always have been, and I'm sure you'll stay that way."

Rose shrugged. "Yeah, but I figured, why take a chance? Might as well make the move now while I still know where I'm going."

"I guess. So, who bought your house? Who are our new neighbors?"

"A very nice couple."

The cagey expression on Rose's face belied her bland description. This roused Mia's curiosity, but not enough to quell her hunger pangs. She could practically smell Elisabetta's eggplant parmigiana from Rose's house. "I better get going. If you give me the number of your movers, I'll arrange for them to deliver everything. I can't thank you enough for this, Rose."

"Please, I'm happy to help. Especially after what you've been through with that husband of yours, that Grosso character. They still haven't found his body, have they?"

"No." Mia winced, recalling the awful weeks she'd

endured after Adam's disappearance. When her cheating spouse never showed up to work at one of the restaurants he managed, he was declared a missing person. Palm Beach PD considered Mia a suspect in his disappearance until the wreck of Adam's cigarette boat, along with the body of his cocktail waitress mistress, were found off the shore of Paradise Island. Palm Beach PD declared Adam Grosso presumed dead due to a boating disaster, releasing Mia from suspicion but leaving her emotionally scarred.

"If you ask me," Rose said, "that son-of-a-you-know-what got the death he deserved."

Mia didn't disagree.

The next couple of days were busy. Ravello's accuser never reappeared and Mia assumed her father was right—the woman was a local nut job. Rose's movers dropped off furniture and everything else the senior wouldn't need in her new home, which was pretty much everything from her old home. Mia thanked her benefactor with a beautiful houseplant for her assisted living digs and a two-pound box of Perugina chocolates, both of which were appreciated. "The chocolate may kill me, but I'll die happy," Rose said. Cammie Dianopolis came over to help Mia organize her new wares and make sense of the décor, which Cammie described as "Neapolitan Bordello Chic" after laughing so hard, coffee came out her nose.

At work, Mia found the perfect powerboat to deliver Alice to her reception, a stunning 1956 Cris-Craft Capri, and negotiated a great price for it. She and her father also worked out a system for engaging potential new customers. Ravello did a little glad-handing and gave a tour of Belle View's facilities, then delivered them to Mia, who pitched a variety of packages that would make their wedding-anniversary-Sweet Sixteen-funeral luncheon an event they and their guests would never forget. If she heard the stale joke, "You're making me an offer I can't refuse" from one customer, she must have heard it from ten. She gritted her teeth and faked laughter. She'd live with a little mob notoriety if that's what it took to close a deal.

The night of Mia's first official event, John Grazio's bachelor party, arrived. She opened the Pick-U-Up app on her cell phone and swiped through drivers. No Jamie. Now she wondered if he was avoiding her, and tamped down a sudden rush of anxiety. He's probably busy with classes, she thought, then repeated to herself, *I'm not ready for a relationship, I'm not ready for a relationship.* Having surrendered common sense and allowed herself to be swayed by Adam Grosso's charm and sex appeal, Mia no longer trusted her instincts when it came to men. She chose a portly school bus driver moonlighting on the rideshare app as her driver.

As soon as Mia got to Belle View, she called a meeting in the Bay Ballroom with the bachelor party staff of waiters, bartenders, and general help. Tables were set to accommodate fifty guests. Ravello had contributed his newly acquired napkin folding skills to the event, applying what he called "the Pyramid fold" to each one. Given that his skills were still rudimentary, to Mia's eye the napkins less resembled pyramids than a certain part of the female anatomy. But she kept this observation to herself.

Aside from the suggestive napkins, the only decorations on the tables were centerpieces featuring laminated *Playboy* centerfolds, provided by the groom-to-be himself. Mia assumed they were from John's private collection. "Okay, gang," she told the assembled troops who'd be working the party. "Tonight's event could be tricky. A bunch of horny guys who'll want to get drunk as fast as possible."

"Those napkins won't cool them down." This came from Giorgio, a new hire. He was a wiry guy in his twenties who came highly recommended by another Queens catering venue. But he packed so much attitude into his small frame that Mia wondered if his previous employer had simply grabbed an opportunity to unload him. Giorgio pointed to a napkin. "They look exactly like a woman's va—"

"Back to the drinks," Mia said quickly. "Antony and Zeke, don't make them strong, even if people complain." She pointed to a brawny waiter with a buzz cut. "I'm promoting Cody to floor supervisor for the night. He'll have a headset so he can reach me right away if there are any problems."

"I'm on it, ma'am." Cody, a former Marine in his early thirties, saluted her. Mia gave her father props for hiring through a local returning veterans program. Guadalupe and Cody were proving the program to be a great source of dedicated, trustworthy employees.

"These guys better be good tippers," Giorgio muttered.

"Concentrate on doing your job," Mia said, trying to keep the annoyance she felt out of her voice.

The staff dispersed to their stations while DJ DJ—

the conveniently named Derrick Johnson—set up his equipment. A few of the party crew lingered behind to watch DJ. "He's a total legend," whispered Missy, a nineteen-year-old who waitressed and worked in the kitchen doing prep and plating meals for Guadalupe. "He DJs at all the cool clubs in Manhattan. He even changed his name so his initials spell DJ. And he's hot."

Mia checked out the DJ and had to admit Missy was right. He had the chiseled bone structure of a romance novel cover hero, and the body to match. His shaggy black hair and bedroom eyes completed the picture. She guessed he was around her age and, for a split second, wondered if he had a girlfriend. A nauseous feeling in her gut instantly replaced this thought as Mia recalled the trauma of discovering her husband's infidelity. Adam, running late to work, had left his cell phone behind on the kitchen counter. She was about to drive it over to him when the naked image of Laurel, a cocktail waitress who worked at Tutta Pasta, popped up on the screen. Mia could still visualize every sickening second of picking up the phone and seeing the come-hither image of the woman's surgically enhanced body, down to the bright fuchsia lipstick on her filler-plumped lips. *Not a flattering color, it clashed with her cheapo orange-hair dye job, and the fact that this image is still emblazoned on my brain means I am so not ready for a relationship.*

"It's awesome Cammie was able to book him," Missy said.

"I guess that means we're pretty awesome, too." Mia cringed at how lame her response sounded. Missy gave a polite smile and retreated to the kitchen.

"Check, check," DJ said into a microphone. He

followed this with a blast of sound that made Mia's
ears ring. She checked her watch, a delicate gold one
her parents had given her for high school gradua-
tion. It was eight P.M. Bachelor party go time.

Cody proved to be expert at keeping John's guests
under control, even preventing a few from losing
their liquor in the ballroom by escorting them into
the bathroom. This freed up Mia to manage the
other event happening at Belle View that evening, a
reception following a couple's renewing their vows
on their fiftieth anniversary. She fumed when she saw
a familiar face deposit a large present on the gift
table—Felicity Stewart Forbes. *She probably figures there
are a lot of homeowners with a clock on them at a fiftieth
anniversary party,* was Mia's dark thought. She ap-
praised the agent's wardrobe of von Furstenberg
wrap dress, Louboutin heels, and Dior purse, and
pegged them all as fakes. She'd learned to separate
the real from the fraudulent at Korri Designs—as well
as in the basement of her family home, where her
brother once ran a thriving business selling designer
knockoffs imported from China.

Mia took a break from the anniversary celebration
to watch the Koller brothers arrive in a limo from
Manhattan for the bachelor party. John Grazio worked
in the security department of Koller Properties, one
of the city's most well-known real estate development
companies. Bradley and Kevin Koller, WASP-y looking and in their mid-thirties, had inherited the company after their father died of a heart attack on one
of his many golf courses. Mia considered personally
welcoming the famous duo to Belle View, but she was
put off by the air of arrogance emanating from the
brothers. Their host, John, practically tumbled down

the staircase in his rush to greet and fawn over them. "Guys, thank you for coming. I can't tell you what it means to me. I'm honored. Deeply, deeply honored."

"Glad to be here," Bradley said, his tone patronizing. Kevin merely gave a slight nod. Mia wondered why the brothers even bothered to grace the outer borough and John's party with their presence.

"The action's upstairs," John said. "It's a good time. Except the drinks could be stronger, but we're working on that." He directed the last comment at Mia. She responded to his angry glare with a look of innocence. "You got the best seats in the house. You're at the Playmate of the Year table. You gotta see the napkins. They're a work of dirty art."

John gestured for the brothers to follow him up the stairs, and Kevin started after him. "Uh, *hello*," Bradley snarked. Kevin stopped where he was and let his older brother precede him up the stairs. A slideshow of expressions crossed the younger brother's face: fury, resentment, embarrassment, and finally, a look of vulnerability. To Mia's surprise, she found herself feeling sorry for Kevin Koller.

She shook off the moment and returned to the vow renewal reception, passing Felicity Stewart Forbes, who was handing out business cards to a nonplussed knot of senior citizen guests. "Like the saying goes, the future is now," she fluted. "Especially when you reach a certain age, if you know what I mean."

"We know what you mean. We're old." A man holding tight to the walker in front of him responded with asperity to Forbes, earning a chuckle from Mia.

She found the anniversary couple posing for photos in the outdoor gazebo where they'd renewed their vows. Flushing Bay lay in the distance, as did

LaGuardia Airport's air traffic control tower. Mia was helping their photographer find a camera angle that blocked out the tower when she heard a loud whoop coming from the Bay Ballroom upstairs. *They must have wheeled in the pop-out cake,* she thought. The photographer finished taking pictures of the anniversary couple and Mia was herding everyone back to the Marina Ballroom when her headset buzzed. It was Cody.

"We have a situation, ma'am."

The tone of his voice alarmed her. "What's going on? And feel free to call me Mia."

"No one jumped out of the cake."

"Did you look inside to make sure someone was in there?"

"Affirmative. I had one of the waiters double-check before we wheeled the cake out. Something must be wrong with the lady inside it."

"I'm on my way."

She hurried out of the Marina Ballroom into the foyer and was about to start up the stairs when an attractive woman in a trench coat burst through the Belle View front doors. "Sorry I'm late," she gasped, out of breath. "They switched the N and R trains and I wound up in Forest Hills."

Mia stared at her. "Who are you?"

The woman opened her coat, revealing a sequined bikini. "Park Lexington. I'm working the bachelor party."

"You're the stripper? Then who's in the—"

Mia's stomach clenched. She raced up the stairs and burst into the Bay Ballroom. John's guests whooped and cat-called. "Yeah, baby, finally!" one yelled.

"I'm not the stripper!" Mia yelled back.

Cody helped her climb to the top of the cake. She threw open the lid and peered inside. A woman lay crumpled on the bottom. It was Angie, the call girl who'd paid Ravello Carina a visit only days before. Mia prayed she was unconscious, but the blood pooling under the knife sticking out of the woman's chest told a different story.

She'd been murdered.

Chapter Four

For a moment, Mia stood frozen. Then she regrouped. "Push this thing into the back hallway, then call the police and report a suspicious death," she whispered to Cody. His eyes widened but he gave a slight nod. He reflexively lifted a hand to salute the order but caught himself halfway.

As Cody wheeled off the pop-out cake, Mia faced the disgruntled party guests. She got right to it. "I have bad news; no one's jumping out of a cake." The chorus of boos was almost deafening. "But," she yelled, waving her hands in the air to get their attention again, "I also have good news. We're making the drinks way stronger." This was met with cheers and a rush to the room's two bars.

As Mia headed for the door, John grabbed her arm. "Hey, what the hell is going on? Where's my entertainment? And how much are these stronger drinks gonna cost me?"

Mia detached her arm from John's hand. "There's been an incident but it's under control. A reminder that you requested stronger drinks. But not to worry, we'll cover any extra charge you incur."

She bolted out the door, pretending not to hear John as he yelled after her, "What about my stripper?"

Mia ran down the stairs. She stepped outside as the police screeched up to the front of Belle View. Luckily, the cacophony of beats from DJ DJ coupled with the 1960s pop music from the anniversary party drowned out the sirens of the half-dozen cop cars. Mia glanced out a window at the boats bobbing peacefully in the marina. She resisted an urge to hop into one, hotwire it—a skill Posi had taught her when she was ten—and take off out of Flushing Bay. Instead she steeled herself for what she knew was coming.

Detective Pete Dianopolis, Cammie's ex-husband, stepped out of an unmarked car that pulled up behind the black and whites. "Hey, Mia. Not exactly a great welcome home, huh?"

"My dad had nothing to do with this," she blurted. "He's not even here."

Dianopolis gave her a skeptical look. He banged on the unmarked car, eliciting a surprised yelp from whoever was still inside. "Wake up, Hinkle, let's go."

"Coming."

"My new partner," Dianopolis said to Mia. "He and his wife had a baby two weeks ago."

Hinkle emerged from the car. He was a younger, slightly leaner version of Dianopolis, who was in his mid-fifties and sported a paunch that looked like he'd swallowed a bowling ball. Hinkle yawned and rubbed his eyes as if he'd woken up from a nap, which Mia assumed he had. "We're here already?"

"Yeah, we're here," Dianopolis said, annoyed. "This ain't a road trip; the station's two minutes away.

Take the boys and secure the area." He turned back
to Mia. "So, what've we got?"

"Upstairs is a bachelor party. When the stripper
didn't jump out of the cake, I looked inside and
discovered she was deceased, possibly by unnatural
circumstances," Mia said, trying to sound as business-
like as possible. She didn't mention she recognized
the woman as an unwelcome visitor to Belle View,
having learned at an early age that when talking to
law enforcement, less was definitely more. "Downstairs is a fiftieth anniversary party. I'm running both
events with my staff."

"Then we're talking a hundred people, maybe
more." Dianopolis didn't look happy about this, and
Mia couldn't blame him. They were all in for a very
long night. "Gutierrez and Abadie, take the front
door. No one leaves until we got their statement and
contact info. You, let's see the body."

It took Mia half a second to realize the last comment
was directed at her. "This way," she said, motioning
for him to follow her. She passed Park Lexington,
who had seated herself in one of the chairs decorating the foyer and was checking her cell phone. "You
want me to do my thing?" the stripper asked, barely
looking up from her phone.

Mia shook her head. "Keep your clothes on," she
said. "For now."

Dianopolis ascended the stairs behind Mia. "So,"
he said, "Cammie here tonight?"

Mia saw right through the detective's forced attempt
at a casual inquiry into his ex-wife's whereabouts. The
detective had a second career—although he was
the only one who ever called it that—as mystery
author Steve Stianopolis. When he'd self-published

his first novel three years prior, he foresaw the career of a Joseph Wambaugh or Michael Connelly for himself. Explaining to Cammie that he needed freedom to enjoy the fame and fans he'd soon garner, Dianopolis asked for a divorce. Cammie gave him one, along with a literal kick out the door. When neither *F* materialized for "Steve," he begged Cammie to reconcile. However, it turned out she was the one who needed freedom from her self-centered husband, so the answer was a loud "no," accompanied by a host of Greek expletives. Three years later, Dianopolis was still trying to woo her back. Convinced that every man found Cammie as alluring as he did, the detective was furious when she accepted a job with "that trolling goombah mobster," as he called Ravello. While Cammie found this hilarious, Mia feared it put her father in the detective's jealous crosshairs.

"Nope," she said, "Cammie's not here tonight."

"And neither is your father," Dianopolis said, glowering.

"Hey, did Cammie tell you Dad has a girlfriend? Someone he met on a cruise. I hear she's great and he's nuts about her." Mia chattered anxiously as she led the man down the hall that connected the Bay Ballroom to a small secondary prep kitchen. "There."

She pointed to the pop-out cake, which was already cordoned off by police tape. Dianopolis snapped on latex gloves and ducked under the tape. He climbed onto the first layer, flipped back the lid on top of the cake, and stared inside. Then he hopped down. "While CSI does their job, let's you and me talk. Somewhere private."

"We can go to my office. But I need to talk to my

staff. We still have two parties here, which means two very unhappy, trapped groups of guests."

Afraid Dianopolis might try and stop her, Mia darted out of the room and down the stairs to the foyer, where she ran into Cody. "The Marina Ballroom guests were asking a lot of questions, ma'am—Mia—so I told them what's going on is all part of a big murder mystery event courtesy of Belle View Banquet Manor."

"Great stall, Cody. I need to meet with everyone in the big kitchen."

He responded with a half salute and spoke into his headset. "Ten-hut! All employees to the kitchen, repeat, all employees to the kitchen. *Now!*"

Mia dashed down the hall and burst into the kitchen as the banquet hall's employees streamed in. She took a deep breath and then, trying to reveal as little as possible, she began to speak. "Thanks, everyone. We have a situation that required the help of law enforcement."

"The stripper got stabbed dead with a knife and the cops need to find out who murdered her." Missy, the nineteen-year-old kitchen helper, jumped in.

"You can relax," Guadalupe said to Mia. "We all know. Everyone knows. Even the guests." Evans, her sous chef, nodded.

Mia released a breath. "Okay then. It looks like we'll be here a while. The police need to talk to everyone and get contact information. I have no idea how long it's going to take."

Giorgio, the unpleasant new hire, shrugged. "What do we care? We're being paid by the hour."

Mia found herself wishing it was Giorgio at the bottom of the pop-out cake instead of Angie. "Use those hours to give our guests anything they want. This is a crazy situation, but we need everyone to leave happy. Got it?"

"Got it," the staff chorused.

"You're the best," she said, finding the restraint not to throw an "except for you" at Giorgio.

Mia left her employees and made her way back up the stairs and into the Bay Ballroom, where a sea of angry faces greeted her. She grabbed a mic from DJ DJ and plastered on a smile. "Hey, everyone, what a night, huh?" There was dead silence. Perspiration beaded on her forehead. Mia had never given the term *flop sweat* much thought. Now she was living it. "I'm sorry about everything. But look at it this way. Plenty of guys have bachelor party stripper stories. *Boring*. But how many guys have bachelor party crime stories?"

"Did you say bachelor party stripper stories?" chimed in Park Lexington who, unnoticed by Mia, had followed her into the ballroom. "I've got those, and then some. I'll never forget the guy who rented a Ferris wheel . . ."

Seeing that the stripper had everyone's attention, Mia handed her the mic and muttered under her breath, "Keep talking." She slipped away to the back hall, prepared to meet her fate with Dianopolis. He was gone, replaced by a swarm of crime scene technicians. "Where's Pete?"

A technician motioned with a gloved hand. "He brought a couple of guys downstairs to talk."

This time Mia took the back stairs that connected the first and second floor work areas. If nothing else, she was getting in her steps for the day—and then some, as Park Lexington would say. She dashed through the kitchen and down the hallway that led to her office in time to see Pete Dianopolis escorting the Koller brothers out of it. "Thank you, both," he said as he walked them toward the manor's front door. "I doubt we'll have any other questions, but if we do, I promise we'll be respectful of your time."

The brothers disappeared into the foyer without a backward glance at the detective. "All that sucking up wasted," Mia said, shaking her head.

Dianopolis crooked a finger and motioned to her. "Your turn."

He stepped into her office and took the seat behind her desk, forcing Mia to take one of the metal chairs. "I wonder if everyone's getting that 'respectful of your time' line from you," she said. "I hate when people get a pass because they're rich."

"Good-looking rich guys like that don't need to knock off a stripper."

"Seriously?" Mia said, irked. "There are a million books about rich people doing shady stuff like knocking off strippers and getting away with it because people like you let them."

"Rich people . . . shady stuff . . . secrets." Dianopolis scribbled in a notepad.

"I'm glad you're at least listening to me."

"Oh, that's not for the investigation. I'm a little stuck on my next Steve Stianopolis mystery and"—he tapped the notebook—"there might be something here." He stuck the notepad into one jacket pocket and pulled a different pad out of another. "So, tell me about our vic. Did you recognize her?"

It was the question Mia feared and hoped to dodge. But she knew it wouldn't help her father if she lied. "Yes," she said. "Angie showed up here out of nowhere a few days ago." She filled the detective in on the late call girl's bizarre accusation, ending with, "but I believed my father a hundred percent when he said he had no idea who she was."

"Oh, you believed your father. Well, that does it for me. Moving on to the next suspect. That was sarcasm."

"Really?" Mia said, then added, "So was that."

Dianopolis ran a hand through a thick thatch of salt-and-pepper hair. He was so vain about this attribute that Cammie told a story about how she once threatened to shave it off during a fight and he retaliated by taking out a restraining order on her, despite the fact they shared a matrimonial bed at the time. "We have an accusation, a dead call girl, and a nervous mob boss."

"Are you talking about a possible Steve Stianopolis novel?" Mia asked, hoping against hope.

"No, that's the case in front of me. I'll be putting a call in to your father."

Ravello Carina appeared in the doorway. "No need, I'm right here."

"Dad!" Mia, overcome with relief at the sight of him, jumped up and threw her arms around her father.

"Guadalupe called and told me what was going on. I figured I better get over here pronto." Ravello separated from his daughter. "I told the anniversary party that everyone's getting a bottle of Montepulciano from the Boldano family's Abruzzo vineyard. I'm going upstairs and offering the same to our bachelor party guests."

"I have some questions for you," Dianopolis said.

"And I'm happy to answer them. When I'm done." Ravello's tone was polite but with enough of an undercurrent to make the detective back off.

Ravello and Mia took the banquet hall's small elevator to the second floor. They entered the ballroom, where they found a room of extremely drunk men entranced by Park Lexington as she worked the room like a professional comedienne, only one clad in gold spike heels and a sequined bikini. ". . . So I said to the groom, 'You may be a lawyer, but you're not the only one here who knows how to get people off.'" Her appreciative audience whoo-hooed and laughed as DJ DJ punctuated the joke with the sound effect of a rim shot.

Mia strode over to the stripper. "Thank you so much, Park. I hope, I mean, I'm sure you have a lot more stories. But first, my father has something he'd like to say."

She turned the mic over to him.

"Hello, I'm your host, Ravello Carina," he began.

There was a murmur in the room as his name sunk in. "Is he *the* Ravello Carina?" Mia heard one attendee ask another. His friend nodded. "Whooaaaa." Both partygoers instantly sobered up.

"We apologize for any inconvenience caused by this . . . unfortunate situation," Ravello continued. "I would personally like to make it up to you by gifting each of you with a free bottle of Boldano Family Vineyard's world-renowned Montepulciano red wine. There's a truck outside now. When the police have finished doing what they need to do, visit the truck for your gift. Thank you all for your patience."

"Thank *you*, sir," a voice called out, prompting a chorus of thanks, along with applause. Mia marveled at how much goodwill a cheap bottle of wine with notes of notoriety could buy. She took the mic from her father and handed it back to Park, who launched into another salacious bachelor party tale.

"Now take me to the body," Ravello said to Mia.

She led her father through the swinging doors to the ballroom's back hall. Guadalupe, Evans, and some of the waitstaff were already there, watching as Angie's body was removed from the cake. "I don't think whoever we rented that cake from is gonna want it back," Guadalupe said.

"Nope," Mia said. "We'll have to eat the cost." Her mood went from glum to glummer as she tallied up the ballooning bills for the evening's events. "Too bad the cake's fake. We could eat it for real and save some money on groceries."

Ravello walked over to Angie and examined her as attendants from the coroner's office laid the late woman out on the body bag resting on a gurney. "Did you tell Pete about how she showed up here and what she said to me?" Mia nodded. "Good. No lies. They're more dangerous than the truth. At least in this case."

Everyone watched in silence as an attendant began to zip up the body bag. The swinging doors suddenly swung opened. John Grazio stepped inside, followed by one of his guests. "Hey, hi, I was wondering, since it was my party that got ruined, maybe I could have an extra bottle of wine or something."

"You can have a case," Ravello said. "And there'll be no charge for tonight's event." Ravello walked out of the hallway through the swinging doors, past the two men and back into the ballroom. Mia flinched. This was proving to be one very expensive evening for Belle View Banquet Manor.

"Thank you, sir, thank—whoa." John stared at Angie's corpse. His eyes widened.

"Holy—is that—" his friend stuttered.

Their reactions set off flare guns for Mia. "Do you know her?"

"What? No," John said. "We were just like, is that the body?"

"Yeah, that's what we meant. Is that like the body, the body of the dead person?"

"We definitely never seen her before, right, Chris?"

"Right. Oh man, I'm gonna be sick again."

Chris bolted from the room. "I better make sure he's okay," John said.

He took off after his friend. As Mia watched them go, she thought to herself, *Those are a couple of really bad liars.*

Chapter Five

Mia's initial impulse was to take off after John and his drunk friend and pepper them with questions. But she wanted to confirm that her staff wasn't too traumatized by the murder investigation. So far, they were being troupers, but she feared the night might wear them down and the last thing she needed was for the crew to quit on her.

"You know what's traumatic?" Guadalupe responded when Mia appeared in the kitchen and checked in with her. "War."

"I'm sorry, were you talking to me?" Missy held up her phone. "I'm sharing all these amazing photos about the police and stuff. I have, like, a million likes and new friends. I may even trend!"

"No worries," Evans said with a shrug. "It's cool." The sous chef fascinated Mia. She guessed him to be in his early thirties. Then again, he could be in his late twenties or mid-forties. She'd yet to see a hint of a smile on his face, but he seemed totally committed to his job. There was a time years ago when a black man couldn't walk through certain outer borough neighborhoods without being chased off by a gang of Italian or Irish thugs with bats. Did he still feel a lingering sense of not belonging?

She shut down this stream of consciousness and concentrated on the task at hand: taking the heat off her father. "I just wanted to make sure you were all okay. Now I'll check on the guests."

Two guests, really—John and Chris. When they were not in the ballroom, she headed for the men's room. She cracked open the door and saw John standing in front of a stall. His friend was bent over the toilet bowl. John noticed her and left his post. "This is at least Chris's second prayer to the porcelain god tonight. Maybe his third. His name's Chris Tinker but we call him Chris Drinker. Because he drinks a lot. I came up with that."

"Very clever." Mia hoped she sounded sincere and not sarcastic, although she had a feel that sarcasm would sail right over the groom's head. "John, I got a very strong impression that you and Chris knew Angie—the victim. I can understand why you wouldn't want to say anything in front of the investigators. But no one's around now. You can tell me."

Mia put this as flirtatiously as possible but, to her frustration, for once he didn't bite. "No, don't know her. It was just weird seeing a body like that. You know, first time and all. I better see how Chris is doing."

He disappeared back into the men's room. Mia released a profanity, then moved on to Plan B. She'd tell a detective her suspicions—but not Pete Dianopolis. She'd go to his partner, Ryan Hinkle.

She found the young detective snoring as he leaned against a wall in the first-floor hallway behind the Marina Ballroom. He started when she gave him a slight shake. "I'm awake!" he said, snapping to attention.

"Whatevs. Look, I have some suspects for you." Mia shared John's and Chris's reaction to Angie's body and their cagey responses when she pressed them to explain.

"Sounds good. I'll let Pete know."

Mia stifled an annoyed response. "Or . . . you could interview them, find out what they know, maybe even arrest them, and look like a hero."

Hinkle shook his head. "Too much heavy lifting for me right now. But thanks for the intel. I'll pass it along."

"Thank you," Mia said through gritted teeth. She marched off. *Enough with a murder investigation that goes nowhere,* she declared to herself. It was time to do her actual job—making sure all of Belle View's guests were happy enough to leave decent reviews on the internet, despite the circumstances.

Even with additional officers and detectives brought in by NYPD, the interviews dragged on for hours. To ensure the anniversary party's goodwill, Mia decided that on top of the Boldano wine offered by her father, she'd gift them with the pasta forks meant for favors at Alice and John's wedding. They were a pricey guest gift; Alice had definitely one-upped her twin on this score. The Carinas would have to re-order the forks and pay for expedited shipping, adding to the long list of expenses the evening had incurred.

Mia positioned herself in the manor foyer and handed out the forks to departing partygoers, thanking each for coming and apologizing for the unforeseen events. The guests were uniformly gracious. "It was exciting," one senior said from her wheelchair. "For a change, I'll have the most interesting story at Sunday dinner."

Felicity Stewart Forbes was the next one through the line. She kept a firm hand under the elbow of a frail old man as she used her free hand to grab two pasta forks. "I know you feel shaken and disoriented by what happened tonight," she told him. "But there could also be an underlying cause for those conditions. All the facilities I've mentioned offer excellent geriatric care. I've run out of brochures, but I'll drop off a list in the morning. What was your address again?" Mia glowered at the real estate agent's back as she and the old man disappeared into the night.

Having disseminated the favors, Mia, exhausted, started for her office. Her plan to catch a few minutes of rest was waylaid by the sound of yelling coming from the parking lot. Through the glass doors, she saw John Grazio arguing with DJ DJ. Chris Tinker, still unsteady on his feet, looked like he was trying to mediate. Unfortunately, a prop plane chose to land at that exact moment, so she couldn't hear what they were saying. The DJ took a step toward John. Before a fight could break out, a cab pulled up in front of the men. Grazio hopped in, yanking Tinker in with him, and the cab zoomed off. DJ DJ, fuming, watched it go. Mia debated doing a little snooping under the guise of concerned employer, but DJ was already taking long, angry strides to a black Escalade SUV.

He jumped into the driver's seat, fired up the engine, and drove off.

"*Mia, cara mia.*"

Ravello emerged from his office and walked down the hallway toward her. "Dad, *marone,* this night."

"This night," he echoed with a sigh.

Mia's heart lurched at the sight of him. If it was possible to age overnight, he'd done it. His dark eyes were shadowed, the worry creases in his forehead deeper. "What's wrong? I mean, I know what's wrong. Everything. But what else is wrong?"

He looked around, then took Mia's hand and his daughter into her office. He closed the door behind them. "There's a development."

"Another? Haven't we had enough for one night?"

"I wish." Ravello hesitated. "They found a check signed by me next to Angie's body."

Mia stared at her father. "*What?*"

"I sometimes presign checks in the register to speed up the process. I don't fill in the amount until I get an invoice."

"That's a terrible idea."

"I know that now. Anyways, Pete's theory is that the woman was blackmailing me, and I killed her before she could cash the check."

"Which she wasn't," Mia said, fuming. "And you didn't."

"Of course not. To both."

"How much was the check made out for?"

"A million dollars."

If Mia had a drink in her mouth, she would have done a spit take. "Are you serious? A check for a million dollars? That's joke money."

"Yup. It's probably the only thing that kept Pete

from cuffing me. That and the fact he knows Cammie would kill him. He still wants to get back together with her, you know."

"Not gonna happen."

"Well, whatever you do, don't tell him that. She's the only one who can keep him in line and off my back." Ravello opened the door and peeked out. "No one's out there. I'm going up to the bachelor party. I'll entertain whoever's left with some B.S. stories about 'The Family.' They're the kind of crowd that would like those."

Ravello took off to beguile the bachelor party with manufactured—Mia hoped—mob stories. She collapsed onto one of the folding metal chairs in front of her desk. Only a few days earlier, her office had felt like an oasis. Now it felt like a prison cell. Small, windowless, dreary. She fought back tears.

"There you are." Pete Dianopolis poked his head in the room, and then entered. "I was beginning to think you were hiding from me."

"You have an investigation to lead. I have guests to please. Not easy, considering the circumstances."

"You have my sympathy. Sincerely. I mean it."

"Thank you."

Pete maneuvered behind the desk and sat down. "This place could use a little work. Maybe a poster or something to cheer it up."

"It's on my to-do list, after 'get my father off the hook for a murder he didn't commit.' Did your partner tell you about the interaction I witnessed between the host of the bachelor party and one of his guests?"

"Nicely put. You sound like a cop yourself. No, he didn't. The guy's useless. The only reason he came back to work early from paternity leave was to get out of the house. The baby came a couple of weeks early. I hear it's chaos over there. So, tell me, what did you 'witness'?"

Mia told him about John's and Chris's reactions to seeing Angie, adding as much drama as she could to sell it. Dianopolis tapped his upper lip with his index finger. "Hmm . . . interesting. Then again, neither of their names were on the check deposited next to the deceased's body."

"No one writes a check for that much money," Mia scoffed. "Especially a mob—someone like my dad. The banks have to report any transaction over ten grand. Can you imagine the alarm bells a million-dollar check would set off? One with Ravello Carina's signature? And give my dad a little credit. He would never hide a body in plain sight. The pop-out cake may have looked like a good location to an amateur, but a pro would think it through and know that the minute that cake is rolled out, the murder's public knowledge."

"You seem pretty familiar with the thought process of murder."

"I watch a lot of cop shows." It was the detective's turn to snort. "Hey, my dad always told me he never did anything like that, and I believe him." This was kind of true. Ravello did deny ever offing anyone. And Mia chose to believe him. "Come on, Pete. Killing someone and putting them in the one place where the body's guaranteed to be exposed. Leaving a million-dollar check with the victim. Even you have to admit it's a stupid plan, and if there's one thing my father isn't, it's stupid."

"That he isn't," Pete had to admit.

"I bet when you run the check through forensics,

they'll tell you that the signature and check amount were written by two different people."

"While I'm waiting for any forensics results, I'll be checking your father's alibi. The old 'I was home sleeping' doesn't fly with me. Cammie told me that the new family across the street from him, the one where the husband and wife work on Wall Street, put in a fancy new security system. The pricey kind you can work from your phone. She wants one just like it. You can do everything from your phone now, did you know that? Even turn on your coffee machine. I bet those Wall Street people are big into that kinda stuff, making coffee with their phones. Anyway, we're getting the footage off their system, so we'll be able to place the time your father left his house."

"Excellent. I'm sure the footage will show my dad is telling the truth."

"For his sake, I hope so. Now, let's talk about another Carina with a track record who was actually on the premises tonight. You." He added the last word to bring home the obvious point that he was talking about Mia.

Mia crossed one leg over the other and folded her arms across her chest. "You do know I was cleared as a suspect in my husband's disappearance? And he's presumed dead at sea?"

"'Presumed' being the operative word. Maybe your father didn't off this woman who showed up to blackmail him. He has a daughter who loves him very much and would do anything to protect him. And that daughter is *you*."

"Yes, me, I get it, Pete. But like my father, I'm not stupid. And the closest I've ever come to doing anything illegal is jaywalking."

"I go back to that word, '*presumed.*' It's important because it implies doubt. No Adam Grosso body, no final conclusion." Pete had a point, much as Mia hated to admit it. Until her husband's body washed up and an autopsy cleared her of any involvement in his death, she would always be under a cloud of suspicion. "I need someone who isn't you or your father to inventory the knives," the detective continued.

"Meaning because you see us as possible suspects, you can't trust us."

"I was trying to be delicate, but yup. We need to determine if one of Belle View's knives is currently resting in the vic's chest."

"I'll ask our head chef to look into it."

There was a loud knock and Park Lexington appeared in the doorway. Behind her stood one of John Grazio's bachelor party guests. "I wanted to say good night and thanks for a great gig," Park said. "I'm definitely gonna incorporate some comedy into my act. Brendan here's in advertising. He's gonna help me brand myself. The Stripper with a Sense of Humor."

"Congratulations," Mia said.

There was an awkward pause. Finally, Park said, "My check?"

"Oh. Right. We need to pay you."

"Double, if you don't mind, because I basically worked two shifts."

"That you did, ha ha." Mia barked a mirthless laugh as she pulled out a register from her desk and wrote Park a check. *Could anyone on the planet have had a worst first week of work?* she wondered as she handed it to the stripper.

Park and her new business partner-slash-date took off, and Mia turned her attention back to Pete

Dianopolis. The detective was furiously scribbling in a pad. "Notes on the case?" she asked hopefully.

Pete kept writing. "The plot for the next Steve Stianopolis mystery's finally coming together. A boat. A young beauty who may or may not be a widow. A father with a shady past . . ."

Mia liked the "young beauty" part. But she was more determined than ever not to provide Dianopolis and his poorly written books with an ending that pegged her father—or her—as the villain.

Chapter Six

By the time the police completed their business, it was close to four in the morning. Mia had sent the staff home an hour earlier. Ravello insisted on sticking around, but when she found him asleep with his head on his desk, she sent him home, too.

The building and parking lot were pitch-black by the time she locked up. The only light came from the single fluorescent bulb Mia left on in her office. She didn't want to add a huge electric bill to the manor's expenses and figured she could tough it out in the dark until her ride showed up. Still, the quiet and solitude made her nervous. She was relieved when a familiar silver Prius pulled up to the front of Belle View. She didn't care if Jamie Boldano was manipulating the Pick-U-Up app. She was just profoundly happy to see him.

"It's so late," she said as she climbed into the back of the car. "I can't believe you're still up."

"First of all, get out of the back seat and get into the front." Jamie pushed a bunch of textbooks off the passenger seat onto the floor. Mia followed his order. "Now take a swig of this." He offered her a bottle of bourbon.

Mia grinned for the first time all day. She took a slug of the liquor, which burned her throat and warmed her body. "An open bottle? You could get pulled over."

"I think all the cops in Queens were here tonight, and now they're all going home to do exactly what you're doing."

"I guess you heard what happened." Mia didn't bother to ask how. The Boldanos had one ear to the ground of any Family operation.

"The basics. But give me the details."

"This woman showed up on my first day, claimed my dad had a thing with her, and owed her money. We got rid of her and I thought it was over. Then the stripper didn't jump out of the cake at the bachelor party we had booked. I looked inside, and it was the same woman, Angie, and she was dead from a knife stuck in her. But it turns out she wasn't the stripper because the stripper, Park Lexington, showed up late due to the subway switching the N and R trains for some crazy reason. Really, what's happened to the subway system in this city? Anyway, they found a check with my dad's signature next to Angie's body, and it was made out for a million dollars, which is ridiculous. Nobody does that except a kid or a numbnut. But Pete Dianopolis wants to stick the crime on my dad because he hates him, or on me if he can't nail my dad. Does any of this make sense?"

"Sadly, all of it does."

Jamie brought the car to a stop. Mia looked out the window. "This isn't my house. It's your dad's bar."

"One of my dad's bars. I'm guessing you haven't

eaten. Piero, the bartender, also happens to be a great cook."

"It's so late. Don't bars in New York still close at four?"

"They do. Except for my dad's bars."

Jamie jumped out of the car and opened Mia's door. He took her hand, and she felt a surge of emotion and desire. *Put a lid on it,* she told herself. *It's only because it's been such a long, horrible night.* Jamie helped her jump over a puddle on the sidewalk, then dropped her hand. He opened the door to the bar, and she stepped inside. It was a timeless place of dark wood and red Naugahyde, the scent of cigarette smoke still hanging in the air despite an almost-twenty-year ban on smoking in buildings. A group of men populated one table. She knew them all and responded in kind to their warm greetings and welcome homes.

"*Ciao,* buddy." The bartender, a middle-aged bald man Mia assumed was Piero, waved to Jamie with a rag he was using to dry a glass. His was the only unfamiliar face in the room.

"Hey, Piero, this is my friend, Mia."

"Ravello's daughter?" Piero's craggy face broke into a smile. He gave a slight bow in her direction. "It's an honor."

"What've you got tonight?" Jamie asked.

"I kept it simple. Baked manicotti. Pasta's homemade, but I gotta warn you, the gravy's out of a jar."

"Bring it, *mio amico.*"

"*Va bene.* You got it."

As Piero headed into the bar's kitchen, Mia noticed that his right leg was gone, replaced by a prothesis. She threw a questioning glance at Jamie, who had gone behind the bar and was pouring them each a shot of bourbon. "Piero was my dad's last driver," he said, picking up on her look. "Then he lost his driving leg to bone cancer, so my dad set him up here." He handed her a shot glass and they relocated to a table near the kitchen.

"That was nice of your dad," she said.

"When Piero couldn't drive anymore, my dad tapped into another skill of his. Mixing drinks. The cooking's just a bonus." Jamie knocked back his shot. "My dad's smart that way. He could run a company."

He sounded sad. Mia sympathized. She felt the same way about Ravello. He and Donny were smart men who, for whatever reason they'd never share with their children, had chosen "the life." Belle View Banquet Manor at least offered her father a chance to use his intelligence in a legitimate way, and Mia was determined to make the career change stick.

The kitchen door swung open and Piero came out. He deposited a basket of warm Italian bread on Mia's and Jamie's table, then returned to the kitchen. Mia helped herself to a chunk of the bread. The outside was hard and crusty, the inside so soft it almost melted in her mouth. "This is delicious."

"Piero makes it himself. He makes his own breadsticks, too. I used to bring them to the kids at my school. They always pretended to fence with them, like we did when we were kids. Some behavior is timeless, I guess."

Mia finished eating her thick chunk of bread, then reached for a breadstick. It made a snappy, satisfying crunch when she bit into it. "Jamie . . . why did you stop teaching? You don't have to answer if you don't want to. I just wondered."

"It's fine. I don't mind answering. After five years of it, I figured out that a lot of my students would benefit more from a good school psychologist than an okay fifth grade teacher. I could get my master's faster if I went to school full-time instead of at night, so rather than keep teaching during the day, I quit to focus on school."

"A master's. Wow. I barely made it out of high school."

"That's only because you had to spend so much time fighting off all the guys who wanted to date you."

"Hah. Hardly."

"It's true. Come on, Tony Brunetti and Sean Fallows got suspended for going at each other in the hallway when they both tried to ask you out to prom at the same time."

Mia covered her face with her hands. "OMG, it was so embarrassing. They'd both seen the same picture on the Internet where someone spelled out 'Prom Me' in pepperoni on a pizza."

"Who hit who with their pizza box first? Do you remember?"

"No. I blocked the whole thing out. Thanks a lot for making me relive it. I didn't want to go with either of them." *I wanted to go with you,* Mia managed not to say. But instead of asking her, Jamie, being the gentleman that he was, had taken his ex-girlfriend so she wouldn't miss the prom.

Jamie chuckled. "Sorry. But it's hard to forget when two guys are beating on each other and pepperoni pizza's flying everywhere. Salambini's pizza, too. Good stuff." There was an awkward pause. "So," he said, changing the subject, "are there any real suspects in the murder?"

Mia threw up her hands. "There were a ton of people at Belle View, there could be a ton of suspects. But I can point a finger at two. John Grazio and Chris Tinker."

She filled Jamie in on the men's suspicious behavior. He pondered what she shared. "I took a criminal psychology class last year. I thought it would be interesting and maybe give me some insight into my family. Unfortunately, it was only one of those things—interesting." He sat back in his chair. "I learned that murders are usually motivated by passion, profit, or ego, meaning someone has suffered a humiliation so wounding it drives them to kill. So that's the motive. Then you have to factor in means and opportunity."

"So, all I have to do is figure out which of the hundred people at the event—make that more, because I shouldn't rule out the staff, I don't know any of them that well—had a motive, as well as means and opportunity."

"It's not up to you, it's up to the police."

"Two words, remember? Pete Dianopolis."

"Oh, right. Then it is up to you. With me helping."

"No." Mia shook her head vehemently. "I'm not dragging you into this. You're doing such a great job of making your own life, Jamie. I don't want anything getting in the way of that."

"But I don't want you doing anything dangerous."

"Don't worry about that. I've got a lot of people looking out for me. A whole Family." She gestured to the table of men off in a corner of the restaurant. They smiled and waved at her.

"Be careful, okay?" Jamie took her hand and gave it a gentle squeeze. "And thank you."

"For what?"

"Believing in me. That I can do what you said. Make my own life."

"Of course."

Mia squeezed Jamie's hand back. They shared a bond that few others could understand or relate to. Holidays spent without fathers because Ravello or Donny was in jail. Classmates pointing and whispering to each other, or worse, forming a friendship with one of them only so they could brag about being "connected." Siblings who followed in their parents' dubious footsteps. But Mia and Jamie always had each other, at least as friends. There was no denying that Jamie was cute, with his hazel eyes, chestnut hair, and light smattering of freckles across a surprisingly straight nose, considering the sturdy Italian honkers on both of his parents. Mia was beginning to second-guess her second-guessing about the relationship. Maybe it was time to let it move out of the friend zone into a sexier space.

The energy surging between the couple was interrupted by Piero's arrival. He held up two plates of steaming baked manicotti. "*Ecco*, you two. Straight from the oven."

Mia inhaled the rich aroma of tomatoes, meat ragu, and herbs. "I had no idea how hungry I am. Don't judge me if I lick the plate."

Jamie laughed. "I've had Piero's manicotti. I may join you." He held up his empty shot glass. "To your health. *Alla tua salute.*"

"*Alla tua salute.*"

The two clinked glasses, then dug into their food.

* * *

By the time Jamie dropped Mia off, it was six A.M.
Elisabetta, wearing a purple track suit with gold trim,
greeted her at the door. Hero, still wary of her,
greeted Mia with a half bark, half growl. "Ravello
called and told me what happened," she said, planting her fists on her hips in a gesture that had earned
her the secret family nickname of Little Mussolini.
"Nobody's arresting my son under false pretenses."
Elisabetta yelled this into the street as if the words
would carry to the local precinct and stop the police
in their tracks.

"Don't worry, Nonna, I'm gonna do everything
I can to keep Dad from being framed for what happened."

"That's my girl." Elisabetta hugged Mia and pinched
her cheeks hard enough to leave red marks. "Go get
some sleep. You'll need it TO FIGHT THE LIES!"
She hurled this comment into the ether as well, following it with a loud sneeze.

"You okay?" Mia asked, concerned.

Elisabetta waved her hands dismissively. "I'm fine.
I got a little cold. I'll live. Go. Sleep. *Va dormire.*"

She pushed her granddaughter through the vestibule to the door that led to the second-floor staircase.
Mia, feeling the all-nighter she'd pulled, didn't need
any additional prompting. She dragged herself up
the stairs, maneuvered around the boxes still crowd-
ing the apartment living room, and fell onto the
carved and gilded bed she'd inherited from Rose
Caniglia. A bird chirped a morning greeting outside
her window, reminding Mia of her missing parakeet.
She pulled her cell phone from her purse and checked
for messages. There were none responding to the
flyers she'd posted about Pizzazz. "I'll make some

calls later," she mumbled into her pillow before falling asleep.

Mia woke up several hours later feeling, if not refreshed, at least functional. She checked her schedule and made an executive decision to move the Rotary Club monthly meeting, scheduled for the Bay Ballroom, to a new location. She had no idea if the police had left Belle View in operational condition and didn't want to take the chance that they hadn't. She put a call in to Ravello's favorite hangout, Roberto's Trattoria, and the manager said yes before she even finished asking for the favor. He even offered to pick up the tab. Whether or not he would have done this for a patron who wasn't connected didn't matter to Mia. It was one less financial burden to carry, even if it left her with two boxes of preordered Danish.

After alerting the Rotary Club president to the change in venue, she called a few of her old Palm Beach neighbors to see if any had spotted Pizzazz. None had, which left Mia feeling dispirited. She missed waking up to the little bird's cheerful chirps. "You packed a ton of personality into your tiny little body," she said to the empty cage. "Pack, not packed," she corrected, refusing to consider that Pizzazz might be gone forever.

Mia showered and put on a casual outfit of tapered black pants, a silk purple T-shirt, and black ballet flats. There were no appointments on her calendar, so she was free to dress casually. As she applied a light touch of makeup, she heard her grandmother talking to someone. Curious, she went downstairs. To her displeasure, she found Elisabetta in the middle of a conversation with rapacious real estate agent Felicity

Stewart Forbes. Hero was by Elisabetta's side, on the alert, ready to protect his human. The agent wore a Chanel jacket—again, a knockoff—over a cream silk top with a pussy bow, and dark camel slacks.

"Ask your friends. They swear by my homemade chicken soup," Forbes said, handing Elisabetta a small plastic container. Hero growled and barked at her and she recoiled, catching herself before she tumbled backward down the stairs. "Good doggy. What a cutie pie, huh? Anyway, drink that soup. You don't want that cold turning into pneumonia."

"It won't," Elisabetta said. "I had the shot."

"Yay." Forbes fist-pumped the air. "Good for you," she said with all the sincerity of a beauty pageant first-runner-up congratulating the winner. "I taped my card to the top of the container, which you are welcome to keep."

Elisabetta examined the container. "Your picture is on this." She held the container up. The front was plastered with a label featuring Forbes making her signature "Number One" gesture.

"Yes, the label has my photo, so you don't forget who I am, along with my contact information in case you lose the card." Forbes stuck her finger in the air, mimicking the pose on the label. She noticed Mia. "Hello," she said in a tone that defined the word *perfunctory*.

"Hi," Mia said. "We met last night." Forbes gave her a blank look. "At Belle View Banquet Manor."

"Of course. Now I remember," the agent said with a wide smile she must have assumed would hide her obvious lie.

"Mia's my granddaughter," Elisabetta said. "She moved in upstairs."

"Really? Well, isn't that wonderful for you. You won't be alone and lonely." Forbes did her best to mask her disappointment.

"Or need to sell," Elisabetta said. "Thank you for the soup."

Elisabetta closed the door on Forbes. She took the lid off the soup, smelled it, then poured the container into the potted flax plant next to the vestibule radiator. "Witch. I wouldn't be surprised if she doctored up that soup. Here's hoping it doesn't kill my plant. But if it does," she added darkly, "we'll know."

Elisabetta marched into her first-floor apartment with Mia right behind her. *"Che strega, mi piacerebbe portarla su una scopa e mandarla a volare fuori da Astoria."*

Mia translated her grandmother's diatribe in her head. "I know you'd like to shove her on a broomstick and send her flying out of Astoria, but since you can't actually do that, how about ignoring her?"

"No!" Her grandmother shook a fist in the air. "I'm not gonna ignore the woman who's ruining my neighborhood. *Capisce?*"

"Yes. I understand."

The women made their way to Elisabetta's kitchen. She pulled out a chair from her 1950s-era dinette set. "Sit," she ordered her granddaughter. Mia sat. Elisabetta placed a plate loaded with eggs, peppers, and sweet Italian sausage in front of Mia, then assumed her Little Mussolini pose. "Eat."

Mia ate.

After breakfast, she decided to bike to work. Mia had barely been home a week and her pants were already feeling tight. Riding a bicycle was one of her favorite activities. It was easy in Florida, where a hill wasn't to be found for miles, but a little less easy in

Queens, where the terrain, while hardly rugged, was more varied. Still, for Mia, there was nothing like pumping up a steep road and then flying down the other side of it as the wind whipped her hair away from her face. She passed homes and shops familiar to her from the rides of her childhood. The trip brought back memories, particularly of trying to talk Posi into riding bikes instead of stealing them. He'd pimp the stolen bikes with streamers and decorative paint jobs, then sell them back to their original owners for the price of his supplies. While the parents might complain—but mostly didn't because they feared the Family—kids loved Posi's handiwork, and the Carinas often found bikes in their front yard from kids hoping Posi would work his design magic on them.

Mia slowed down when she reached flatter ground. It was a gorgeous early spring day, the kind where the air was soft and the leaves the bright green of new growth. As Mia pedaled toward Belle View, she reviewed the previous night's events. Angie's body in the fake cake, John's and Chris's mysterious reactions, that stupid million-dollar check.

Mia slammed on her bike brakes to avoid hitting a parked car as a thought about the check occurred to her. Who better to frame for murder than a mob capo with a rap sheet? But what if it hadn't been placed in the pop-out cake *by* the killer? What if someone saw what happened and took advantage of it to get Ravello Carina in trouble? A killer . . . and a possible witness. Instead of merely protesting that her father was innocent, she finally had a theory she could share with Pete Dianopolis.

Encouraged by this potential new investigative

path, Mia soared up one last hill and coasted down it. When she reached Belle View, she chained her bicycle to the gazebo and walked toward the facility. Something stuck to her shoe. She reached down and peeled off a piece of police tape. She stood up and let out a startled cry. A young woman stood directly in front of her. The woman held her cell phone a few inches from Mia's face. Mia saw that the voice memo app was open.

"Hi, I'm Teri Fuoco, investigative journalist for the *Triborough Tribune*," she said. "I'd like to ask you some questions about the recent murder at Belle View."

Chapter Seven

The press. Great. Mia muttered a few vulgarities in her head, then plastered on a polite smile. "No comment."

She threw back her shoulders and strolled toward Belle View, suppressing the urge to race inside and lock all the doors. The reporter followed on her heels, which was no surprise. She was an "investigative journalist." Translation: a dog with a bone, the bone being "reputed crime figure, Ravello Carina"—the first three words being the description that generally preceded her father's name in the unwanted press coverage he received. The concept of names triggered a buzz in Mia's names. *Fuoco,* she mused. *Fuoco. Why does that sound so familiar?*

"Was the victim known to your father?" Mia ignored Fuoco and walked faster.

The reporter followed, shooting a rat-a-tat-tat of questions at her. "Is her death related to the acquisition of Belle View by the Boldano Family? Was it ordered by Donny Boldano? The family claims Belle View is a legal enterprise, but did the victim know differently? Was her death part of a cover-up operation?"

Mia halted her walk and turned to face her adversary. Not expecting this, Fuoco bumped into Mia and stumbled. Mia scrutinized the reporter as the woman regained her balance. Age-wise, the two appeared to be in the same ballpark. Physically, they parted ways. Fuoco's body type leaned toward lumpy while Mia's bordered on skinny. The reporter's dirty blond hair hung to her shoulders in no discernible style. She was clad in a pink polo shirt and khaki pants, giving her the look of a 1980s preppy or a young Connecticut housewife. "You know I'm not gonna answer one single question you throw at me," Mia said. "So save us both a lot of wasted time and go away. Far, far away." She opened the door to the Belle View lobby. "Follow me in here and I'll have you arrested for trespassing."

She stepped into the lobby and pulled the door shut, coughing as her senses were assailed with the smell of disinfectant. A cleaning crew was scrubbing down Belle View's interior. She jumped out of the way as a guy pushed a floor waxing machine past her into the Marina Ballroom. Cammie Dianopolis waved to her from the office hallway. "Morning. I got the crew out here to get rid of the police stink."

"Thank you for that."

Cammie beckoned to her. "Come to my office. I'll fill you in on a couple of things, and then take off for the day."

"It's not even eleven o'clock."

Cammie ignored her. Mia walked down the hall and joined her co-worker—if Cammie could even be called that—in her office. "Shut the door," Cammie said, pointing to it with a sparkly pink lacquered fingernail enhanced with a rhinestone surrounded by the intricate illustration of a rose.

"Nice manicure."

"Spa Castle does good work."

Mia shut the office door. Since the folding chairs had been relocated to her own office, there was nowhere to sit, so she leaned against a wall. "You got another office chair."

"This was your broken one. Pete fixed it for me. And while he was here, I got a little dirt out of him. The chick who was murdered? The medical examiner puts the time of death between six and nine P.M."

"That's not much help."

"The coroner can only offer a three-hour window."

Mia released a frustrated groan. "Between prepping the two parties and running them, that was the busiest time of the night. Pretty much everyone was here at some point during that block of time."

"True. Pete said it didn't allow them to establish alibis for too many people."

Mia twisted a lock of hair around her finger, a nervous habit since childhood. "A reporter hit me with questions outside." She twisted the lock tighter. Her index finger began to pulse.

Cammie nodded. "Teri Fuoco. *Triborough Trib*. Picking up where her father left off."

"Huh? Explain, please."

"Jerry Fuoco. He was a *Trib* reporter, too. Made a lot of noise about the Boldano family about twenty years ago."

"Ah," Mia said, nodding. "That's why her last name sounded familiar."

"Yup. He kept throwing spaghetti at the wall to see what would stick, but nothing did. Donny made sure of that, which ticked off my Pete, let me tell you. He was on Team Fuoco. Anyway, the *Trib* finally stopped being obsessed with the Family and Fuoco faded away. But now it's nex-gen Fuoco, as in his daughter."

"Here's hoping she meets the same fate as her father." Mia caught herself. "Which wasn't . . ."

"Deadly? No. He just got moved to another beat on the paper."

Mia released the finger held captive by her hair twirling. "I need to give Pete a call. I have an idea I want to run by him."

"I can do you one better." Cammie tapped out a text with her beautifully manicured nails. "I told him my chair's a little wobbly. Money says he'll be here in ten minutes. Or less."

"In the meantime . . ." Mia leaned her chin on her hand as she thought. "Adam managed a restaurant in Palm Beach."

"Your presumed-dead-husband-that-we-hate Adam?"

"Yes, that Adam." Mia wrinkled her nose like she'd bumped up against a bad smell. Then, feeling guilty, she said, "Am I a terrible person for never defending him? Like, for not saying he had a good side?"

"Did he?" Cammie asked, skeptical.

Mia looked down at the room's faded carpet. "You know what's sad? I can't say yes for sure. Maybe he was always playing a game with me. The kind where the minute I committed to him, he started to get bored and antsy. He'd won, but the game was over. I can't just blame him, though. I'm not a victim. I'm an adult who made a choice. A dumb choice but one I gotta own."

Mia swallowed and blinked back tears. The two women were quiet for a moment. "You were saying about managing a restaurant," Cammie gently prompted.

Mia snapped back from her depressing side trip. "Right. I remember some of the waiters at Tutta Pasta joking that a lot of guests assumed they were invisible, so they overheard some great gossip that way. I wonder if our waitstaff brought anything back to the kitchen. I have to talk to Guadalupe and Evans."

"They're here."

"Really? Why? We don't have an event for a couple of days."

"What can I say? You have a dedicated staff. Except for me, of course."

Mia shook her head, amused. "I'll be right back."

She left Cammie for the kitchen, stopping to adjust a few photos in the hallway knocked askew by the vibration of an airplane on approach to LaGuardia. She pushed through the kitchen's swinging double doors. Guadalupe was rearranging her massive collection of pots while Evans perched on a stool, thumbing through a book of recipes. "Thanks for coming in, guys. And Guadalupe, sorry for sticking you with the police's inventory request last night."

"No worries," Guadalupe said, effortlessly transferring a pasta pot half the size of Mia from one shelf to another as she talked. "By the way, I told the police our equipment is so disorganized that I have no idea how many knives we have, so I can't tell them if anything is missing."

"Is that true?"

"It is now." Guadalupe pulled out a drawer and turned it upside down. An assortment of kitchen utensils clattered onto the stainless-steel countertop. "In case they don't believe me and want to look for themselves."

"Great," Mia said, relieved. "A million thanks." She turned her attention to Evans. The sous chef was so engrossed in his recipe book that he hadn't even looked up when the utensils made a racket. "Whatcha got there, Evans?"

He held up the book. "*The World's Great Desserts.*"

"Yum. Count me in for sampling whatever you make."

"He wants to be a dessert and pastry chef," Guadalupe said. "We're just a stop on the way."

"Or . . . we're his final destination because we have the best dessert and pastry chef in Queens."

This earned a smile from the laconic man. "I like that."

Mia gave herself an imaginary pat on the back for good management, then focused on what brought her into the kitchen. "I was wondering, did the waitstaff happen to bring any stories from the parties back into the kitchen? I know they sometimes hear things and then discuss them."

"You mean pick up dirt and gossip about it," Guadalupe said.

"Well . . . yes."

Guadalupe and Evans stopped what they were doing to think for a moment. "Nothing really from the anniversary party," he said. "That was pretty much your standard old folks and family event. But there was talk about the bachelor party."

"You know, like, who hit on some of the waitresses, who was crazy drunk," Guadalupe said. "Who cracked jokes, who seemed nervous or scared—"

Mia held up her hand. Here was a road to a possible suspect. "Okay, that. Who was nervous or scared?"

"Missy was going on about the groom and this one friend of his, this guy who kept throwing up. She said he was sweating like crazy, too. Went through a couple of napkins."

"I remember she didn't want to bus his table," Evans added. "Said he was gross."

It has to be Chris Drinker, I mean Tinker. "Thank you," Mia said. "This is really helpful. If you remember anything else, let me know. And Evans, make whatever's on the cover of that book."

He closed the book and examined the cover. "Pavlova. From New Zealand. Will do."

As Mia returned to her office, her phone pinged a text from Cammie: Pete's in my office. Made it in less than five minutes.

She found the detective on the floor under Cammie's chair, tightening the wheels with a screwdriver. "You should be good now." He rose to his feet with much creaking and groaning, taking a minute to smooth down his hair. "Oh," he said, noticing Mia and not looking very happy about it, "you're here."

"Am I interrupting something?"

Pete opened his mouth to reply, but Cammie got out a "No, it's all good" before he could say anything.

"Pete, I have a scenario I want to run by you."

He checked his watch. "Sorry, I have to—"

"Listen to what she has to say, Peter."

The tone in Cammie's voice was enough to make the detective quickly respond, "Okay, shoot."

"We have a body. We have a check." Mia paced as she talked, then stopped for dramatic effect. "What if the killer and the person who left the check are two different people? Person A killed Angie. But Person B found the body and grabbed a chance to get my father in trouble. In which case, you're looking for a murder and a . . . get-someone-in-trouble-er. I don't know what the criminal name for that is."

"False incrimination, obstruction of justice. Maybe a few others. But I gotta say, that seems far-fetched to me."

Mia was about to retort that the only reason it seemed "far-fetched" to the detective was his vendetta against his perceived competitor for Cammie's affections when Cammie stepped in again. "In case I haven't made it clear to you, Pete, I have zero interest in Ravello. I do not find him even remotely attractive, not the teeniest, weensiest, tiniest bit—"

"Okay, that's a little extreme," Mia said, feeling compelled to defend her father.

"I'm trying to get my point across to my ex here. If the universe said to me, you have to date Ravello Carina, or you'll never see another tube of Frosty Pink Passion lipstick again . . . I would say good-bye to the lipstick."

Pete gaped at Cammie. "Wow. You'd say good-bye to Frosty Pink Passion? That is some serious stuff there." He turned to Mia. "Your scenario isn't terrible. I'll look into it."

She released a breath. "Thank you." Pete bent down to tie his shoe and she mouthed a "thank *you*" to Cammie, then blew her a kiss. Cammie winked at her. The sound of conversation wafted in from the foyer. Cammie glanced in that direction. "The groupers are here."

"The who-pers?"

"I forgot to tell you, the place came with some preexisting clients. Groups that use the bridal lounge for meetings. I think it was a way for the old owner to squeeze a few bucks out of a room that sits empty a lot."

"What kind of groups?"

"A.A., Debtors Anonymous—pretty ironic, considering how Ravello got the place off a bad bet. I guess the owner didn't bother to drop in on those meetings." Cammie checked a calendar on her wall. "Right now, a pet grief support group's got the room."

"Those are all non-profit groups. They shouldn't have to pay rent."

"They'll love you for that. Usually they collect it in an old coffee can. I once had to roll two hundred pennies."

Mia left Cammie's office for the first-floor bridal lounge. She had an idea and detoured to the kitchen, where she removed the large white boxes of Danish meant for the relocated Rotary Club meeting. "Evans, would you mind putting out a coffee and tea setup in the downstairs bridal lounge?"

"No problem." Evans put down his book and got to work.

Mia carried the boxes into the bridal lounge. Around ten men and women of assorted ages were sitting on folding chairs arranged in a circle. More than a few were red-eyed and clutched tissues. "Gerald, did you want to share?" a slim woman wearing horn-rimmed glasses asked an older man in a gentle voice. Mia assumed she was the group leader.

Gerald hesitated and looked toward Mia. The others followed suit.

"Sorry to interrupt," Mia said. "We had these pastries for an event that didn't happen, and I thought you might like them. We're also setting up some coffee and tea for you."

"That's so nice," a girl about Mia's age said, then burst into tears.

"I'm so sorry, I didn't mean to upset you," Mia said, feeling terrible. "Here, have a chocolate croissant." She handed the girl the croissant, then the whole box. "Why don't you pass that around, along with the napkins?"

The box went around the circle and returned to Mia empty. Evans came in pushing a cart with carafes and coffee cups. He helped Mia distribute beverages, departing to the sound of profuse thanks from the meeting attendees. "Everyone here has suffered a loss, so a little comfort and kindness goes a long way," the group leader explained to Mia.

"Of course. And by the way, you don't have to pay rent for the room anymore, either."

Three more people joined the young girl in weeping. Even the group leader's eyes misted up. "Thank you for that, too," she said, her voice husky. "By the way, I'm Vivien T."

"Mia Ca—Mia C. And I can sympathize with all of you." She noticed an empty chair and sat down. "I have a beautiful cat, Doorstop. I call him that because he's so lazy he might as well be one. I adopted him from a shelter, so who knows what kind of life he had before I got him. I figure he's earned a rest."

"Adopt, don't shop," Vivien T. said with approval.

"But I also have—had—a parakeet." Mia's own eyes grew misty. "Pizzazz. She was a pistol, let me tell you. Chirped out songs, bossed around Doorstop."

"Did she cross the Rainbow Bridge?" Vivien asked, her voice soft, her tone caring.

"No. When I was moving back here, someone jostled me, her cage door opened, she got frightened, and flew away." Mia couldn't restrain herself any longer and burst into tears. "My poor, sweet baby."

Vivien put her arm around Mia's shoulder. "It's all right. You're with people who understand."

"I know." Mia gulped and sobbed, "Not one of you said, 'It's just a bird.'"

Mia emerged an hour later with ten new friends and a commitment to join the group. "I'm gonna call all my friends in Florida," Betty, a large woman in her sixties, promised. "I know a ton of people who retired there. We'll get the word out about Pizzazz all over the state, honey."

"Thanks, Betty," Mia sniffled, accepting Betty's hug.

The pet bereavement group left. Mia was drying her eyes with a napkin when Cammie, dressed in a workout outfit, a gym bag slung over her shoulder, appeared in the foyer. "I'm off," she said. "I'm a little worried that if I don't leave now, I'll end up clocking in a full day of work."

Mia waved her off. "Go. You got Pete to listen to me. You've earned your keep today."

Cammie was about to leave when the glass doors that fronted Belle View Banquet Manor flew open. A tall, zaftig woman dressed in a black pantsuit flecked with gold, dripping with jewelry that might or might not be costume, strode into the room. With her teased black hair and cat's-eye black eyeliner, she resembled an upscale witch. "I'm Barbara Grazio, mother of John Grazio," she announced in the gravelly register of a heavy smoker. "Which one of you is handling his wedding?"

"She is," Cammie said, and then literally raced out the door, leaving Mia face-to-face with the dreaded mother of the groom.

"He-he-hello," she stammered. "Welcome to Belle View. How can I help you?"

John Grazio's mother, a head taller than Mia—and probably half a head taller than her own son—bent down so that the two women were eye level. Mia could feel hot breath on her face. "We need to talk," the woman said, her tone ominous. "*Now.*"

Chapter Eight

Don't let her scare you, Mia thought to herself. She held the woman's glance. "Of course. It's a pleasure to meet you, Mrs. Grazio. Why don't we talk in my office?"

Mia tried to make small talk as they walked, but the imposing woman wasn't interested, responding either monosyllabically or with grunts. The news about the bachelor party debacle had obviously reached her. Mia made a mental list of the ammunition she'd need to defuse the tension—apologies, refunds, cases of the Boldano Family wines. They reached her office and she sat down behind the desk. "Mrs. Grazio, I can't tell you how sorry my father and I are about the . . . incident at your son's bachelor party."

"Oh, you mean the murder? Pfft, old news." The woman put her hands on the desk and leaned in toward Mia. "I heard a rumor that the bride's family is gonna arrive by boat, but not the groom's."

"Oh," Mia said, a little disconcerted, but relieved that a deceased call girl wasn't Barbara's biggest problem. "Alice and John only booked one boat."

"Book another."

"I'll have to run the cost by the bride and groom."

"No, you won't." Barbara Grazio reached into her designer purse, pulled out a top-of-the-line credit card, and slapped it on Mia's desk. "I want a boat. A big one. On that boat, I want some guys with trumpets playing announcement music—"

"A fanfare."

"Whatever. And I want a big corsage, one that covers my shoulder." She gestured to said shoulder. "And I want it in this color." She reached into her purse and pulled out a fabric swatch in the brightest shade of blue Mia had ever seen. "It's from the dress we buried my mother-in-law in. The dress was hideous, but I loved the color, so I snipped a swatch before they closed the coffin."

"It's . . . stunning. But it might overwhelm the bride's color scheme of peach and pearl."

"You say that like it's a problem."

"I'm also a little concerned that this color doesn't exist anywhere in nature."

"That's what the Web is for. It's in the name: *double-u, double-u*. Worldwide. So go out in the world and find it."

"O-okay."

The woman reached into her purse again. Mia flinched, afraid of what she might pull out next. Fortunately, it was only a lipstick and compact. "I'm sure I'll have other ideas," she said as she reapplied a bright shade of orangey red. "When I do, I'll need to get in touch with you."

Mia fumbled in her drawer for a business card. "Here you go. All my information is on it."

Mrs. Grazio took the card and dropped it in her

purse, along with the lipstick and compact. "One last thing."

"Yes?" Mia said, uneasy.

"After you find my flowers, I want that swatch back."

Barbara Grazio strode out of the room. Mia dropped her head on the desk. After a minute, she lifted it up and then typed two e-mails, one to Alice Paluski and one to her fiancé. She explained about the additional boat but chose not to mention the electric blue flowers in case she was able to find a substitute that would make John's gorgon of a mother happy. To her relief, the responses were a "Whatevs" from John and a "She's paying? I'm good" from Alice.

Mia considered her next move. She had no appointments scheduled for the afternoon. By now, Ravello was done with lunch at Roberto's and on his way back to Belle View. He could handle any walk-ins. She texted her father that she was leaving for the day, then biked home. After a quick shower and change of clothes, she took a cab to the Triborough Correctional Facility. Henry Marcus, the guard on duty in the visiting room, greeted her like an old friend, which at this point she was. "I heard you were back in Queens. Welcome home."

"Thanks, Henry. How's the family?"

"Good, very good. My oldest had another kid, a boy. Here." He took out his wallet. "I'm old-fashioned, I like real pictures, not ones on a phone."

Mia examined the photo of a cherubic infant. "Adorable."

"Hey, how's your father? We haven't seen him in a while."

"He's doing something different now. Running Belle View Banquet Manor."

"Keeping his nose clean, huh?" Henry held a finger to the side of his nose. "Good for him." He glanced behind Mia. "Frank brought in your brother. You've got thirty minutes. Tell Ravello I send my best. He's a good man. Always remembers us on the holidays. Even when he's not here."

"I will. And congratulations on the newest Marcus." Mia crossed to a table and took a seat across from Posi. "Hi, and no, you're still not trending."

Posi frowned and cursed, earning a finger shake from Frank, the guard who escorted him into the room. "Sorry, Frank. So, sis, what's up?"

"You know how that woman Angie came and accused Dad of owing her money for sex? Well, we had a bachelor party the other night and found her in the pop-out cake dead with a knife stuck in her."

"Go on."

"Turns out you were right about how Dad's typo took him to a bad site. I don't think he ever did anything on the site, but he was too embarrassed to admit he was considering a little online dating. Anyway, it was Angie at the bottom of the cake and not the stripper, and next to her was a check signed by Dad for a million dollars."

"Clearly a plant."

"I know so, and you know so, but tell it to Pete Dianopolis."

"Pete's an idiot but he's not an idiot. He knows. He's just being a pain in the—" Frank cleared his throat and gave Posi an admonishing look. "Tushy."

"Still, Dad's the number one suspect and I guess

I'm number two, thanks to Adam Grosso still being M.I.A. I swear, if he wasn't presumed dead, I'd kill him."

"You'd have to get in line for that honor." Posi threaded his fingers together and cracked his knuckles. "Okeydoke, let's look for other suspects. What's the deal with the staff?"

"The waitstaff was hourly hires who only came to work the parties. They all seemed fine except for this Giorgio character, who was a real—" Frank cleared his throat again. "Jerk. As to full-timers, there's Guadalupe Cruz, the head chef, and she doesn't strike me as the type who would kill and hide the body. She was in the military. I don't see her taking anyone out without a good reason, and then I see her owning what she did. Evans, the sous chef, is odd. I don't get him, but that doesn't make him a killer. Or maybe it does, I dunno. Then there's Cammie, of course, but she calls Pete when she has to kill an ant, so I don't see her taking a knife to someone."

"Okay. Let's talk guests now."

"I think the police ruled out the anniversary party guests, although there was a real estate agent there who's like the Grim Reaper of Astoria senior citizens, trying to get them to sign a sales contract with her before they croak. I can totally see her speeding up that process, but I don't know what connection she'd have to Angie."

"There might be one. It's an avenue. What about the bachelor party? Were those Queens guys? Anyone I might know?"

"John's from Bayside, not Astoria. No one looked familiar to me. They were mostly younger, mid-twenties. The only names you might know are the Koller brothers."

"From Koller Properties?"

"Yeah, John works security at their corporate head-quarters in midtown."

Posi stroked his chin. "That's interesting. Their names came up around here the other day. The city is thinking of selling this dump. Now that the Astoria and Long Island City real estate markets are so hot, the land it's parked on is worth a shi—a boatload. The Kollers are some of the people who wanna build in Queens. Dad said Belle View's got a great view. Maybe they've got their eye on it."

"That would explain why they came to the party. To check out the land and location. But what would that have to do with Angie's murder?"

"You're making me think. Too much thinking hurts my brain and then I frown, and I get lines on my face, and that's not good for my future as a hot convict."

"Sorry," Mia said, her tone dry. "I'll think for you. There's one thing I forgot to tell you. When John and this friend of his, Chris Tinker, saw Angie's body, they definitely reacted to it. Not in a 'Holy sh—'"

"Ahem," said Frank.

"Not in a 'Holy *shoot,* a dead body!' way. In a 'Holy sh-oot, we know her!' way. They denied it, but I'm pretty sure they were lying."

"Hmmm . . . The guards here took your phone when you checked in, right?"

"Yes."

Posi turned to his guard. "Hey, Frank, you mind looking something up for me?"

"Sure, no problem." Frank took out his phone.

"Type in Happy Hour Bar and Grill and tell me if there's one in midtown Manhattan."

Frank tapped on his phone. "Yup. One-fifteen and a half East Fifty-first Street."

"I thought so," Posi said. "Thanks, buddy."

"I don't know what's going on," Mia said.

"When I was starting out in the Family, Donny had me do some liquor deliveries to that particular Happy Hour Bar and Grill, which is across the street from Koller's main office. Donny had a line on a decent rum from Puerto Rico for a good price."

"You mean a fell-off-the-truck price."

"You're going off topic. Anyway, the place has a real popular bar scene, especially with people from nearby businesses like Koller. And because of that, it's full of working girls, like the late, unlamented Angie. My money's on this John and Chris knowing her from there."

"That's great stuff, Posi. I'd hug you, but I'm afraid Frank would pull his gun on me."

"That I would," Frank said, nodding. "It's my job." His phone dinged. "Hey, I just got an alert on you, Posi."

Posi put a hand on his heart. "You set an alert for me? No joke, I'm touched."

"Yeah, well, we get a lotta lowlifes here, but not a lot of celebrity lowlifes."

Posi beamed at his sister. "You hear that? I'm a celebrity." He turned his attention back to Frank. "So, what is it?"

"Something from the *Triborough Tribune*."

Mia grimaced. "Uh-oh."

Posi raised an eyebrow. "What?"

"Nothing. We had a visit from a *Trib* reporter. Daughter of a reporter who had the Family in his crosshairs. Someone named Fuoco."

"Jerry Fuoco?" Posi waved a hand dismissively. "He's been off the beat for years. I heard he passed on. Doubt his kid can make any noise. What's it say, Frank?"

The guard squinted at his phone. "I need my readers." He took a pair from an inside pocket and perched them on his nose. "'Murder at the Manor.' Hah, sounds like one of those mysteries by little old English ladies." He continued to read. "'A party entertainer was found dead inside a jump-out cake during a bachelor party being held at Belle View Banquet Manor. The manor is now under the stewardship of reputed mob lieutenant Ravello Carina, who insists the business is being run as a legitimate enterprise. Our heart goes out to the family of the late victim, Carina says. The police report that Carina, father to jailed convict Positano Carina and one-time murder suspect Messina Carina, is being cooperative with investigators.'"

Mia considered the story. "At least she used the word *reputed*. It could've been a lot worse."

"True," Posi agreed. "Frank, any chance you can share my mug shot with the hashtag, another hot convict?" The guard gave him a "you're kidding, right?" look and Posi shrugged. "Had to ask. Every missed question is a missed opportunity. Ooh, that's a good one. I gotta write it down. I'm thinking I might be a motivational speaker when I get out of here."

Frank tapped his watch. "Visit's over. Time for bye-byes."

Mia said good-bye to her brother. She promised Henry to pass on his thanks to Ravello for the baby gift he'd sent Henry's son and daughter-in-law, retrieved the personal items she had to surrender before the visit, then left the facility. Rather than call a ride service, she decided to take the subway to Ditmars Boulevard and walk home from there. Late afternoon was turning into early evening, on the cusp of rush hour. She swiped her Metro card and ran up the stairs, reaching the platform as a train pulled into the station. She jumped onto the train and managed to find the last seat on a subway car.

As the train rattled from one station to another, Mia thought about her conversation with Posi. She recalled John Grazio's obsequious behavior with the brothers Koller. Mia couldn't imagine them taking it well if they discovered their security maven was consorting with call girls. She couldn't imagine John's fiancée, Alice, taking it well either, or his horrifying mother. Mia could see a predicament like this pushing someone like John over the edge. Then there was John's friend Chris. What exactly was his story? He reminded her of the guys in high school who were all booze and braggadocio, then wound up managing a McDonald's. Noble work, to be sure, except that for them, it was less of a career choice and more of an only option.

As the subway lurched into the Ditmars stop at the Queens terminus of the N train, Mia vowed to do a little digging and see if she could uncover a secret that would drive Chris Tinker the Drinker to murder.

Chapter Nine

On the mile-long walk from the subway to her grandmother's house, Mia was distracted from analyzing potential murder suspects by the Easter decorations still clogging the tiny front yards of home after home. Her street, 46th Place, wasn't the only one where the neighbors duked it out for the honor of most over-the-top holiday outdoor décor. She passed her family church, Our Lady of Perpetual Anguish, where she'd attended school from kindergarten through eighth grade. Mia never understood why the Catholic church forced such depressing names on their parishes. Then again, she'd earned a nice chunk of change selling her "Perpetual Anguish" volleyball T-shirt on the Internet to an ironic hipster.

Mia picked up a chocolate bunny foil wrapper someone had discarded on the street and placed it in a trash can. She recalled the giant Easter baskets she'd woken up to, some her size, some even larger. Her mother, unable to let a mythical creature get credit for the huge haul of chocolate and toys, dispelled the myth of the Easter Bunny early on. *At least Mom let us have Santa,* Mia mused as she made the left onto 46th Place and trudged up the steps to her front door. *Well, until I was seven.*

She entered the two-family home's tiny vestibule and heard a cacophony of voices coming from Elisabetta's first-floor abode. She tracked the voices to the kitchen, where her *nonna* and a half-dozen friends were all talking and yelling at the same time. "What's going on?" Mia's question was lost in the Tower of Babel-like mix of English, Italian, and Greek angry sentiments and surprisingly foul language coming from the mouths of eighty-plus-year-olds. "YO!" she yelled. This silenced the room. "What's going on?" she repeated.

Nonna shook a furious fist in the air. "That *strega,* Felicity Little Miss Two Last Names, talked Andrea Skarpello into selling her house. The Giannellis, the Alexopouloses, Rose Caniglia, now Andrea? Where will it end, Mia? *Che doloro,* I won't have a friend left in the neighborhood. It'll only be coffee and high heel stores."

"Okay, I don't think there's even such a thing as a high heel store. But I'm as angry about this as you are. I'll talk to Andrea and see if I can do an end run around whatever line Felicity used to scare her into selling."

"*Grazia, bella bambina.*" Elisabetta affectionately pinched her granddaughter's checks.

"Ow."

The other *nonnas* and Greek grandmothers surrounded Mia, expressing their gratitude with hugs and more pinches. Her face was sore by the time she managed to extract herself and go upstairs to her apartment. She took off her shoes and rubbed her feet, which ached from the post-subway trek. Then she padded into the kitchen to see what she could scrounge up for dinner. Mia opened her refrigerator door to find a shelf of leftovers from Elisabetta, all in repurposed ricotta and mozzarella containers. She heated up a bowl of meatball soup in the microwave and devoured it, using a thick slab of Italian bread to sop up any liquid left in the bowl. Fortified, Mia retrieved her laptop from the bedroom and parked herself on the couch, which crunched under her as she sat down because she'd yet to remove the plastic encasing the cushions.

The laptop whirred to life. Her screensaver appeared, an image of Pizzazz staring down at Doorstop who, intimidated, was skulking away from the bird. "Pizzazz," she murmured, then forced herself to focus. She typed "Chris Tinker" into the search engine. It was a common name and a long list of possible Chris Tinkers popped up. On a whim, she typed in "Chris Drinker" and was rewarded with a page of images of John Grazio's buddy in a variety of inebriated states. She had to page through a few social media sites, but finally found contact information for him, a telephone number for the cell phone store he managed on Steinway Street.

Mia yawned, worn-out from the long, stressful day. She'd get in touch with the louche Tinker-Drinker tomorrow. The thought of a twelve-hour sleep was too appealing to pass up. She copied the Tinker-related link and sent it to her cell phone. After powering down her computer, she tapped a telephone number into her phone.

"Hi, Mia." The response came from Noah, the eight-year-old who'd lived next to her in Florida.

"Hi, Noah. I wanted to check in and see if you've seen Pizzazz."

"Nope. I seen a gator, though. It came up into the McNarys' backyard. Mrs. McNary was screaming so loud. A guy came and caught it. It was awesome."

"Cool. But no Pizzazz."

"Nuh-uh." Noah paused. "Maybe the gator ate him."

Mia scrunched up her face to banish the unpleasant image. "I hope not."

"Noah, sweetie, who's on the phone?" she heard Marie, Noah's mother, call to him.

"It's Mia," Noah called back, loud enough to make Mia's ears ring. "It's about Pizzazz."

"Again? For heaven's sake, it's just a bird."

"I heard that," Mia muttered.

"Should I tell her?" Noah asked.

"No. But thanks."

Mia ended the call with a heavy heart. She put down her phone and called up another photo on her computer screen. Pizzazz, her head tilted slightly, a mischievous look on her face, perched on the head of the small St. Valentine's statue that once decorated Mia's Palm Beach bedroom dresser. The statue had been a gift from Adam. "The patron saint of happy marriages," he'd told his thrilled wife when he presented it to her. St. Valentine's hair appeared white in the photo. Closer examination revealed the white color wasn't hair. It was Pizzazz poo. Mia had printed the photo and included it with the divorce papers she delivered to her philandering spouse.

Mia plugged her phone and computer into chargers, then slumped into the bedroom. She changed into a sleep tee, and crawled under the heavy, bright-red crushed velvet comforter that came with the bed she'd inherited from Rose Caniglia. Doorstop, sensing her sadness, leaped onto the bed and wrapped his lean body around her head. "Pizzazz isn't 'just a bird,'" Mia said to the cat as she drifted off. "She's *our* bird."

The long sleep gave Mia the energy she desperately needed. After a breakfast of leftover soup, she readied herself for the day ahead, which would include a visit to Chris Drinker during her lunch break. When she left the house, she noticed her grandmother hiding behind her Virgin Mary grotto, peering down the street with a pair of binoculars.

"Nonna? Uh, what exactly are you doing?"

"Spying on the new neighbors." Elisabetta adjusted her position. "There's a stroller, which means kids, which is a good thing. But there was a woman going over plans with a guy who looks like a contractor, and that's a bad thing. She's all thin and dressed in a nice suit with that shiny hair you see in shampoo ads. She looks like one of those City types." Elisabetta's tone dripped with scorn.

"A reminder that Queens *is* the city."

"*Vero, si.* But you know what I mean. The people who come here and rip apart the neighborhood, then flip-flop for a quick buck."

"You mean they flip the houses for profit. Let me see." Mia scampered halfway down the stoop stairs and opened the chain link gate to the front garden. She bent down next to Elisabetta behind the Virgin Mary and borrowed the binoculars. What she saw didn't please her. A definite "city type" of a woman pointing to the blueprint that a man who appeared to be a contractor was holding. The woman tossed a dismissive gesture at Rose's sturdy but unprepossessing two-family home. Mia handed the binoculars back to her grandmother. "Let's not panic . . . yet."

Mia decided to mix things up by taking the bus to work. Transportation charges were adding up and she didn't want Jamie dropping everything to chauffeur her around, which she was afraid he might do. The last thing Mia wanted was to distract him from his studies. The bus meandered its way to Belle View, passing homes that hadn't been touched in sixty years and ones gussied up by gentrifying new arrivals. The bus lumbered onto a commercial block that told the same tale. A poster slapped over the faded lettering of a butcher shop trumpeted the summer opening of a store with two words Mia never expected to see in the same sentence in Astoria: *vegan gelato.*

The bus eventually deposited her a block or so away from Belle View. When she got to the catering manor, she went straight to Ravello's office, where she found him finishing up a phone call. As she waited, she noticed a glass vase filled with an arrangement of pale lavender flowers and baby's breath on his desk. Her father must have paid a visit to his florist "friend." "Okay, Detective Hinkle," he said into the phone. Mia's stomach lurched at the word *detective.* "Thanks for the update," Ravello continued. "I appreciate it." He ended the call, got up, and came around his desk to give his daughter a kiss. "*Ciao,* sweetheart."

"What's up? Why were you on the phone with Hinkle?"

"Trying to find out if there's any new intel on the check they found with the body. Nothing yet."

"You know forensics will show that the million dollars is written in someone else's handwriting."

"Doesn't matter." Ravello gave a defeated shrug. "A guy like me, they're always gonna be looking for something."

"Well, then, boy, are they in for a disappointment when they find nothing," Mia said with vehemence.

"I'm sorry, *bella*."

"For what?"

Ravello threw his arms open. "This. All of it. I never would have dragged you back from Florida for an *incubo*, a nightmare."

"Okay, first of all, you didn't 'drag me back' from Florida. I was *so* done with that place. And second, this isn't a nightmare. I mean, it's not *not* a nightmare, but we've been through worse. You doing time, you and Mom splitting up, me and the whole Adam thing. You being framed for murder? It's nothing. Okay, maybe not nothing, but at least not something we can't get through together."

Ravello, his eyes misty, gazed at his daughter with affection. "I'm so proud of you."

"Don't be proud of me yet. Save it for when this whole . . . *incubo* . . . is over."

Mia gave her father a supportive hug, then went to her office. A red light blinked on the desk telephone, alerting her to messages. She pressed a button and played them back.

"Hello, this is Ira Metzger. We have a bar mitzvah booked for August thirteenth. I'm calling to say we won't need the facility anymore. . . ."

"Hi, we had my daughter's quinceañera scheduled for July ninth. We wanted to let you know you can release that date . . ."

"Hey there, I'm calling about the retirement party we were planning to throw on June fourteenth . . ."

Mia groaned and collapsed into her chair. Angie's murder had put a *malocchio*—a curse—on Belle View.

It took a few hours but by making a rash of promises Mia had no idea if she could make good on, she managed to save the bar mitzvah and quinceañera. As to the retirement party, it turned out the honoree had passed away in his sleep. Mia convinced the man's boss to turn the event into a celebration of his late employee's life, thus salvaging the third event. After she finished the last phone call, she leaned back and closed her eyes, exhausted. She shook it off and stood up. "I'm going to lunch," she called to her father, then realized he was probably already at Roberto's, digging into their special of the day. She factored in how long it would take by bus to get to and from the cell phone store where Chris Tinker worked and called a cab. *I really have to learn how to drive,* she thought to herself as she waited for her ride.

The cab deposited Mia in front of a store that had once been Kidz Town, a children's clothing store, and now housed an authorized dealership for a range of cell phones. She looked inside. The shop was empty of customers. Chris Tinker lolled against a counter, checking his phone. He wore a light blue polo shirt with the store's logo on the breast pocket. Mia faltered for a moment. Then she repeated a mantra that her Miami yoga instructor had her students repeat at the end of each class—*I am smart, I am strong, I am all I need to be*—and stepped inside the store. "Hi. Chris, right?"

Chris looked confused and then it came to him.

"The girl from Belle View. Sorry, I didn't recognize you right at first."

"No worries. It can be weird seeing someone out of context." Chris responded with a blank look. Mia got the feeling he had maxed out on his intellectual potential. "You mentioned at the bachelor party that you worked at this phone store."

"I did?"

"Yeah." Mia knew Chris had too few specific memories of the night to call her bluff. "I've been thinking about getting a new cell phone and thought I'd see what you're selling here."

"Cool." Chris picked up the exact phone Mia already owned. "We've got a great data plan going with the model. If you add an extra line, which you don't even have to use, you get rollover minutes that you can apply to a credit or your balance . . ."

Tinker droned on with the kind of cell-phone-sales-speak that made Mia's eyes cross. She pretended to listen and understand what he was talking about while looking for an opportunity to steer the conversation to the bachelor party. "I like the whole data thing you're talking about. I burned through a lot of it at the bachelor party, dealing with everything that was going on." Mia affected her best dim Barbie doll attitude. She leaned toward Chris and said in a stage whisper, "Can you believe what happened that night?"

Chris hesitated. Then he said, also in a stage whisper, "Can you keep a secret?" He didn't wait for Mia to nod yes. "John and me knew that chick, the one in the fake cake. We ran into her at this bar in the city—"

"Queens *is* the city."

"I'm talking about Manhattan, the real city. She came on to us and John made out with her a little—

you know, getting it out of his system before the wedding—and she invited him home with her. But when he found out she was a hooker, he passed. I mean, he's got Alice. Why pay for what you can get for free, right?"

Mia was saved from calling him out on his sexist attitude by a customer entering the store. As Chris went over to offer help, Mia was struck by his odd gait, which she hadn't noticed at the bachelor party when he was staggering drunk. He walked duck-footed, as her mother would call it, with his feet facing out at a forty-five-degree angle. Mia flashed on a memory. When she was eight, her mother enrolled her in ballet classes, which Mia loved, and beauty pageants, which she hated but Gia loved. The two extra-curriculars proved antithetical to each other because the dance classes gave her the duck-footed gait that so many ballerinas had once they got offstage, the result of spending years in first position. Since this was not the stride of a pageant winner, the ballet classes went away. Mia recalled with smug satisfaction how the pageants went away when she was eight, after she reached the end of a runway during the Little Miss Astoria contest, pulled down her pants, and mooned the audience.

While Chris waited on the customer, Mia pretended to browse. She mulled over the new information he'd shared. What if Angie approached John a second time and he didn't pass on the chance for a premarital fling? Could she have pulled a version of the stunt she tried to pull on Ravello? Coitus first with John, an unexpected bill later. Angie showed up on the same night as the bachelor party. Was that coincidence or a plan?

She wandered back to the counter, where Chris was completing a transaction. "If you're paying cash there's a five-dollar service fee on all prepaid telephone cards," he told his customer, a feral-looking guy whose twitchy behavior indicated a drug problem. Mia instantly recognized Chris's scam. Someone bought a prepaid phone card; he entered the legitimate amount into the store's system while pocketing the cash "service fee." The corporation never saw a "service fee" charge to question and the clients doing business in cash weren't the type to ask questions. She knew several Family wannabes who had run this racket, "service fee-ing" themselves into designer duds and pricey wheels. Higher-ups like her father didn't take too kindly to these low-levels blatantly bilking the poor.

A new angle to Angie's murder occurred to her. Being that Angie was a lady of the evening, Mia assumed she ran an all-cash business. What if she'd tried to buy a phone card from Chris, caught on to what he was doing and one grifter to another, demanded a piece of the action to keep her mouth shut?

Chris's dubious customer darted out of the store and he turned his attention back to Mia. "So, where were we? Would you like to continue this conversation over lunch? I can hang up the CLOSED sign and we can go over to Roberto's Trattoria. They have great daily specials. A daily special for a girl who's special daily." Chris punctuated this lame line with a suggestive grin and a wiggle of his eyebrows.

"I know Roberto's. My father eats lunch there every day. Maybe you've met him. Ravello Carina?"

Chris's eyebrows froze, and his grin disappeared. "You're—you're—Ravello Carina's daughter?"

Mia flashed an angelic smile. "Yes. He's Belle View's new owner and my very overprotective daddy."

Beads of sweat sprouted on Tinker's forehead. "Uh . . ." He typed away furiously on a computer. Mia peeked and noticed he wasn't even writing actual words. "Hey, I found a great special. The phone is free, and so is everything that comes with it. You can't beat that, huh? Please tell me you can't beat that."

A half hour later, Mia ambled toward the exit carrying two bags that included a new phone plus every available accessory; she didn't even know what some of them did. "Thanks, Chris. Oh, and you might want to knock off that 'service fee' scam of yours. My father wouldn't be too happy about it." She left the store before Chris could respond.

Mia decided she'd earned herself a treat. She popped into La Guli Pasticceria, a Ditmars Boulevard institution. She was enveloped by the scents of sugar, vanilla, anise, chocolate, and a dozen other delicious pastry aromas as soon as she stepped inside. Each scent brought back memories of every family event she went to before moving to Palm Beach; all featured an array of La Guli's delicious Italian sweets.

"Ciao, Mia," Julie, the woman behind the counter greeted her. Julie, a buxom woman in her sixties, had been filling the Carina family's orders and stomachs for decades. "Welcome home. What can I get you?"

"Ciao, Julie. Let me see. So many choices." Mia perused the dark wooden cases, original to the eighty-plus-year-old store. They were filled with a dazzling assortment of cookies and pastries: biscotti, butter, pignoli, and tri-color cookies, sfogliatelle,

mille foglie, and of course, cannoli shells, some
dipped in chocolate, some not, all waiting to be filled
with sweet, fresh ricotta cream and dotted with tiny
chocolate chips. "Let me have a cookie assortment to
bring back to Belle View. And a cannoli for me."

"You got it." Julie pulled out an empty cannoli
shell and piped it full of filling. She dipped the ends
into chocolate chips, then handed the cannoli to
Mia, who bit into it. Heaven. "I heard your dad took
over Belle View. That's a very, very good thing."

Something about the way Julie said this sent an
alert to Mia. "I think so, but I'm his daughter. Why
do you?"

"The guy who he got it from? Bad news. His name
was Boris or Bouras or something. My cousin went to
an event there, a twenty-first birthday party, and she
said the guy was a lowlife who was running the place
into the ground. Of course, being that it was a twenty-
first birthday party, everyone was too blasted to notice.
But my cousin, she noticed. Anyway, we're all glad it's
back in good hands."

"Thanks, Julie. What do I owe you?"

"Nothing. Consider it a business-warming present."

Mia was about to argue when her cell phone rang.
She hastily ate the last bite of cannoli, then dug her
phone out of her purse. She recognized Guadalupe's
number. "Hi, what's up?"

"You need to get back to Belle View." Guadalupe's
voice sounded strained. "The police are here. They
cornered Giorgio, who stopped by to pick up his
check."

"I'm on my way."

Mia thanked Julie, grabbed the cookie assortment,
and typed in a rideshare request as she raced out

the door. When she got to the catering hall, she ran inside and was greeted by the sight of Detectives Dianopolis and Hinkle leading a handcuffed Giorgio out of the main kitchen. He looked more angry than terrified, and Mia got the feeling this wasn't the first time he'd found himself in cuffs. "I told you a million times, I didn't kill the chick."

Dianopolis snorted. "You're in the system, Giorgio. We got your prints on the check. Seems to me like you did it, right, Hinkle?"

"Right," Hinkle said through a yawn.

"Close the book, my friend Giorgio, 'cuz that's all she wrote," Pete said. "Ooh, good line. I gotta put it in one of my mysteries."

"No, no, you're wrong," Giorgio insisted. "Yeah, I tried to frame Carina, but I swear on my own grave, I did not kill that girl."

"Lucky for you, they axed the death penalty in this state. But my partner and I have made our peace with that. We'll be happy with a nice life sentence without the possibility of parole."

Now Giorgio looked terrified.

Chapter Ten

Mia stepped aside to let the detectives pass with their charge. Then she ran into the kitchen, where she found Guadalupe and Evans.

"Are those from La Guli?" Guadalupe asked. She took the assortment from Mia and ripped open the cellophane. "Excellent. I need to do some stress eating."

"And here's a new cell phone," Mia said. "I'm fine with the one I have. Take whatever you want." She emptied the bags from Chris's store onto the counter. "Tell me everything that happened."

"Like the detective said, Giorgio was already in the system," Guadalupe said, her mouth stuffed with cookies.

"Yes. Pick up the story from there."

"They took him into your father's office, which backs up against the wall next to the oven, so I can hear everything."

"If she holds a cup to the wall and listens through it," Evans chimed in. He held up a phone accessory. "I need a new case. Can I have this?"

"All yours."

"I'll take the phone," Guadalupe said. She opened the box and looked inside. "Oooh, it's rose gold. Pretty. Where were we?"

"Holding a cup to the wall," Mia prompted, "You heard everything. Then what?"

"Giorgio told the cops that our man Cody asked him to make sure the stripper was in the pop-out cake, and when he looked inside it, he saw Angie. He figured out she was dead and saw an opportunity to frame your dad."

Mia scrunched her face, trying to make sense of what she was hearing. "Why? Why would he want to frame Dad?"

"Turns out Giorgio is the nephew of Andre Bouras," Evans said. "The guy who had to give up this place to your dad as payment for some serious gambling debts."

Her face cleared. "Ah. Giorgio was trying to get revenge on his uncle's behalf."

Guadalupe nodded. "He ran down to Ravello's office and found a check Ravello had signed but not filled out. He wrote in a number, then dropped it in the cake next to Angie."

Note to self: get a better lock for Dad's door. Second note to self: tell Dad never, ever do that check thing again. And possibly have him tested for early onset dementia.

"Plus," Guadalupe continued, "it also turns out Giorgio has a rap sheet. Small stuff, shoplifting, disorderly conduct. But it put him in the system."

Third note to myself: never take another employee recommendation from the catering place that recommended Giorgio.

"So," Guadalupe said, "the police came, then left with Giorgio. I guess that's it. Murder solved."

"Right."

Guadalupe eyed her. "You don't sound convinced."

Mia sighed. She picked up a chocolate biscotti, put it down, then picked it up again. "Since I touched it, I guess I have to eat it." She took a bite and chewed. Guadalupe poured her a glass of milk and she took a few sips. "Here's the thing. I've spent my whole life watching people lie. My father, my brother, their friends, their 'associates,' other relatives. This has given me kind of a superpower to separate lies from the truth. The cops were bringing Giorgio out when I was coming in. I heard them say they had his prints on the check, which was stupid on his part, but makes sense if a person makes an impulse move to frame someone. But I didn't hear the cops say anything about his prints on the knife—you know, the murder weapon. Giorgio thought to wipe off the weapon and then blew it by not doing the same for the check? While I'm happy to see the heat off my father, any halfway decent lawyer will point out that this is a big hole in the police's case. Giorgio said he dropped the check in the cake to get back at my dad and denied killing Angie. I think he was telling the truth when he said both those things."

Guadalupe and Evans exchanged a look. "Then if Giorgio isn't the killer," Guadalupe said, "who is?"

Mia threw up her hands. "I wish I knew. Because as soon as Giorgio's released for lack of evidence, the heat is right back on my father."

Mia ended the day with a win, locking down a lavish engagement party. But with the cloud of what she considered an unsolved murder hanging over Belle View, she couldn't enjoy the booking. She went into the kitchen for a comfort snack and found one pignoli nut cookie left from the La Guli assortment. Clearly, she wasn't the only employee who felt a need to self-soothe with food.

She left the catering hall and economized by taking the bus home. It dropped her at the corner of her street. But rather than go to Elisabetta's, Mia took a detour down the street to Andrea Skarpello's house. She rang the doorbell and saw an eyeball through the peephole. There was the familiar sound of a half-dozen locks being unlocked. Then Andrea threw open the front door.

"Glykiá píta!" Andrea said, which Mia remembered translated to "sweetie pie."

"Come in, come in." The 46th Place residents had a habit of offering this invitation twice, possibly because they assumed their elderly neighbors didn't hear it the first time.

Mia took Andrea up on her invitation and followed her down a short hallway, then through the living room. "I'm so sorry about Stavros. He was a lovely man."

"Thank you, sweetie. I hoped we'd see our sixtieth anniversary together, but that wasn't God's plan." They arrived in the kitchen and Andrea motioned to Mia to take a seat at the room's small table. "Your *nonna* said you might stop by, so I made spanakopita and baklava."

Andrea pulled a baking pan of spanakopita out of her circa 1970s avocado green oven and cut a large slice that she placed in front of Mia. Mia took a forkful of the spinach and feta pie. The crispy phyllo dough crumbled in her mouth. "Amazing," she said.

"It's nice to have a visitor," Andrea said. "I miss

that." The widow's tone was wistful, her loneliness palpable. Her children had dispersed to other parts of the country, with one son posted to Japan through his job in the State Department. Elisabetta had told Mia that Andrea moving in with any of them wasn't an option, at least not at the moment.

"Didn't you have a couple living upstairs?"

"They saved and bought a place in Jersey." Andrea took Mia's empty plate and replaced it with a plate of fresh baklava. Mia vowed to increase her bicycling to burn off the calories she was enjoying, courtesy of Andrea.

The older woman sat down across from her. She put an elbow on the table and rested her chin on her hand. "Such a lovely couple they were. I felt safe with them here. Now, it's not the same."

"It's a wonderful space, Andrea. You could find another great tenant. Wouldn't that be better than uprooting your whole life?"

"I don't know. The real estate lady had a point when she said I'm—"

"Not getting any younger," Mia chorused with her.

"It's true."

"Nobody is. You're not, I'm not, the real estate lady isn't. Unfortunately, we can't age backward."

"It's so quiet here now. At least in assisted living, there'd be people around. Until they die. But then, new people come in. Rotate out, rotate in."

Mia put her fork down on her second empty plate of the night. "Andrea, please don't do anything yet. I'm going to find you a great tenant. Give me a little time because I have to solve a murder first—"

"I understand."

"But then I am all about keeping you on this block."

"*Eísai énas ángelos pou stálthike apó ton ouranó.* You're an angel sent from heaven." This effusive statement was accompanied by a hug and the requisite cheek pinches.

Mia left with spanakopita and baklava in a to-go container, which was de rigueur on 46th Place. To send a guest off without a healthy second meal of leftovers was considered terrible form. As she walked down Andrea's steps, she noticed the slim, well-dressed woman she'd seen before at Rose's old house, deep in conversation with a workman. *Time to meet the new neighbors and maybe welcome them with Andrea's delicious food,* Mia thought. She crossed the street and waited politely while the woman and workman completed their conversation. He got into a pickup truck and drove off; the woman turned her attention to her phone.

Mia stepped forward. "Hi, I'm Mia Carina. I live up the street."

The woman looked up. "Hi. If you're worried about construction noise, we have a permit for work to take place from seven A.M. to four P.M. We'll respect those hours." She flashed a dismissive smile, then refocused on her phone.

Mia steamed at the woman's attitude but remained polite. "Thank you for that."

"Is there something else?" The fake cordiality was gone, replaced by full-on annoyance.

Mia extended the leftover container. "I thought you might like a treat. Homemade spanakopita and baklava from Andrea, who lives across the street. Sort of a 'welcome to the neighborhood' gift."

The woman gaped at Mia, then laughed. "Oh, you think *I'm* the one moving in here." She raised her hands and shook them as if warding off germs. "No, no, no. I'm the interior designer. I live in NoMad. That's in the city. It means North of Madison." The woman said this slowly, as if Mia might be mentally challenged.

"Queens *is* the city and I know what NoMad means." Mia said this through gritted teeth. "I hope whoever *is* moving in here shows up with a lot less attitude."

She stomped back across the street and up the block to Nonna's house. When she got inside, she slammed the front door behind her, eliciting a startled cry from Elisabetta and an equally startled bark from Hero. Her grandmother came into the vestibule. "*Ma, cosa sta succedendo?* What's happening?"

"The and-it-rhymes-with-witch across the street is not our new neighbor, thank God. She's the new owner's interior designer and a total horror." Mia handed Elisabetta the container of leftovers. "Here. From Andrea."

"You stopped by and talked to her. *Va bene.* That's my baby girl."

Elisabetta reached up to pinch Mia's cheek, but she pulled back. "No more tonight. I need to let the bruises from Andrea's pinching heal."

Her grandmother cast an angry look past her, to the street. "Interior designer," she said in a mocking tone. "Design *this.*" She shook a fist in the direction of the new neighbors, then brought her other hand down on the crook of her elbow in a karate chop gesture that was the Italian equivalent of flipping someone off with a middle finger. "I bet whoever bought Rose's place is gonna 'fix it up,' then sell it for more money. I'm telling you, the crummiest building in Astoria is worth a fortune to some developer. They knock it down and throw up these 'luxury apartments' no one here could ever afford. Your father's lucky Belle View's still standing. With those views, I'm surprised there's not a load of condos sitting on that land, even if your backyard is the LaGuardia runway."

"Nonna, your blood pressure. You need to calm down."

"I know. I'm gonna take a shot of Amaretto. You want some?"

"No, thanks. It's been a long day. I'm gonna go upstairs and chill before I go to bed."

Mia kissed her grandmother and went upstairs to her apartment, almost tripping over Doorstop, who was in the doorway living up to his name. She fed the cat, changed into her jammies, then collapsed on the couch. She'd inherited a TV from Rose Caniglia, a twenty-year-old model that came with a remote and not much else. Mia put on the show she usually unwound to, a reality mash-up of travel and real estate that let her armchair-travel all over the world. However, given the current real estate turmoil of 46th Place, Mia didn't find the show relaxing and she switched it off.

She rested her head on an ugly decorative pillow that came with the couch and replayed her conversation with Elisabetta. She didn't think her grandmother was exaggerating when she said the Belle View land was worth a fortune. If, as Posi said, the Koller brothers were sniffing around the Triborough Correctional Facility, which was in a much less scenic part of town, the thought of what they could park on the catering hall's property would make them salivate.

Could Angie's murder somehow be tied to a real estate deal?

A few hours later, Mia woke up on the couch in the same position where she'd passed out. Her cell phone rang loudly and insistently. She turned it off and rolled over, too tired to move into the bedroom. Suddenly, the landline Nonna insisted on keeping let loose with a loud, even more insistent ring. She exclaimed a few choice words as she got up and marched to the phone. "*What?* And if this is a telemarketer, I swear, I will hunt you down."

"It's your father."

"Dad." Mia's tone instantly switched to apologetic. "Sorry." She noticed the time on Rose's dusty old cuckoo clock. "Why are you calling me at one-fifteen in the morning? What's wrong?"

"Bad news," her father said. His voice sounded husky. "There's been a fire at Belle View."

Chapter Eleven

The cab Ravello sent for his daughter arrived moments after she threw on jeans and a T-shirt. Fire engines were parked at the front of the catering hall, so the cab driver dropped Mia off in the parking lot. Mia was overcome with relief to see the building still standing, but the air was acrid with the scent of smoke. She looked around for her father but didn't see him. A few firemen were next to the hook and ladder truck winding up hoses. "Is it safe to go inside?" Mia asked.

"Yeah, the fire was contained to the back of the kitchen," one responded.

Mia dashed into Belle View and ran to the kitchen, where she found Ravello talking to the fire captain. "Dad," she said, going to him. The two hugged. She stepped back and surveyed the room. There was a hole big enough to fit a man where a wall used to be. In the distance, Mia could see the blinking lights of the LaGuardia runway. The stove next to the new hole seemed to have sustained the second-most amount of damage in the room. The fire had spread to it, igniting the grease trap. The smell of burnt, rancid grease made Mia's eyes water. She realized Ravello was talking to her and forced herself to focus.

". . . So he basically saved the place."

"Sorry, Dad, I missed that."

"I was saying that Evans was just leaving when the fire broke out. He called it in and then battled it with a couple of our extinguishers."

"Thank God for that. But what was he doing here so late?"

"All he said was he had to finish some stuff. I don't care. He's a hero."

"Where is he? I'd like to thank him."

Ravello glanced around. "He's not here? I guess he took off."

"We've got an investigation team on the way, but I'm not putting myself on the line when I say that if this isn't arson, I should turn in my badge," the captain said. "I have some paperwork I need you to fill out."

"We can't do it in my office," Ravello said. "It's too close to the fire and reeks."

"Try my office," Mia said. "Maybe the smoke didn't get that far."

Ravello took the captain to her office. Mia stayed behind. She pulled a dish towel out of a drawer and held it over her mouth as she opened the kitchen windows. She did the same for every window in Belle View. She found a few large fans in a storage facility attached to the side of the building and dragged them inside, positioning each one so it blew any lingering smoke out of the building and into the chill of the night air. Then she went to her office.

The captain was gone, but Ravello was still seated behind her desk. He was on his phone. "That's great,

Tulio, I appreciate it. . . . Sure, I'll be here at seven. I don't know if I'm even gonna go home."

Mia took the phone from her father. "Hi, Tulio, this is Ravello's daughter, Mia. He won't be here at seven because he'll be getting some much-needed sleep—" She held up a hand to quell her father's protest. "But I'll be here. What will I be here for?"

"Oh." The man on the other end sounded nervous. "I'm uh, a friend of your father. I owe him a couple of favors. I'm gonna have a crew there in the morning to fix your kitchen wall. And, uh, there's another friend of your dad's who owes him a favor. He'll be dropping off a new stove. We'll hook it up for you. You should be up and running again in a day or two, once the plasterwork on the new wall dries."

"That's fantastic, Tulio. My dad and I are very grateful to you."

"Oh boy, I sure hope so." Tulio didn't sound any less nervous. "Tell your dad if he needs anything else, I am here for him. Very, very here for him."

"I will." Mia ended the call and handed the phone back to her father. "Wow, he must owe you a bundle."

"Oh yeah. What he's doing for us'll put a dent in it. A small one." Ravello rubbed his eyes and sighed. "I'm starting to think I had it easier running games for the Family."

"No!" Mia practically yelled this at her father. "You are *not* going back to that. We're gonna make this work or die trying."

"Came close to that tonight," Ravello said, his expression wry.

"It's a figure of speech. Luckily, we don't have any midweek events. If what Tulio told me holds, the kitchen should be functional again by the weekend when we really need it. In the meantime, if anything comes up, we can improvise in the upstairs secondary kitchen. Now go home. Get sleep. I'm gonna spend the night here."

This energized Ravello. He stood up and slammed his fists on the desk. *"Non c'è modo all'inferno!* No way is that happening! What kind of father do you think I am, leaving my daughter alone in a dangerous place like this?"

"The kind of father who recognizes that his daughter is a mature, grown woman who can take care of herself!"

The two stubborn Carinas faced off, each refusing to budge. Ravello broke first. "Fine. But not until I make a call."

"Are you comfortable? You don't look it." Mia addressed this to Jamie Boldano who, a half-hour after the call from Ravello, was stretched out on an improvised bed made of couch pillows on the floor next to the bridal lounge daybed where Mia lay. The room was dark, lit only by ambient light coming from the LaGuardia facilities.

"I'm fine." Two pillows separated as Jamie switched positions. He shoved them back together.

"Again, you really don't have to do this."

"I was afraid your father would hurt me if I didn't." Jamie said this with a chuckle. "He may be a legit businessman these days, but he's still pretty intimidating."

"That may come in handy if any of our customers

try to welch on their bills." Mia pulled the plaid afghan that was meant for decoration up to her chin. "Are you cold? Do you want me to close the windows?"

"I'm good," Jamie said. "I like the air. You can't smell the smoke."

Mia wrinkled her nose. "That smell is so hard to get rid of. Why did someone do this? Were they sending a message? Or did they want to burn the place down?"

"I honestly don't know. Do you think it's related to the murder?"

"Absolutely. Look at what we grew up with—the Life. A murder at a place, a fire at the same place. When would those two things not be related?"

"Never."

"Exactly." Mia said this with emphasis. "It lets Giorgio off the hook, the waiter the police arrested for the call girl's murder. He's sitting at Rikers right now, waiting for his arraignment."

"What's the deal with that Evans guy?" Jamie asked. "What was he doing here so late?"

"My dad was vague about that. Evans is a weird guy, but he doesn't seem dangerous or anything. Still, who knows anymore?" Mia pondered the latest turn of events. "I think it's all about this place. Not the building, the land it's sitting on."

"It's the land, Scarlett, the land," Jamie intoned.

"Huh?" Mia, confused, sat up. "What is that? And why are you talking with a Southern accent?"

"It's from the movie *Gone with the Wind*."

"Never saw it."

"Scarlett's dad says it to her when she disses the family land. He says it's the only thing worth fighting and dying for because it's the only thing that lasts."

"Hmmm . . ." Mia thought about this. "Maybe it's also worth killing for."

"Maybe."

The two lapsed into a companionable silence. "Remember our sleepovers when we were little?" Mia said after a minute.

"Are you kidding? They were some of the most fun times of my childhood. My favorites were when we pitched my Cub Scout tent in the backyard and pretended we were camping in the wilderness."

"With your mother yelling to us every ten minutes, 'You okay?' And your father yelling at her, 'Leave 'em alone, they're playing!'"

"Then he'd order food and have a guy deliver it to us in the tent." The two laughed at the memory. "And we'd get bored and yell to my mother to bring us my computer. When the battery died, Dad would run an extension cord to the patio outlet, and we'd watch videos until we fell asleep."

"Sometimes I miss how easy life was as a kid."

"Selective memory."

"Uh-oh, here comes your psych degree again."

"Seriously. We handpick our memories and archive the ones we don't want to dwell on. They're not gone, they're tucked away."

"I know. Like the times your father wasn't around to order us food because he was off doing business. Or doing time. Like my dad." They lapsed into silence again, both dwelling on the more painful memories of their childhoods. Jamie yawned. "You yawned," Mia said. "Go to sleep."

"I'm not tired."

"Yes, you are. So am I. I'll go to sleep if you will."

"Deal. 'Night, Mia."

"'Night, Jamie."

Within minutes, the rhythmic sound of Jamie's breathing indicated he'd fallen asleep. Mia, however, was wide awake. She kept hearing Jamie's words: "'It's the land, Scarlett, the land.'" The more she analyzed the recent dire events, the more it looked like the real estate developer Koller brothers might be the connecting link between Angie's death and the fiery attack on Belle View. She needed to pay the brothers a visit and see if she could ferret anything useful out of them. Mia feared Belle View might not survive the wrong turns and glacial pace of the police investigation, now complicated by an added arson investigation. She'd call the Koller office in the morning and make an appointment with Bradley and Kevin, using the ruse of pitching the brothers on hosting future events at Belle View.

Satisfied with her plan and feeling safe with Jamie at her feet, Mia fell asleep.

When she woke up in the morning, Jamie was gone. A wave of insecurity washed over her, but Mia remembered that he had an early class and assumed he didn't want to wake her up. She showered in the lounge's shower and changed into clothes she found in one of the room's drawers. Cammie had told her that bridal parties often left stray pieces of clothing that the Belle View staff washed and folded, then packed away until it was claimed. Few items ever were, so Mia was able to dig out clean undergarments and jeans. The only shirt that fit was one that said I LOST MY MONEY AND LUNCH IN VEGAS. She hoped the day didn't bring any drop-in potential customers.

Mia went downstairs. The first item on her agenda was calling Belle View's small staff of full-timers and letting them know they had the day off. She left a message for Evans. When she told Guadalupe what happened to her kitchen, the chef vowed to water-board the perpetrator. "You thought I was coming in?" said Cammie. "That's adorable."

Once this task was completed, she turned her attention to setting up a meeting at Koller Properties. She located a telephone number through an Internet search and pressed it into her cell phone. After navigating a hellacious list of voice commands, she finally reached a human being who put her through to Bradley Koller's assistant. "Bradley Koller's office," a voice chirped on the other end of the line.

"Yes, hello, my name is Mia Carina. I'm the assistant general manager at Belle View Banquet Manor. Mr. Koller and his brother were here the other evening for an event, and I'd like to set up a meeting to discuss the possibility of utilizing our facility for a future Koller event." *I sound so professional,* Mia bragged to herself.

"Thank you, but we're not interested." The assistant hung up on Mia.

Mia uttered a frustrated exclamation. Then she redialed, once again working her way through the voice commands.

"Bradley Koller's office."

"Yes, hi, this is Mia Carina. We were just speaking. We got disconnected."

"I'm sorry, we don't take solicitations over the telephone." The call ended.

Mia let a string of cuss words fly. Then she punched

in the telephone number, muttering a profanity with each stop at the voice commands.

"Bradley Koller's office."

"Ravello Carina, *my father,* would really like to see a meeting with Bradley and Kevin Koller happen."

There was a pause at the other end of the line. "How's one this afternoon?"

"Perfect."

This time Mia had the satisfaction of ending the call.

Chapter Twelve

The Koller meeting set, Mia sat back in her office chair and debated what to wear. The goal was to sell herself as a hip, upscale businesswoman. If the brothers had any suspicions about an ulterior motive for the appointment, it would be rendered useless.

She did a quick mental inventory of her wardrobe and decided a shopping trip was in order. Mia walked through Belle View to make sure no one else was there, and locked up the building, hoping both that and her father's mafioso reputation would deter miscreants from finding their way into the catering hall through the large hole in the kitchen. Then she took a cab to Steinway Street. The one positive of gentrification was that a couple of high-end clothing and shoe stores had sprouted up in the Astoria business district. She went into a store that once housed a video rental business and now sold the kind of outfits that transformed a Queens girl like Mia into a trendy Manhattanite until she opened her mouth and honked out a few sentences in her distinctly outer-borough accent.

Within an hour, Mia had outfitted herself in a

form-fitting button-down white shirt, a navy blazer, and slim-fit pants in a subtle navy and dark gold pattern. She finished the look with platformed black pumps that were stylish, yet comfortable. Mia used her phone to transfer funds from her dwindling savings account to her debit card and paid for her purchases. She noticed a text from the DJ who'd worked John Grazio's bachelor party. "Hi. Wondering about my check." Mia slapped her forehead. She'd forgotten to pay him that night. She texted him back. "So so sorry. I'll get it to you ASAP." DJ sent her back a thumbs-up and smiley face. Mia relaxed. At least something could be solved with relative ease.

A Prius with the Pick-U-Up magnetic logo on its door stopped in front of the coffee shop and dislodged a passenger. Mia smiled when she saw the driver was Jamie. "Hey," she called to him, and waved.

Jamie's face lit up. "Hey." Mia walked over to the car. "I was going to call you and check in. See how you're doing. You look great."

"Thanks. You think I look good enough to impress the Koller brothers?"

"The Koller brothers?"

"I set up a meeting with them on the pretext of pitching Belle View as a party venue for them. What I really want to do is see if I can suss out any dirt on development plans they might have for the neighborhood." Jamie opened his mouth to speak. "Don't you dare do that thing where you tell me to be careful and not do something dangerous. I'm a thirty-one-year-old woman who survived a cheating husband, the investigation into the disappearance of same cheating husband, and a couple of hurricanes, so I think I can take care of myself." She took a breath.

Jamie smiled. "I was gonna offer you a ride into Manhattan."

"Oh. I'll take it."

As usual, Jamie's front seat was covered with textbooks, so Mia climbed in the back seat. Her phone rang. She didn't recognize the number but took the call. "Hello?"

"This is Barbara Grazio. John's mother."

Mia stifled a groan. "Hi, Mrs. Grazio. How can I help you?"

"I haven't heard back from you about the blue flowers. I need to see a sample."

"Yes, of course. I'm working on it and hope to have that sample for you by tomorrow. I'll text you as soon as I get it."

"Do that," the woman said, and ended the call.

"I saw your face in the rearview mirror," Jamie said. "What was that about?"

"The mother of a groom, and she is the *worst*. You've heard of a bridezilla? This woman is a groom's-mother-zilla. I don't think I've ever met a needier person in my life. You'd think she was the one getting married. Cammie warned me. She said, make the groom's mother happy. Then she cut and ran."

"Weddings can be hard on a groom's family. They're more tolerated than embraced. If this woman's Italian—"

"Oh, she's Italian. *Molto, molto Italiana.*"

"You know us Italians love our weddings. Maybe she doesn't have a daughter. Or the groom is an only child. This is her one chance to shine in a big way. The more she can celebrate and feel like an important part of the event, the easier it is to accept that there's another woman in her son's life. One who's meant to supplant her."

Mia was awed by Jamie's insights. For a reason she couldn't explain, she choked up. "James Francis Boldano," she said, her voice thick. "You're gonna make the best effing therapist in the world."

"I need to pontificate around you more often," Jamie said with a grin.

"To be honest, I'm not sure what that means, but go for it." Mia's phone rang again. "Oh, please don't be groom's-mother-zilla again." She looked at the number. "It's not. Phew. Hello?"

She heard a man's voice. "Yeah, is this the number to call about the missing bird?"

"Yes," Mia said, excited. "Yes, it is. You found her?"

"Yeah. I saw your flyer. And then this little bird flew by. You still offering a reward?"

"Yes." Now Mia was wary. "I want to confirm you have the right bird. Green with a yellow head?"

"That's it."

"Liar!" she yelled into the phone. "Pizzazz was—is—yellow with a green head. What kind of human being are you, scamming someone who lost a beloved pet? You can go straight to—hello? They hung up." Mia slammed her phone on the seat and wiped away a few angry tears.

Jamie shot her a dark look and muttered a few choice descriptions of the scammer. "I'm tempted to call one of my dad's goons and have him track down whoever was on the other end of that call."

"You're so sweet. Believe me, the thought crossed

my mind. But we can't go there. Once we do, we can never come back."

"You'll find Pizzazz, Mia."

"I hope so. But I'm beginning to think I may not." Tears bubbled over her lower eyelids. She pulled a tissue from her purse and blotted them away.

Jamie glanced at her through the rearview mirror, his gaze filled with compassion. "Should I put on some music?"

"Thank you, I'd like that."

Jamie put on a soft rock station, which played comforting classic hits as they crossed over the Queensboro Bridge into Manhattan. He deftly navigated midtown traffic and pulled up in front of the Koller Properties headquarters, a dull office tower on Third Avenue in the Fifties. "I'm sorry, I can't pick you up. I have stuff going on tonight."

"Please, don't worry about it. I can get myself home." Mia started to unbuckle her seat belt. She paused. "Jamie . . . does your father have people looking into what's going on at Belle View? My dad may be running the place, but it's still a Boldano Family business."

Jamie sighed. "My dad stopped talking to me about family business once I told him I wasn't going into it. Not to be mean, to protect me. What I don't know can't hurt me. I'm sure he's got people keeping an eye on what goes on at Belle View. But that's because he has to keep it a clean operation. The Feds are always breathing down his neck. They can't wait to throw him back in jail, and the rest of the Family with him. Dad needs Belle View to stay legit. If there's any hint of involvement . . ."

Mia finished his sentence. "It's over."

"Yup."

Mia resumed unbuckling her seat belt. "This meeting better pay off." She got out of the car and waved Jamie off, then turned to face the Koller building. Mia closed her eyes and murmured a mantra a new age-y friend once shared with her to help overcome stress: *I am having a safe, uneventful journey.* Whether the journey was physical or emotional, Mia discovered repeating the simple sentence a few times did create a sense of calm. She threw her shoulders back and marched into the building, hoping she exuded a confidence she didn't fully feel.

The lobby, whose salmon-colored marble walls, floor, and ceiling were meant to convey luxury, felt oppressive. Mia approached a uniformed guard sitting behind a gilded rococo station that would have been at home with Rose Caniglia's gaudy furnishings. "Hello. I have an appointment with Bradley and Kevin Koller."

"Sign in and I need to see ID."

Mia signed in and handed the guard her Florida ID card. The guard, who looked like a former drill sergeant, eyed it suspiciously. "I don't drive," Mia explained. "And I only moved back to New York a couple of weeks ago."

The guard passed the ID card through a scanner. A few beeping noises later, a machine produced a nametag featuring Mia's ID photo. He attached it to a lanyard. "Fifty-third floor. Second elevator bank. Swipe this over there," he said, pointing to a row of what looked like subway turnstiles. "Then wear it during your stay here."

"Yes, sir." Mia suppressed the urge to salute him.

She approached the turnstiles and followed the guard's instructions. The turnstile arms retracted and an elevator in the second bank opened its doors to her. Mia stepped into an elevator decorated with hints of salmon-colored marble and was whisked to the fifty-third floor, where the elevator doors opened onto a reception area covered in . . . salmon-colored marble. *Italy must have sacrificed an entire mountain for this place,* Mia thought as she stepped off the elevator. She approached a receptionist wearing a headset. "Hello, I'm Mia Carina," she said in her most officious voice. "I have an appointment with Bradley and Kevin Koller."

The receptionist, a well-dressed woman in her forties with a demeanor as cold as the building's omnipresent marble, spoke into her headset. "Their one o'clock is here." She addressed Mia. "You can take a seat over there. An assistant will be with you in a minute."

Mia took a seat on one of the creamy leather couches the receptionist pointed to. She sat all the way back. The couch was so deep her feet dangled over the edge, half a foot off the floor. Feeling like a kid at the grown-up's table, she perched on the edge of the couch, firmly planting her feet on the marbled floor. An impossibly thin and tall woman in her late twenties walked down the hallway toward her. To Mia's horror, she saw that they were wearing the same blazer. She pulled hers off and slung it over her arm. "Mia?" the woman said. She managed a condescending smile that reeked of doing Mia a favor.

"Yes, hi," Mia responded, standing up.

"We spoke on the phone. The Kollers are ready to see you."

The young woman led Mia through a maze of cubicles to a giant conference room with a spectacular view across the East River to Long Island City and beyond. Mia could see a plane taking off from LaGuardia Airport. "I can practically see where I work from here," she said, awed by the panoramic vista.

The assistant didn't respond and departed without bothering to introduce herself. Left alone, Mia went over her game plan. Small talk first—lots of flattery, apologies for the "terrible event" at Belle View, a segue into gossip about the murder, where she hoped to catch a flicker of guilt on either of the Kollers' faces. Then a pitch for Belle View—because if neither Koller was a killer, it wouldn't hurt having them as clients. The office wall was glass and Mia could see the brothers approaching. She noted how Kevin resembled an off-brand version of his older brother; a few inches shorter and a few pounds heavier, with the same sandy, thinning hair, but less of it. However, their facial expressions were an exact match. They wore the same smug, arrogant looks on their faces that Mia remembered from the bachelor party.

Since they were sans nameless assistant, she put her blazer back on. "Hello. Thank you so much for meeting with me," Mia said with a bright smile. She stood up and extended her hand, taking turns shaking with each brother. Both offered limp, slightly clammy grips. The three took seats around the coffee table. "First of all, I can't tell you how thrilled we were that the Koller brothers were at our venue." Mia cringed inside at how thick she was laying it on, but the smirk on Bradley's face showed the unctuous

approach was working. "And I'm glad I get the chance
to apologize in person for the horrible incident at the
bachelor party." She subtly scanned the men's faces
but much to her frustration, their expressions were
impassive. "I can't believe someone was brutally
murdered on our property." Mia added a shudder for
effect.

"Stuff happens," Kevin said with a shrug.

"You wanted to talk to us about Belle View's catering services?" Bradley said.

"Right, yes." Mia took a deep breath, then launched
into her pitch: "As you saw for yourself, Belle View
offers gorgeous views from both its luxurious ballrooms, and everything from linens to food is top-of-
the-line. What you don't know is that all of this comes
at an incredibly affordable price."

"But all of that comes in Queens," Bradley said
with a snort. "And we're not going to be holding a
Koller party in Queens."

"Do you do outside catering?" Kevin asked.

Bradley turned to his brother. "Excuse me."

Kevin looked embarrassed, yet resentful. "Sorry. I
thought I'd ask. For the future, maybe."

Bradley, annoyed, said, "What my brother means
is, do you cater events not held at Belle View?"

*Which is exactly what Kevin asked but with different
words*, Mia refrained from saying. "Absolutely," she
said, having no idea if this was true. "We can provide whatever you need, wherever you need it." *I hope,
I hope.*

"Before we'd commit to any large-scale events, we'd
need to do a test run," Bradley continued. "Kevin's
throwing a party for his girlfriend this weekend, here

in our Koller event space. We'll replace the people he hired with you and your people."

"We will?" Kevin said. He didn't seem too happy about the idea and Mia didn't blame him. "I, uh, wasn't thinking that we'd, uh . . ."

"I'd be happy to do a small event, like a dinner for you, as a test run," Mia said, jumping in. "Small" meant closer contact with the brothers. "I wouldn't feel right taking work away from a company you already hired."

"Too late." Bradley had pulled out his phone while she was talking. He held it up. "I texted them they're out."

"You did?" Kevin and Mia both responded weakly.

"Get me a list of everyone employed by Belle View and our security team will vet them. We'll let you know if there's a problem. We have strict security standards for anyone who might be involved with any Koller project or event, even peripherally."

Mia's heart sank as she saw a primo opportunity to spy on the brothers slipping away. "About that. I should tell you that my father's done a couple of stints in prisons, my brother is finishing another sentence, and Donny Boldano, my dad's boss, is both a godfather and my actual godfather."

Bradley and Kevin shared a look. "You know what?" Bradley said. "Let's just call your group vetted."

"Sounds good to me," Mia said, relieved.

"Let me get my girlfriend. It's her birthday; she should have some input into what happens." Kevin shot a dirty look at his brother and typed out a text.

"Let the girls do their party planning thing, Kevvo," Bradley says. "We have work to do."

"We 'girls' do love our parties," Mia couldn't stop

herself from saying. Luckily, the brothers took this as fact and not sarcasm.

Bradley got up and left the room without a good-bye. Kevin scurried behind him. He stopped in the hallway to talk to a heavily made-up tiny doll of a young woman with shiny flaxen hair extensions that hung down to her waist. She wore tight designer jeans, a beige cashmere turtleneck that was tight across what Mia pegged as enhanced breasts, and platformed brown leather boots with a six-inch heel and the designer red sole that indicated they cost five figures. Whatever Kevin was telling her, which Mia assumed was about her birthday party switcheroo, was making the girl very unhappy. Kevin put a hand under her elbow and steered her into the conference room. She crossed her arms in front of her chest and glowered at Mia. "This sucks," she said. "You suck."

"Cimmanin! Don't say that." Kevin motioned to Mia with a small move of his head and added, sotto voce, "Her father's in the mob."

Cimmanin's face cleared. "Really? Cool." She sat down at the table.

"You gals have fun," Kevin said, and darted out of the room.

There was an awkward pause, then Mia recovered and introduced herself. "I'm Mia. Mia Carina."

She extended her hand and Kevin's girlfriend shook it with a grip stronger than either of the brothers. "Cimmanin Doonan. Sorry if I was rude. It was before I knew you were interesting."

Mia detected a slight accent she couldn't place. "Not a problem. Cimmanin, that's an interesting name. What nationality is it?"

"This one. Like, America." Cimmanin twirled a

bleached extension around her finger. "It was supposed to be Cinnamon, but my mother could never say it or spell it right. It kept coming out 'Cimmanin.' So that's what they put on my birth certificate."

Mia picked up on the dropped *r*'s in Cimmanin's short speech and in a flash, got who she was: An Outer Boroughs girl masquerading as a Manhattanite. She didn't have a foreign accent; she was trying to hide the one she brought with her over a bridge or through a tunnel from Brooklyn, Staten Island, Queens, or the Bronx. Mia relaxed. Now that she had Cimmanin's number, she knew how to play her. Only the trendiest of trendy for Miss Cimmanin Doonan. Mia pulled out her elegant and incredibly expensive Korri Designs wallet. The wallet, a freebie going-away gift from her boss, had been paid for but returned by the husband of Palm Beach's most notorious wealthy kleptomaniac.

While Mia pretended to search the wallet for a business card, Cimmanin's eyes traced her moves. "Is that the Korri N'Est Plus Ultra?" Kevin's girlfriend asked, practically drooling.

"Yes. You know how they say something feels like butter? Feel this."

Mia handed the wallet to Cimmanin, who gave it a gentle, reverent stroke, then handed it back. "I am so putting that on my birthday wish list." Cimmanin said this with a feverish intensity.

Mia put the wallet away as slowly as possible, making sure her new client saw every angle of the impressive object. "Cimmanin, I know this change is big and very sudden. What I want to do is keep everything about the party you liked and take anything where you were 'meh,' and kick it up."

"Awesome." Cimmanin smiled a big smile that showed off a mouth of perfectly installed veneers. "The food and booze are all fine, I can have Kevin's assistant Becca get you a list of what's what so you can work off it and add anything you think would be cool. For the décor"—which Cimmanin pronounced as 'day-coo-hua'—"it's supposed to be super elegant. Like, orchids and stuff."

"*Vogue* says 'simple is the new black.'" Vogue hadn't said this, but Mia was vamping. For her, "simple" meant less to decorate, which was key to pulling off a big party in less than a week.

"I love *Vogue*," Cimmanin said with reverence.

"Don't we *all*, girlfriend," Mia said. She held up her hand for a high-five, then feared she'd gone too far. However, Cimmanin responded with a hearty slap. "Now, how many guests are you expecting?"

"I dunno. A hundred? Two hundred?" Mia blanched. "Becca has the list. She's supposed to be helping with the party. She's a pain, though. Acts like she doesn't even want to be doing it."

Recalling the snobby uptown girl who escorted her to the conference room, Mia thought it was safe to assume Becca despised being her boss's girlfriend's lackey. "I'll talk to her. What was the plan for music?"

"Becca booked some friend of hers." Cimmanin got a devious look on her face. "But I think that's a place where you can kick it up a notch, like you said."

Mia had a sudden flash of inspiration. "I know DJ DJ."

Cimmanin gasped. "You do? He is *so* lit. But can you get him? He's like, everywhere."

The thought of DJ being unavailable hadn't occurred to Mia, but she hid her concern. "That won't be a problem." *I hope, I hope, I hope.*

"Okay, now I'm excited." Cimmanin used her hands with their perfectly polished nails to push herself up from the table. "If you got—have—any questions, call the office, Becca'll put you through to me. If you need anything, she'll be glad to help you."

"No, she won't."

"You're right. She'll be miserable. So call her a *lot.*"

The two Outer-Borough girls exchanged a conspiratorial grin. "By the way, I have to ask," Mia said. "Where are you actually from?"

"Sunnyside. You?"

"Astoria."

"Queens girls, represent!" Cimmanin put a hand on her hip, held the other in the air, and Nae-Nae-ed her way out of the office.

Mia picked up her shoulder bag, surprised that she was being allowed to let herself out of the Koller building. Whether the brothers trusted Mia or had forgotten about her didn't matter. The lack of security offered a great opportunity to poke around the office. She took a leisurely stroll in the opposite direction from the reception area, eyeing each office she passed. All were either occupied or a glass wall would put her in plain view of anyone who walked by. She gave up and turned around. Cimmanin's party would give her an opportunity to see the Koller brothers in their natural habitat. Since it was an evening event, she might also be able to sneak off and search their offices for any evidence that might link them to suspect real estate dealings in Queens. Now all she had to do was put a call in to DJ DJ.

Mia sat by herself at a two-top table in the back corner of the Happy Hour Bar and Grill, the restaurant across from Koller Properties that her brother, Posi, pegged as the possible location where Angie had met up with future groom John Grazio and his bestie with a drinking problem, Chris "Drinker" Tinker. An actor-waiter handed Mia a menu. "Welcome to Happy Hour Bar and Grill, where every hour's Happy Hour."

"Thank you. I'll need a few minutes. But can I get an iced tea?"

"You got it." The waiter practically sang this and danced off. As Mia ate a buttery garlic knot from a basket he'd placed on the table, she wondered if his chipper demeanor was a by-product of the fat tips generated by a constantly inebriated clientele. She pulled out her cell to call DJ DJ and suddenly felt nervous. Texting would have been the easy, impersonal way to go, but it would be harder for him to say no to her actual voice. She took a deep breath, released it, then tapped in his number.

"Hi, Mia."

Mia was thrown for a minute. "Oh. My name came up on your phone."

"Yeah, I put your number in my contacts when you texted me back. If I don't see a name, I don't take a call."

Mia realized she'd never heard the DJ speak. He had a low, melodic voice—like that of an actual radio DJ. She found herself glad that he hadn't wanted to miss a call from her. "I know this is a long shot, but I'm doing Kevin Koller's girlfriend's birthday party on Saturday, and I was wondering if there's any chance you're free to DJ it. You can pretty much name your price." This was a guess on Mia's part, but given how Kevin Koller's eyes turned into big hearts, and animated songbirds danced around his head when he gazed at Cimmanin, she figured it was a safe bet.

"You might want to buy a lottery ticket because it's your lucky day."

"Really?" Mia's heart beat a little faster.

"I was supposed to do a first-year anniversary for"—Kevin named the previous year's Oscar winner for Best Actress—"but she decided to divorce her husband instead, so the party's off. I picked up another gig, but I can pass it off to someone else. I'd like to get in the Koller orbit."

"Oh, DJ DJ, that's fantastic. Thank you so much. You're saving my life."

"That reaction's a little extreme, but I'll take it. And call me Dee. DJ DJ's my working name."

"Dee. Much better. One of our waitresses said you'd changed your name so that it gave you the initials *DJ*. Being the nosy person that I am, now I want to know what your real name is."

"Let's just go with Dee."

"Oooh, a mystery man."

"Mystery Man. Maybe that'll be my new pseudonym." He chuckled a low, sexy chuckle. "But yeah, I find being a little mysterious makes me way more interesting to party planners than the boring real story. Hey, are you okay? You sound stressed."

"It's kind of hard not to be when there was a murder at your new business."

"Right. That's raw."

Mia flashed on the argument she saw between the DJ and John in Belle View's parking lot. The direction of her conversation with Dee offered a chance to bring it up. "That was such a horrible night. What happened affected everybody. I saw you and the groom get into it in the parking lot."

"Ugh, that guy is a giant d-bag. I asked for my check and he refused to pay me. He said I hadn't finished the gig. Worse, he said he hated my playlist, so he wasn't going to pay me anyway. What a deadbeat. And that friend of his. Total drunk. He kept saying, 'It was her, it was her.' I thought he was going to barf on my boots."

"I should warn you, Grazio will be at the Koller party. He's head of security."

"No bigs. He texted me that you got stuck with all the bills. Sorry about that."

"Don't be." Mia was assuaged by Dee's explanation of the fight, but something still bothered her. "You're one of the most famous DJ's in the city. I love our place but it's not exactly high-profile. Why did you take the job?"

"It was a new venue for me. You never know when someone's going to book your place for a Super Sweet Sixteen. You would not believe what people pay me to be a trophy hire, a name that their little princess can use to show up all the other Sweet Sixteen parties in her crowd."

"Got it. I'm glad you haven't written off Belle View."

"Are you kidding? Never. It's a great location."

"Thank you. We think so." Mia couldn't contain her emotions. "It's new to us, too. My dad's only been running it a few months. He's doing such a good job. I don't want that stupid murder messing things up for him. I'll do anything to help him and keep the business going. *Anything*."

"Wow. He's lucky to have a daughter like you."

Mia regained her composure. "Sorry, I didn't mean to get like that. Back to Cimmanin's party—"

"Cimma what?"

"Long story. Anyway, it's at the event space in the Koller Property headquarters on 51st Street. I'll text you the address. I can bring your check then, too."

"I've got a better idea. Are you free Friday night?"

I'm free every night there's no party at Belle View because I don't have a life, Mia thought but didn't say. "I think so. I need to double-check my calendar."

"I'm DJing over at this club called The Union in Union Square. Do you know it?"

"I could try to be cool and say, 'No, doesn't sound familiar,' or I could say, 'Uh yeah, it's only the hottest club in New York.'"

"If you're not doing anything, come by."

"I'll never get in. The doorman will ID me as B and T—Bridge and Tunnel."

Dee released another low, sexy chuckle. "Don't worry. You'll get in. I'll see you then."

"Maybe. Oh, who am I kidding? Union? *The* club? I will so be there."

"Excellent. See you around ten."

Mia managed not to blurt out, "That's so late!" Instead, she went with a simple "Bye."

Dee signed off and Mia suppressed the urge to do a little happy dance in her chair. Her waiter reappeared. "Somebody's smilin', and that puts me in a good mood."

"You may be in a less good mood when I tell you I filled up on the rolls."

"Don't worry about it. I already made a ton of tips from the morning drinkers."

He refilled her iced tea and Mia took a sip. "Thanks . . ." She checked out his nametag. ". . . Ricky."

His smile grew wider. "You called me by my name. Just for that, the iced tea is on me."

He winked and headed to another table. Mia vowed to return with a crowd and an appetite, and request Ricky's station. She glanced around the restaurant. It wasn't even two in the afternoon and the place was packed. The floor was tile, the booths wood, and the hard surfaces amplified the cacophony of chatter. She noticed a pretty girl in her twenties clinging to the arm of a soused middle-aged business-man. She was dressed in sort-of office attire, less like a real outfit than one of those Sexy Secretary cos-tumes in Halloween stores. Her thoughts wandered to the late Angie. She'd worked the crowd, like this girl. Mia wondered if Angie had seen or heard some-thing at the Happy Hour Bar and Grill that led to her murder, although overhearing anything in the noisy restaurant would take the sonar sense of a bat.

Mia tapped a number into her cell phone. Cammie answered the call.

"Hi."

"You sound out of breath."

"I'm on the elliptical."

"Oh. Any chance you can take a break and see if you can finagle the late Angie's address from Pete?"

"I don't need a break to do that. Call you back in a sec."

Cammie ended the call. A minute later, she rang

back. "It's 641 West 87th Street, number 10D. Roommate's name is Sofeea Sloan, first name spelled *S-o-f-e-e-a,* God knows why, probably some Millennial who has to be 'different.' She's still living there."

"Thanks. As you were."

"Oh, I'm done with the elliptical. I was killing time until my facial. Bye-yee."

Today's my day for weird names, Mia thought as she scribbled the name and address Cammie had given her onto a cocktail napkin. The next item on her agenda would be paying Angie's roommate a visit. But first, a little research. Mia typed "Sofeea Sloan" into her phone's search engine. The unusual spelling provided a quick result: "Sofeea Sloan Public Relations." Mia clicked on the link to Sofeea's website. The image of a stunning redhead wearing glasses she probably didn't need graced the site's home page, which featured the tagline, "We know how to handle your business." "What does that even mean?" Mia muttered. A few testimonials followed the tagline, all of which spoke highly of Sofeea's efforts. Mia clicked on a link for pricing packages, which had cutesy names like "Newbie" and "Flying High," ranging from least to most expensive. Mia was impressed. Belle View might benefit from a PR maven like Sofeea. In addition to digging up whatever she could on Angie, she'd get some information on the "Middle of the Road" package, which had a price point she could live with.

Mia stuffed her phone and the napkin into her purse. She left a tip equaling the price of her iced tea for Ricky, then departed the Happy Hour Bar and Grill. Although it was spring, the April day had a chill to it, so as soon as Mia got outside, she put on her blazer. She buttoned it, then looked up and saw an unexpected visitor being greeted with familiarity by the Koller Properties doorman and ushered inside the building: real estate agent and despised 46th Place interloper Felicity Stewart Forbes.

Chapter Thirteen

Mia watched as Forbes disappeared into the Koller lobby. *Now that's interesting. What is she doing here?*

There was only one way to find out. Mia dashed across the street, ignoring the honk of a cabbie who was blowing a red light but had the nerve to be annoyed at her. No one had asked her to return the temporary Koller ID, so she flashed it at the reception desk guard. "I left something upstairs. What a ditz, huh?"

"Okay," he said, nonplussed.

"I'll sign in again."

"You don't have to."

"I insist. I wouldn't want you or any of the guards to get in trouble." Mia wasn't about to miss the chance to see where Forbes was headed. She scribbled her name under the real estate agent's flowery signature. As Mia guessed, she was headed to the fifty-third floor, home to the Koller brothers' offices. And now, so was Mia. She hurried to the turnstile and swiped her way into the elevator bank.

Moments later, she was back in the fifty-third floor's marbled reception area. "Hi, I'm doing Cimmanin's birthday party, we had a meeting an hour ago, and I left my favorite sunglasses in the conference room."

"Oh. No problem, I'll have someone get them for you."

The receptionist went to push a button on her console. Mia waved her hands. "No! I need to go myself. I lost other stuff, too. My purse fell and God knows what rolled out of it." She leaned forward and whispered, "possibly a feminine product."

The receptionist hesitated. "Well . . . I guess it's okay. Go on back."

"Thank you. You're the best."

Mia flashed a smile that she hoped relayed a relaxed self-confidence she didn't feel. She refrained from adding a wink, figuring that would be overkill, then scurried down the hallway toward the conference room. It was occupied by Forbes, who appeared to be arguing with the Koller brothers. *I have to hear what they're saying*, Mia thought. She checked out the office closest to the end of the room where the three were standing. If she could get into it, she could try listening to the conversation through the common wall. Luckily, the office occupant was familiar to her.

Mia opened the door halfway and stuck her head inside. "Cimmanin, there you are." She stepped inside. "I've been looking for you. I have a great idea for your party."

Cimmanin put down the copy of *Vogue* she'd been thumbing through. "Awesome. I can't wait to hear it."

And I can't wait to have it. Mia saw the wall between the conference room and the office sported a dry erase board. She grabbed a marker. "Picture this," she vamped. She drew a giant X on the board and leaned into it. All she could hear from the conference room were murmurs.

"Uh-huh."

"It's . . . your seating plan." Mia added a flurry of small x's on the lines of the big X. "The little x's are the tables. This arrangement creates not one, but four different dance floors." She tapped each area with her marker.

"Huh," Cimmanin said.

"I know you're having trouble visualizing this, so close your eyes," Mia said, using Cimmanin's lack of enthusiasm to her advantage. The birthday girl closed her eyes. "Imagine the party venue set up with a big X of tables. Then imagine DJ DJ spinning awesome tunes while four different sections of the room are filled with your friends dancing, having the best time of their lives. Take a minute to really see this in your mind."

As Cimmanin did so, Mia pressed her ear to the dry erase board. ". . . Deal . . ." Felicity was saying. ". . . Land . . . best price."

Cimmanin opened her eyes and Mia stepped back from the board. "I totally see it. And I *love* it."

"Great. Now, let's talk about centerpieces." Mia heard the conference room door open and close. An angry Felicity Stewart Forbes marched down the hallway. Mia dropped the marker, bent over, and clutched her middle. "Oooh, my stomach," she said, grimacing. "I don't know what's wrong with me. I need a bathroom."

"There's one two doors down."

Mia yanked open the office door. "I only go at home," she called to Cimmanin as she made a run for it.

"But you live in Astoria," Cimmanin called back.

Mia made it to the elevator and managed to jump inside with Felicity Forbes as the door was about to slam shut. If Forbes was surprised to see her, she hid it well, replacing the stormy look on her face with a big, fake smile. "Hello, there. What a coincidence."

"Yes. A big one."

"How is your grandmother feeling?"

"Healthy as a horse. She's gonna live forever." Mia couldn't resist rubbing that in. Then she got down to business. "So, what brings you to the Kollers?"

"I could ask you the same question."

"But I asked it first."

"I saw them at Belle View and thought I'd use that as entrée for a cold call to see if they have any real estate needs I might bc ablc to help them with."

"Wrong." Mia pulled the emergency button. The elevator slammed to a stop, throwing them off-balance. She put a hand on a wall to steady herself. "Alrighty, let's talk. I know you're lying. Why are you really here and why did you kill that stripper?"

"*What?*" The agent seemed legitimately aghast. "I didn't kill anyone, I swear."

"Then why are you meeting with the Koller brothers? I heard the words *deal* and *land* and *best price.*"

Felicity narrowed her eyes. "Were you spying on me?"

"I was in the office next door and have excellent hearing. It runs in the Carina family. And think of that as 'family' with a capital *F.*"

The older woman sagged against a wall. "Curse my drive to outsell all the other loser agents. I even took up bocce ball so I could schmooze the old Italian papas. I got two sales and a marriage proposal out of it. But I had to keep pushing, pushing, pushing. And now . . ." She sighed a heavy sigh.

"I'm waiting."

"I was doing some work for the Kollers. Help them target vulnerable sites in Astoria. Underutilized land, businesses that might be in trouble."

"Places owned by senior citizens."

"Oh, that has nothing to do with the Kollers; that's my own business model. But for them, I put in a ton of hours, assembled a terrific list, made some calls. Did all the legwork. And you know what Bradley just did? Fired me. He told me they're going with someone in Manhattan."

Manhattan. Always the eight-hundred-pound gorilla in the Queens room. "That list you put together. Is Belle View on it?"

Felicity nodded. "Number two. Right after the Triborough Correctional Facility. That site is perfect for mixed use. Belle View, though . . . I can see luxury condos with marina views, underground parking with two spots per unit, double-paned windows to cut the sound of the airport."

Mia glared at the avaricious agent. "Stop drooling."

"My bad." The agent straightened up. "I don't know anything about the murder. You have to believe me. When I heard the Kollers were coming to Belle View, I got myself invited to the fiftieth anniversary party, which wasn't hard because that husband is a major flirt. I don't know how that couple made it this long. My plan was to show the brothers around Belle View and really get them excited about the property."

"And sell it right out from under us."

"I'd be doing you a favor. You know Belle View's a money pit."

"But it's *our* money pit. And it's gonna stay that way. *Capisce?*"

Felicity looked nervous. "Yes. Yes, I understand."

Mia knew an exit moment when she saw one and pushed an elevator button. Nothing happened.

"You pressed the emergency button before," Felicity pointed out.

"I know. But I figured if I pressed a floor button, it would go again," Mia said, pressing button after button.

"They don't work that way. Press the red button, the one that's blinking, to get help."

Mia, embarrassed, did so. A voice came over a loudspeaker. "There you are. We've been trying to reach you. Do you have an emergency?"

"We did, but we're okay now," Mia said into the intercom. "We just need to get out of here."

"We'll get right on that."

An hour later, Mia and Forbes were freed. The real estate agent was so eager to escape Mia's company that she gave her four-inch spike heels a workout running in the opposite direction. Mia took in big gulps of air, a relief after the torture of managing her claustrophobia for the last hour. She pulled out the napkin with Sofeea's address, turned it over, and drew a diagram of Cimmanin's table setup. It was a good idea, whether she came up with it accidentally or not, and Mia didn't want to forget it. Then she walked to the Number 1 train on the West Side.

As she rode uptown on the Broadway local, she ran through the events of her time spent in and around Koller Properties. She didn't hate Cimmanin; in fact,

she liked her, and working on her party might prove
to be fun. But there was something hinky about the
Koller world. Or maybe that was the New York real
estate development world in general. The construction industry was known to be mobbed up. On any
given project in the city—all five boroughs—you
couldn't swing a dead stool pigeon without hitting
someone who was an "associate" of one Family or another. But so far, when it came to recent events on
her own home front, she saw no evidence of a deal so
treacherous it might lead to murder.

The subway rattled into the 86th Street station and
Mia disembarked. She scampered up the steps and
onto Broadway. Despite the nip in the air, the trees in
the median boasted tiny, hopeful leaves. A few elderly
citizens and their caregivers were seated on benches,
bundled up, but welcoming the hint of a season
change. Mia headed up the wide boulevard and
made a left onto 87th Street. She checked the street
numbers as she walked. Like all odd numbers in Manhattan, 641 West 87th Street was on the north side of
the street, at the end of the block. It was a respectable
dowager of a pre-war building, typical of the area but
lacking the doorman that came with its fancier neighbors. Mia entered the vestibule and scanned the di-
rectory until she found Sofeea's intercom number.
She entered the code and it rang. "Tomas?" a woman's
voice said. "You're early."

"This isn't Tomas. It's Mia Carina of Belle View
Banquet Manor. Where your roommate, Angie . . .
expired. My father, Ravello Carina, asked me to stop
by and express my condolences in person." Mia considered the irony of how she'd avoided trading in on

any connection to her connected family for years, yet now she tossed out her father's name like a practiced nepotist.

"I have a break in my schedule. I'll buzz you in."

A loud buzz startled Mia. She pulled the interior door open and stepped into the building's lobby, a study in the kind of New York faded elegance that belied four-to-five-digit rents. She got on the elevator, relieved it only went up ten stories. After her Koller elevator adventure, the less time she spent in one, the better. When she got off, she found herself right in front of Sofeea's apartment. She buzzed, and after a minute the door was opened by a drop-dead gorgeous redhead with perfect height, perfect features, and a perfect figure. She introduced herself with a perfectly dimpled smile. "Hi, I'm Sofeea. Come in."

Mia stepped into the apartment living room. Sofeea, the renter—or owner, if the building was a condo or co-op—might be a perfect beauty, but she had nothing on the view, which was breathtaking. Below lay Riverside Park, in all its newborn green glory. Beyond the park was the majestic Hudson River. As if on cue, a sloop floated by, then a darling tugboat. New Jersey hugged the other side of the river's shore. "What a view," Mia said. "You must get some amazing sunsets."

"I do. It's almost worth the rent."

Mia gave a polite laugh. She took in the room's odd arrangement. The entryway had been transformed into an ersatz office. A door that didn't look original to the apartment could be closed to separate the office from the large living room which, in addition to a couch and coffee table, featured a large bed and a swinging cocoon chair suspended from the ceiling. "Is this a studio apartment?"

"Oh no. It's a three-bedroom."

Mia choked. "A three-bedroom in Manhattan? On the Upper West Side? I don't want to think about what that costs."

"It's not easy but I manage. Here, let's sit down."

They entered the living room. Mia took a seat on the couch. Sofeea folded herself into the cocoon chair, gently swinging back and forth. The cell phone in her hand lit up, indicating a call or a text. Sofeea ignored it.

"My dad and I wanted to say how sorry we are for your loss," Mia began.

"That's very nice, but not really necessary. Angie and I weren't very close, and she only lived here about a month. We were acquaintances in high school— we're from Ohio—and she needed a place to live when she moved to New York. She wanted to be a tattoo artist, the kind who celebrities go to, but she wasn't that good. Instead, she drifted around and was having trouble coming up with the rent. I was pretty much over her. But," she hastened to add, "please tell your father how grateful I am for his concern."

"I will. It was so awful how she died. Being murdered and all. I'm sure the police have talked to you."

"Yes. Two officers from Queens. One seemed like a moron, the other kept dozing off."

Pete and Ryan. "I bet they poked around all over the place." Mia affected an annoyed attitude.

"They wanted to," Sofeea said with a sly smile, "but I made sure my lawyer was here to restrict their search to what was approved in the warrant, which was Angie's bedroom. Well, the one where she was crashing."

"Do you know if they found anything?" Mia asked, replacing annoyance with a gossipy tone.

"If they did, they didn't tell me. I'm guessing there wasn't much to find. Angie basically showed up with a carry-on suitcase. And it's not like she had the money to accumulate stuff once she was here. Except for what she could mooch off me." For a brief second, Sofeea's sophisticated demeanor cracked and she sounded peeved.

"Uh-huh," Mia said. She was distracted by the redhead's phone, which kept blinking on and off. Who was that insistent on connecting with her? "I'm sorry, but I'm really thirsty. Would you mind getting me some water?"

"Oh. Sure."

Sofeea gracefully unfolded herself from the swinging cocoon chair. She put her phone down on the coffee table and left for the kitchen. As soon as she was out of sight, Mia grabbed the phone. She pressed a button. The screen lit up with messages from half a dozen men. That screen disappeared, replaced by one requesting a passcode. Mia put the phone down, careful to position it the way Sofeea had left it. A door opened, and the beautiful woman glided back into the room. Mia wondered if she'd been a dancer in a former life.

Sofeea handed her a glass with a minute amount of water. She checked her smart watch. "I hate to rush you, but I have a client due any minute."

"Of course." Mia downed the water. "You're in public relations, right? I'd like to talk to you about that when you have time. I was thinking we could use a campaign for Belle View. Put the fact it's under new ownership to use for some publicity."

Sofeea seemed uncomfortable. "The thing is, I don't handle businesses. I'm a personal publicist. I work one-on-one with individual clients."

"Ah, got it." Mia handed back her empty glass. "Thanks for the water. And again, you have our sympathies."

Sofeea let Mia out and watched her get on the elevator. As Mia waved good-bye, the other woman closed her apartment door. Mia pressed the button for the ninth floor. When the elevator stopped, she darted out. She ran down the hall to the building's emergency stairway and bounded up the steps back to the tenth floor. Mia positioned herself at a bend in the hallway that allowed her to observe the entrance to Sofeea's apartment while remaining hidden from its occupant. The elevator opened, and a middle-aged man emerged, accompanied by a flashy-looking blonde. They rang Sofeea's bell, then disappeared into the apartment.

Mia watched the same scenario repeatedly play out for the next two hours. Hard-looking young women and a range of men coming and going on the hour and half hour—sometimes on the quarter hour, confirming the suspicion Mia had from the moment she met Sofeea. She thought about the package descriptions on her public relations website: "Newbie," "Middle of the Road," "Flying High." All worked as innuendos for sexual activities.

Sofeea Sloan wasn't just Angie's roommate. She was her madam.

Chapter Fourteen

At five P.M., the flow of visitors to Sofeea's apartment abruptly stopped. *Banker's hours,* Mia thought wryly. She shook out some of the body cramps she'd gotten from being on alert for a couple of hours, then strode to the phony publicist's door and rapped on it.

"We're closed," the woman called from within.

"I think you're gonna want to talk to me, Sofeea," Mia called back. The ominous note in her voice worked. The door opened. Mia didn't wait for an invitation to enter the apartment. "I know what's going on here."

"I have no idea what you *think* is 'going on here,' but whatever it is, you're wrong." Sofeea was defiant. "I happen to be an extremely hardworking, independent businesswoman."

"No argument there. But all that hard work isn't going into public relations. Relations, yes. But the private kind, not the public. No wonder there's a bed in the living room." Mia pointed to the cocoon chair with distaste. "And God knows what goes on in that thing. I'm just relieved I didn't sit in it."

"I-you-I—" Sofeea sputtered.

"Let's call this place what it is. A bordello. And let's call you what you are. A madam."

Mia planted her fists on her hips and stared down Sofeea, who did the same. There was a standoff, then Sofeea caved. "Okay, fine. I'm a madam. What do you care? Oh, I get it. You want a piece of my business for your father."

"*What?* Absolutely not!" Now Mia was angry. "My father may have done some not great things, but he's no frigging pimp. I care because your business may have led to Angie's murder."

Sofeea's expression changed from combative to scared. "I don't understand."

"It's complicated."

"Let's sit down."

The madam gestured to the couch. Mia held up her hands. "I'm not sitting anywhere in this apartment unless you put down paper first."

"Fine. Luckily, I still get the print edition of the *Times*. A lot of my clients are old school that way."

Sofeea grabbed a copy of the *New York Times* and spread the front section on the couch. Mia sat down on the paper while Sofeea pulled over a side chair. "You know that dark website called Meet Your Match?" Mia asked. "Spelled with an extra *e*?"

"Maybe."

"Which is a yes. And I assume your 'business' links to it."

"Maybe."

"Another yes. You need to hustle a lot of clients to pay the rent on this place. Back to what I think happened. A typo led my dad to the site, Angie responded, but when he realized who she was, he ended the call.

But she knew who *he* was and worked it. If we had her computer, I bet we'd find a search for him."

"She didn't have a computer. She paid me by the hour to use mine."

This was an unexpected break. "Which you never told the police because they would have confiscated it as evidence."

"Yes."

Now Mia was excited. "Fire up that baby. Let's see if I'm right."

The women got up and went to Sofeea's office area. She sat down at the computer. Mia stood behind her. "It takes a while to log on, I have a lot of security."

"I bet."

While Sofeea typed, Mia entertained herself by taking a subtle scan of the madam's work area. A couple of personal photos were placed on the highest shelf above the built-in desk. Some featured kids, most likely nieces and nephews, or the children of friends. Only one photo included Sofeea. She and a man had their arms around each other's waists. The man looked familiar. *Could it be?* Mia wondered. She positioned herself to get a better look at the photo and confirmed the man's identity. He was none other than Bradley Koller.

Mia filed this discovery away for the time being. She didn't want to distract the madam from confirming Angie had targeted Ravello. Sofeea stopped typing. "I just remembered; Angie had her own password. I didn't want her on my account."

"Smart move on your part. Do you know her password?"

"No," Sofeea said, frustrated.

"Think. It could be her old street address, a celebrity

she had the hots for, her favorite saying." Sofeea brightened. She tapped a few letters on the keyboard and a home page opened. The women cheered. "That was pretty short. What did you type?"

"F.M.L."

"Eff My Life?"

"Her favorite saying."

"Well done. Okay, now go to her search history. Look for my father."

Mia peered over the madam's shoulder as she clicked on the drop-down menu for the search history. A long list appeared. Each entry featured the name "Ravello Carina."

Sofeea gaped at the list. "You were right."

"She did her homework." Mia pointed to an article. "I remember that one. It's about whether my dad was senile or acting that way to get out of a jail sentence."

"Which was it?"

"The latter. It didn't work. But I bet Angie thought it was the former. And tried to use his 'senility' to make him doubt his own memory and think maybe he really did sleep with her."

"Hold on a sec." Sofeea opened an article.

"That one doesn't have anything to do with my father."

"I know. It's about one of my clients. Former clients. I haven't heard from him in weeks." The two women scanned the piece, which was about a seventy-year-old CEO fighting to hold on to his position after underlings questioned his mental acuity.

"Drill down in the search history," Mia instructed Sofeea, who did so. A few more articles appeared, each one featuring a wealthy aging man whose wits might or might not be slipping.

"These are all my clients," Sofeea said. "Or were. They stopped booking appointments. It really hit my bottom line. If it weren't for referrals, I'd be out of business."

"Angie may have been a bad tattoo artist, but she was a good grifter. I bet she pulled the same blackmail scam on these guys that she did on my dad. No way they'd come back to you. They were afraid of being exposed."

"But how did she get into my account? I have top-of-the-line security. And my password's not written down anywhere."

"Let me guess. It's your childhood address in Ohio."

It dawned on Sofeea. "Which Angie knew . . ."

"Because you went to school together and lived in the same town."

The stream of profanity coming from Sofeea belied her glamorous image. "I can't believe this." She began typing furiously. "I'm sorry to kick you out, but I have to do some serious damage control."

"No worries, I get it. I'll let myself out."

Mia put her hand on the doorknob. Sofeea stopped typing. "Thanks. I owe you. I really was a publicist. I got tired of the crappy pay. But I'm good. When you're ready, let me know. I'll give you the 'Flying High' publicity package. On me."

"Great, I'll be in touch." Mia shuddered. "But I don't want to know what that package is when you're not talking about publicity."

* * *

As Mia walked back to the subway, she thought about the photo of Sofeea and Bradley Koller cuddling together. Mia guessed they'd met at Happy Hour Bar and Grill. If Bradley knew about his girl-friend's line of work, he probably didn't care. His father was famous for cavorting with call girls and porn stars. Whenever the tabloids had screamed about his latest liaison, the Koller family simply shrugged it off or used it as evidence of the old man's virility, pivoting the story from sleazy to proof that Koller senior was such a stud no one woman could satisfy him.

Sofeea had seemed genuinely shocked by Angie's double-crossing her. But that was a separate issue from Angie's murder. If Sofeea was dating Bradley Koller, and the death was related to a clandestine Koller real estate deal in Queens, there was every possibility that Sofeea knew about it—and might even have set her roommate up.

Mia's phone rang. She checked, saw it was a call from the groom's-mother-zilla, and ignored the call. Seconds later, her phone buzzed a text: **"Where's my blue flower sample?"** Mia groaned. "You're not gonna let up, are you?" she said to her phone. Then she had a brainstorm. **"Name and address of Dad's maybe girlfriend,"** she texted to Cammie, who texted back, **"Lin Yeung, Asia Flora, 452 St. Marks Place."**

She searched "Asia Flora" on her phone. The store was open until seven and it was only five-thirty. Mrs. Grazio's crazy flower demands offered Mia a chance to check out this Lin Yeung woman and evaluate whether she was good enough for her father. Mia joined the mass of rush-hour commuters for a subway ride downtown.

Mia never cared much for the East Village. The rents may have been astronomical, as they were all over Manhattan, but she still found the neighborhood grimy and rundown. But Asia Flora was a revelation. The exterior of the old brownstone was painted a crisp white, with the windows and front door outlined in black. Flower boxes filled with a lovely array of succulents hung below each window. Black planters filled with a combination of lavender and rosemary stood sentry on either side of the front door, perfuming the air with their scents. The building shone like a diamond in a field of cow patties. Not that Mia had ever seen a cow patty, but she'd seen some big, honking diamonds when her brother was arrested for fencing them.

A deliveryman came out of the store carrying a tall, rectangular vase filled with a spectacular arrangement of roses, hyacinths, lilies, and snapdragons. Mia peered through the store window. A tall woman with tawny skin and golden hair was perusing the flower case, her back to Mia. The store phone rang, and the woman stepped behind the counter to answer the call. As she turned, Mia saw she had Eurasian features. "Asia Flora," she heard the woman say. This had to be Lin Yeung. Mia felt embarrassed by her expectation that her father's paramour would fit the stereotype of a tiny, silky-haired Asian woman. She waited until Lin ended the call and then stepped inside the store.

She was greeted with a warm smile. "Hello." Lin spoke with the gentle timbre of a yoga instructor Mia studied with in Palm Beach, a woman whose voice was guaranteed to put Mia to sleep within fifteen minutes. "Can I help you or would you rather look around?"

Mia wanted to get a sense of who Lin was before

she brought up her connection to the woman's possible boyfriend, so she chose to play customer. She pulled out Barbara Grazio's blindingly blue swatch. "I'm an event planner and my client is demanding flowers in this color. I told her there's no such thing. She insists that there is, somewhere on the planet. She's a tough one, so I'm hoping she's right and I'm wrong."

Lin took the swatch and examined it. "You're not."

"Oh boy."

"This shade of blue isn't found in nature. The only way to achieve it is by either spraying white roses or dipping them into a dye. I say roses because they'll look better wearing this color. It's not my usual way to work, but I'd be happy to do it for you, Mia."

Mia turned red, mortified that Lin had seen through her act. "You know who I am."

Lin graced her with another smile. "Of course. Have you ever wondered why your father's wallet is so fat? It's stuffed with pictures of you. That's how we got to know each other. Bragging about our grown children." She pointed to an artistic black-and-white photo hanging on the wall behind the service counter. A handsome man in his late twenties had his arms around the shoulders of an equally good-looking woman who held a baby in her arms. "My son, Alex, and his wife, Caroline, with their little girl, Eliza. My daughter, Olivia, took the picture. She's a fashion photographer."

Mia walked over to the photo and studied it. "You have a grandchild."

"And another on the way."

"We haven't given Dad any grandchildren yet." Mia couldn't help sounding wistful.

"You've got time."

Mia snorted. "Oh, you are *so* not Italian."

"No. Vietnamese and American. My father was a G.I. Classic Vietnam War story. Only mine didn't abandon his mixed-race child. He was killed in action."

"I'm sorry. When did you come here?"

"In 1975. During the Fall of Saigon. I was seven."

"You don't have an accent."

"My mother insisted I take elocution lessons. She didn't want an accent to be a career barrier for me. I was a federal prosecutor until a few years ago, when I retired and opened this shop."

"A prosecutor? Seriously? Does my dad know that?"

"Yes. He also knows I have no interest in dating a gangster, so if he goes back to the Life, we're done."

"Good. The more motivation he has to stay legit, the better."

Lin indicated a teapot and electric kettle on a small glass table. "Would you like some tea? I keep it out for my customers."

"No, thanks. I should get going."

"So, do you approve of me?" Lin's light, almost golden, brown eyes twinkled.

Mia looked sheepish. "Busted. Okay, I did want to check you out. But I also really need these blue flowers. This groom's mother is scarier than some of my dad's 'associates.'"

Lin made a face. "A groom's-mother-zilla? You poor thing. I've run into a few of those myself when I've done wedding arrangements. I'll make you a corsage of blue flowers that will look so real, the woman will think you picked them yourself."

"Thank you," Mia said, relieved. "I better go. It was nice meeting you. Very nice."

"Same here."

"Your store is beautiful, by the way. I can see why my dad likes to come here." Mia, on the way to the front door, noticed a bridge table with several arrangements on it. She detoured over to one that was a riot of color, with orange tiger lilies, purple irises, yellow roses, and hot pink peonies. "I love this one."

"Those are by my students. And that one happens to be your father's arrangement. He said he was using as many of your favorite colors as he could in it." The sight of her father's bouquet, crafted so lovingly, brought Mia to tears. She pressed her hands on her eyelids to make herself stop crying. Lin brought her a tissue and put an arm around her shoulders. "He loves you so much," Lin said. "He's beyond happy you came home, Mia. Every time he came into the shop, he entered with a countdown. 'Forty-nine days!' 'Twenty-one days!' Working with you is a dream come true for him. He so badly wants Belle View to succeed. Not just for us and our future, but for yours. He'd do anything to make that happen. Except kill for it."

"Of course not. Thank you for your faith in him." Mia wiped her eyes and cleared her throat. "I really appreciate you making the blue flowers for me. Let me know when they're ready. I'll come by and pick them up."

Mia left the shop. Twilight was fading into evening. She made her way to the Astor Place Station, and as she shoved herself onto a crowded uptown train, she contemplated the conversation with Lin. One of the Family's unwritten rules was, never let the wife and kids know the details of what you did—especially the wife and girl kids, old school as that might be. Posi swore their father had managed to steer clear of violence, at least the deadly kind. But as Mia changed trains at Union Square for the Queens-bound N train, she couldn't stop wondering . . . motivated by a desperate desire to save Belle View, could her father have been driven to kill someone who posed a threat to it?

Chapter Fifteen

Mia stopped by Belle View before heading home to see how the kitchen repairs were coming along. A brand-new commercial stove, delivered by one of the many gamblers who owed Ravello a favor, sat gleaming and ready for action. Meanwhile, Tulio's work crew had made fast work of repairing the hole in the wall created by the firemen when they extinguished the blaze outside the kitchen.

Mia wrinkled her nose. The air in the room smelled like a combination of fresh paint and smoke damage. But that scent was overwhelmed by another, worse smell. Mia sniffed her way out of the kitchen, trying to track down whatever it was that was giving off the rotting odor. She found the culprit in Ravello's office—the bouquet of lavender flowers on her father's desk, now wilted and shedding petals. She made a move to toss it, then hesitated. Ravello had created the bouquet under the auspices of Lin, his secret girlfriend. Mia felt presumptuous disposing of something her father might have a sentimental attachment to. Instead, she pulled out her cell and texted Ravello. "Time to throw out the flower arrangement in your office. It stinks."

"It does?" he texted back. "I didn't notice." Ravello's nose had been broken a couple of times in ways he'd never shared with his children. The damage left him with an iffy sniffer.

Mia cabbed home, where she passed out as soon as her head hit the pillow. She awoke the next morning to a cacophony of chatter coming from Elisabetta's. "Nonna, everything all right?" she called from her landing to the apartment below.

"No! No, everything is not all right! *Misericordia!*"

Mia learned as a child that when her grand-mother's reactions bordered on the level of Italian opera, it was a personal, not a global crisis. She threw on her bathrobe and padded downstairs. She found Elisabetta and her Army in the kitchen, all in a high dudgeon and talking at the same time. "Yo!" she yelled to get their attention. It worked. They quieted down. "Better. Now, what's going on?"

"The new people, do you know what they did?" Elisabetta's eyes flashed with fury. Her voice was guttural with anger. "Rose's Virgin Mary is gone. Gone! They got rid of it."

"Who does that to the Virgin Mary?" This mournful rhetorical question came from Elisabetta's longtime next-door neighbor, Phyllis Carullo. She crossed herself and the other women followed suit.

"I know how upsetting this is to all of you," Mia said. "But new people bought the house. They can do whatever they want to it. Who knows? Maybe they're Jewish."

Elisabetta shook her head vehemently. "No. The Levines at forty-one-twenty-two? They kept the Virgin Mary that came with their house. They've lived here thirty years with the Madonna in their front yard. You know why? The Jewish people believe in tradition."

"They had the first bible," Phyllis explained to Mia. "The Old Testament."

"I know what the Old Testament is." Mia said this through gritted teeth, her patience worn thin. "Here's the deal. When the new neighbors move in, be nice to them. Welcome them with some of the incredible food you all make. Then explain how important the Virgin Mary statues are to the block. I'm sure they have zero idea about that. Hopefully, they'll understand and replace her. But if not, you have to make peace with their choice. Because it is *their* choice."

There was grumbling in a mix of languages, including Hero's outraged barks. "Fine," Elisabetta said with great reluctance. "This is all that real estate agent's fault, that Felicia two-last-names."

"Felicity Stewart Forbes," Mia said.

"Any chance she murdered that girl at Belle View?" her grandmother asked, looking hopeful.

Mia threw up her hands. "Yes, no, I don't know. Maybe she did, maybe she didn't. I'd love the murderer to be her, I'd love it to be anyone. I just want the whole thing over with."

Mia trudged upstairs. She fed Doorstop, then showered, dressed, and left for the day. Instead of going straight to Belle View, she took a walk to La Guli, where she picked up a box of pastries, comfort sweets for her and some new friends. When she'd checked the day's schedule, she'd seen that the pet grief support group was holding a morning meeting. Mia assumed they'd let her participate in the session but figured a little sugared bribery wouldn't hurt.

"One for the road," her store clerk friend, Julie, said, handing her an anise biscotti. "You look like you could use it."

"You have no idea." Mia chomped down on the hard cookie.

"Here." Julie poured her a cup of coffee. "You gotta dunk those. They're like rocks. Delicious, all-natural rocks."

"Honestly, they're delish either way." Mia dunked the biscotti, then alternated between hard and soft bites. "Why is life so complicated, Julie? I know that somewhere right now, there are people dunking biscotti and reading the paper with their feet up on an ottoman. What does it take to be one of those people?"

"Disposable income."

"Truth."

"But I know you, Mia." Julie waved a hand at her. "You don't wanna be one of those people, sitting around all day eating bonbons and watching the soaps."

"Bonbons and soaps? I'd have to take a time machine back to the nineteen fifties to be that person."

"You know what I mean. I'm trying to say you got too much going on up here." The store clerk tapped her head. "Things'll calm down. And then you and your dad'll be throwing the best parties Astoria's ever seen. Now, go. *Andiamo.*" Julie motioned with her hands to shoo Mia from the store. "Set the world on fire. But not really. You don't need another one of those at Belle View."

"No, we do not."

Mia blew Julie a grateful kiss and left the store. Still feeling emotionally vulnerable, she opened the

Pick-U-Up app. She tapped in a request, hoping Jamie's Prius would pop up. It didn't, so she chose a red mini-SUV, which pulled up in front of the Pasticceria a minute later. Traffic was light and the ride to Belle View quick. She stopped in her office to confirm the day's schedule, then brought her pastries into the bridal lounge to join the support group. She was happy to see that Guadalupe and Evans had set up a coffee station without her putting in a request for one. "Hi, everyone."

"Hi, Mia," the group chorused back.

"I brought pastries. From La Guli." This brought wan smiles from the grieving pet parents. "Is it okay if I join you?" Mia put the question to Vivien, the group leader.

"Absolutely. Do I see sfogliatelle? Yum."

Mia took one of the empty metal chairs that comprised the circle of mourners. She handed her La Guli breakfast sweets to Vivien, who took a custard-filled pastry and then passed the selection on to Betty. "Gerald, you were saying?" Vivien prompted after taking a big bite of her treat.

"Yes, um . . . I looked into cloning Willie, but it's over a hundred thousand dollars. And they can't guarantee they'll create a pup with the same personality as your fur baby. That's what made Willie so special. He was all personality."

Gerald's lower lip began to quiver, and Mia felt her own tears start up. She took a tissue from a box being passed around. She made a mental note to provide more tissues. One box wasn't going to cut it for these meetings.

"Some people decide they can never replace a beloved pet, and that's a perfectly respectable choice,"

Vivien said. "But a lot of us in this group have lost before and adopted again. It doesn't make the loss any easier, but there's comfort in a new addition to the family, and in knowing you're providing a sweet creature with a loving home."

Gerald nodded and wiped his eyes. "I think that will be me. I need time to get there."

"Take as much as you need. Mia, do you want to share anything today?"

Mia sniffed and nodded. "I had a real disappointment this week. A phone call from some scam artist claiming to have Pizzazz. This loser wanted the reward money." As she recalled the incident, she became more indignant. "Who does that? Who lies to someone about their beloved pet? What was he gonna do, go out and buy another poor little bird and try to pass him off as my Pizzazz? Like I wouldn't know my own wingbaby. Is that a thing? A wingbaby 'cuz it's a bird and doesn't have fur? Is featherbaby better? Maybe. Wingbaby kind of sounds like wingman, which is a little ooky when you think of a bird. Where was I? The scam artist, right. I'm sure this a-hole recognized me from when I was a suspect in my husband's disappearance or he saw my name and thought, 'Hey, her father's in the mob; she's good for some cash.'"

The group members exchanged nervous glances. A few paled. "M-m-m-mob?" Gerald stammered.

"Disappearance?" Betty said with a look of shock and a little fear.

Vivien put a hand to her forehead, knocking her glasses askew. "I knew that Belle View had new owners, but I had no idea—"

"Please, don't worry," Mia rushed to assure the

group. "This is a totally legit business. Yes, technically it's owned by the Boldano Family—"

"The Boldano Family?" Vivien repeated, her voice squeaky.

"We might wanna relocate," Betty said to the others.

"No!" Mia cried out. "My father would be so upset."

"For the love of God, don't upset her father!" Gerald yelled this.

"I was going to tell you I adopted a new kitty, so I don't need the group anymore, but now I'm not going anywhere," said the young woman Mia remembered from the first meeting. "No way am I upsetting your father."

Ravello suddenly stuck his head into the room. "*Ciao,* all." Startled, several of the support group members shrieked. "*Mi dispiace,* didn't mean to startle you. I was looking for my daughter."

"Right here, Dad." Mia rose.

"I need to talk to you a minute." Ravello addressed the group. "We haven't met yet, but I want you to know that our home here at Belle View is your home for as long as you need it, rent-free. Please consider yourself part of the family."

"Is that family with a capital *F*?" Mia heard Gerald whisper to Betty, who elbowed him in the ribs to be quiet.

Mia left the room with her father. They went into his office and he shut the door behind her. "I got some news from the Cammie-Pete hotline," Ravello said. "The cops released Giorgio last night. They didn't have enough to hold him on the murder charge."

"I knew it. Not to toot my own horn, which of course means I'm gonna toot my own horn, but the cops around here could learn a thing or two from me." Mia paused. "But . . . does this mean Pete'll be breathing down your neck again?"

"Until someone—anyone—else is made for the murder."

This was it. Mia's chance to put the hardest question of her life to her father. Rather than dance around it, she'd resolved to come at him point-blank. Mia knew her father. She'd be able to tell from his spontaneous reaction whether he was telling the truth. "Dad, did you kill Angie?"

Her father's mouth dropped open. "What?" he said, his face colored with disbelief. "You think I could be a murderer?"

Mia threw her hands in the air. "Yes, no, maybe. Given how little you ever told me about what you actually do, I think that's a fair question."

"I . . . I . . ." Ravello paused. He stared at the ground for a moment. Then he looked up at his daughter. "You're right. It's a fair question and you deserve an honest answer. No. No, I did not kill Angie."

His eyes begged Mia to believe him. And she did. This time. "Okay," she said in a quiet voice. Then she balled up her fists. "Argh. This whole thing is crazy-making."

"Agreed," Ravello said. "But we can only do what we can do. I wish we had a booking this weekend. Anything you can do to keep yourself busy?"

"Yes, and I need to talk to Guadalupe and Evans about it. I finagled my way into being the event planner for Kevin Koller's girlfriend's birthday party. It'll give me a chance to do a little spying on Koller-land. I told them Belle View caters off-site. Do we?"

"We do now."

"Good. I'll tell Guadalupe."

"She'll be happy to be doing something. She starts thinking about re-joining the military when she's just sitting around."

"I'll talk to her, then make some hires for the waitstaff."

"Make sure Giorgio's on the list."

Mia stared at her father in disbelief. "That's a joke, right? Like I'm gonna hire the guy who set you up for murder."

"That's exactly what you're gonna do," Ravello said, a crafty look on his face.

It dawned on Mia that her father wasn't being an altruist. His wiseguy radar was sending out an alert. "You think there's more to what's going on with Giorgio than the police have figured out."

"Oh yeah. There's something off about the guy. According to Cammie, even Pete thinks so. We'll put Giorgio on staff at the Koller party, and I'll keep an eye on him. See if I can pick up anything hinky. It's like that saying, keep your friends close and your enemies closer. The closer Giorgio is to us, the more of a chance we have to find out what he's up to."

"What if he says no? You took his uncle's business. He hates us."

"He's also broke," Ravello said. "I had Carlo, Carmine Bellini's son, do a little digging. He's a computer whiz. Great kid. Got a scholarship to Fordham, a good Jesuit school. He'll go straight, but like a lot of these computer kids, he likes the occasional hacking challenge."

"Then we've got a plan," Mia said. "I'll call Giorgio, make him an—offer him a figure he can't turn down."

"I was afraid you were gonna say, 'make him an offer he can't refuse.'"

"I almost did, God help me," Mia admitted. "I've been hearing it so much on the tours for potential customers, it got stuck in my brain. I'll call him right now."

"*Eccellente*. And *cara mia . . .*" Ravello took Mia's hands in his own. "Thank you. For believing me. And understanding that there are things I'll never tell you. *Ti amo.*"

"I love you too, Dad."

Ravello released her hands, and Mia took out her cell. She searched her contacts, found Giorgio's number, and tapped it in. "No answer. I'll leave a message." She spoke into the phone. "Hi, Giorgio, it's Mia Carina. Glad to hear NYPD couldn't hold you. I have a party coming up, a good one, with the Koller brothers. I'd like to hire you to work it. Give me a call."

Mia ended the call. "Argh, I forgot to tell him when it is."

She redialed the call. Evans appeared at the door. "Hey. Have any of our guests called to say they're missing their phone?"

"No," Mia said. "Why?"

"I was throwing away a bag of garbage and heard ringing coming from the dumpster. I thought maybe someone's phone got tossed accidentally."

Ravello and Mia looked at each other. Their eyes widened as they had the same thought. Mia took off down the hall, with Ravello and Evans right behind her. She ran through Belle View until she reached the building's back door. She threw it open and rushed to the facility's dumpster, which was often used by residents of the marina who ignored the PRIVATE PROPERTY warnings plastered all over it. Mia used a corner of the dumpster to heft herself up to the edge of it, and began hurling out trash bags, heaving them to the ground.

Evans watched, confused. "What's she doing?"

"Don't ask; help her," Ravello ordered.

Evans shrugged, but joined Mia in tossing garbage out of the dumpster. "Call Giorgio's number from my phone," she yelled to her father.

Ravello did so. A loud ring emanated from the bottom of the dumpster. Evans tossed a bag onto the pavement and gasped. "Whaaaa . . ."

A very dead Giorgio Bouras lay at the bottom of the dumpster. Mia stopped pulling bags out of it.

"Now call the police," she said to her father.

Chapter Sixteen

Once again, Belle View Banquet Manor was a crime scene. The parking lot quickly filled with police vehicles, their blue and red lights blinking on and off. Uniformed officers cordoned off the dumpster area with yellow crime scene tape. Crime scene technicians examined every inch of the surrounding area. A coroner's van idled nearby, waiting to retrieve the body.

Mia broke it to the pet bereavement group that there was an "incident," and the police had requested they stick around for questioning. They watched the action in stunned silence. "At least I'm not crying over Willy anymore today," Gerald said. His fellow grievers nodded in agreement.

"The police won't keep you long," Mia said by rote. How many times had she uttered the same phrase to guests when Angie was found dead? She was starting to wonder if her father *would* be better off running numbers and illegal poker games. At this point, they seemed less dangerous. She noticed the young woman who'd adopted a kitten was missing. "Where's Casey?" she asked Vivien.

Vivien held a finger to her lips. "She beat it. She has three hundred dollars in outstanding parking tickets."

Cammie came from around the side of the building, sporting a fresh cut and color and carrying shopping bags. "The cab had to drop me a block away. These heels are for showing, not walking." She saw the law enforcement activity. "Now what?"

"There was a body in the dumpster," Betty said, trying unsuccessfully not to be excited by the extraordinary event. "Mia found it."

Cammie looked at her askance. "And you are?"

"Betty. My Malti-poos Jackson Maine and Ally died within a week of each other."

"You have my sympathy." Cammie turned to Mia. She gestured toward the dumpster with her head. "Anyone we know?"

"Giorgio."

Cammie's mouth dropped open. "Noooooo."

"Yeeeessss."

"Why?"

Mia, feeling as close to a breakdown as she'd ever felt in her life, mimed pulling out her hair. "If we knew that, this whole stupid business would be over."

Pete Dianopolis saw Cammie and excused himself from the investigation. He walked over to them. "Hi, Cammie, I see you've been giving my credit cards a workout."

"Nothing like the workout you gave your 'personal trainer.'"

"I've told you a million times, that's over. Can't a guy have a midlife crisis without getting beat over the head by it?"

Cammie ignored his whining. "What's the deal here?"

"You know I can't tell you that."

She reached into a shopping bag, pulled out black lace thong panties, and held them up. "They were having a two-for-one sale on these lace thongs at Bellissima Lingerie. I've never worn a thong before. I can't wait to see what I look like in them."

"Guy hasn't been dead that long, body's still warm," Pete blurted. "Strangled. Wallet's gone, so either a robbery or faked robbery. My money's on the latter. Too many coincidences with recent events at Belle View."

"That's better." Cammie put away the underwear. "Now, interview the support group members so they can go back to mourning their pets in peace."

Cammie and Mia walked off toward Belle View offices. "Check and see if he's watching me walk away," Cammie said sotto voce to Mia.

Mia sneaked a peek over her shoulder. "Yup."

"Good," Cammie said with a satisfied smile. When it came to Pete, Mia had no idea if her co-worker simply enjoyed torturing her ex or was playing a long game to let him back into her life. Either way, it was currently working for the Carinas.

Once inside the building, Cammie split off for her own office while Mia continued to Ravello's. She found her father behind his desk, head dropped down, face in his hands. "Dad?"

Ravello lifted his head. He looked exhausted. "I asked Evans and Guadalupe to come here for a quick meeting. Can you let Cammie know?"

"Sure." Mia stuck her head into the hallway and yelled, "Cammie, meeting!"

"Coming!" Cammie yelled back.

Evans and Guadalupe came from the kitchen, Cammie from her office. The small staff crowded around Ravello's desk. "First, I want to thank you all for being so patient with the recent events at Belle View," he began. "It hasn't been easy for any of us, but I'm especially sorry to see such wonderful employees suffer any inconvenience or trauma. Which leads me to this. I would understand if any of you wants to quit. You'll leave here with two weeks' severance pay and a glowing recommendation. I'd miss you, that's for sure. But I wanted to give the option. Mia, anything you want to add?"

Mia addressed the group, her tone somber. "Just that you said 'I,' not 'we.' We would both be very sad to see you go, but a hundred percent supportive if that's your choice."

Guadalupe was the first to respond. "If a couple of years in Iraq didn't break me, you think I'm gonna let some low-life, small-time killer take me out? No way. If you want me to go, you'll have to fire me."

"Same here," Cammie declared, quickly adding, "but please don't. I'll never be able to get such a cushy sitch anywhere else."

"Thank you both." Ravello turned to Evans. "Where do you stand?"

Mia couldn't read the expression on Evans's face. "I'm here," he said, without the conviction of the others. Not for the first time, Mia wondered about him. Was he intentionally a cipher as personality choice? Or might he be hiding something?

"I'm relieved to hear you're all sticking with us, but

if you change your minds, that won't be a problem."
Ravello managed a smile. "*Grazie.* Let's all get back to
work and stay out of the police's way unless they have
questions for us, which they probably will."

Guadalupe, Cammie, and Evans departed, leaving
Ravello and Mia alone. A thought occurred to her. "I
was wondering, did the original employee applications come with this place when it was turned over to
you?" she asked her father.

"I don't know. I never looked. If they did, they'd be
in that file cabinet." Ravello pointed to a gray metal
four-drawer cabinet. "Why?"

"I wondered about Evans's background. I get a
weird vibe from him."

Ravello considered this. "I met with Guadalupe
and Evans separately when I first got the place, to
make sure we could all work together. Guadalupe
only said great things about Evans. He's an odd-
ball, that's for sure, but I wrote it off to one of those
spectrum-y things everyone's always talking about
these days."

"Could be that," Mia acknowledged. "Still, I
wouldn't mind double-checking his background."

Ravello gestured to the file cabinet. "Have at it."
He checked his watch. "It's noon. I'm gonna be late
to Roberto's. If the police want to talk to me, they
know where to find me." He kissed his daughter on
the top of her head as he passed her on the way out
of the office.

Mia struggled to pull open the top drawer of the
file cabinet, which was rusty and rickety. She stood on
tiptoes to thumb through the folders, which were
filed in no particular order. "Andre Bouras was a
lousy gambler *and* businessman," she grumbled as

she blew dust and wiped cobwebs off files in the second drawer. Mia found what she was looking for in the middle of the bottom drawer: a fat file marked EMPLOYEE APPLICATIONS.

She extracted the file and retreated to her office, closing and locking the door behind her in case anyone in the casual work environment of Belle View chose to enter without knocking. Mia paged through years of applications that had been haphazardly shoved into the folder. She was about to give up when she landed on the application for Evans Tucker. Mia carefully perused the document. The sous chef's contact information showed a home address on the Upper East Side in Manhattan. She Google-Earthed the building number and wrinkled her brow. It was hard to imagine the Evans she knew living in such a pricey town house. Under "Previous Employment," he'd listed two restaurants near the address he'd listed for his home. Mia put a call into the first one, a place called Colette's Brasserie. The familiar tone of a non-working telephone number came up, followed by the message, "The number you have reached is no longer in service." She called the second restaurant, a place in Brooklyn with the pseudo-hipster name of The Diner, and got the same response.

Mia leaned back in her chair. The restaurant business was notoriously brutal. There was every possibility both restaurants had gone out of business, leading Evans to a less interesting but steadier gig at a catering hall. There was also the possibility he'd purposely listed restaurants where his employment would be difficult to verify without tracking down owners or employees of the closed businesses. Stymied, Mia closed her search engine and left to make herself useful.

She spent the next two hours helping Guadalupe prepare and serve lunch to everyone at Belle View, including the police. Pete Dianopolis pulled her aside on the way to delivering another platter of sandwiches to the pet bereavement group. "Wanted to let you know we got what we needed from the grief group. Man, some of those stories are heartbreakers. I thought Hinkle was gonna burst out crying when he heard how that lady's Malti-poos died within a week of each other. He's tired from that baby of his and it makes him vulnerable. I'll take him another sandwich to cheer him up. And one for me, too."

Pete lifted two heroes off Mia's platter, and she continued into the lounge. She placed the almost-full tray next to an empty one. "You'd think a murder investigation would make me lose my appetite," Betty said as she put a third veggie hero sandwich on her plate. "Instead, I'm starving."

"The good news is that the police told me you're all free to go," Mia said.

"We will," Gerald said. "Right after dessert. Is that chocolate mousse?"

"Yes, and the cannolis are homemade." Mia took one and chomped down on it. "I could use a little comfort food myself right now."

The group polished off everything on the dessert platter, then departed. Mia was cleaning up the room when Cammie strode in. She looked anxious. "I need to talk to you."

Mia excused herself from the bereavement group and stepped into the hallway. "What's happening?"

she asked, concerned. "Did you get an update from Pete?"

"No. He's being tight-lipped all of a sudden. I sent a picture of me wearing the thong, okay, a couple of pictures, and he didn't even respond." Cammie, looking worried, bit her lower lip, then released it. "Is it me? Have I lost it? I'm no model but I thought I looked pretty good in them. Tell me what you think."

Cammie pulled out her phone and called up her photos. Mia examined them and frowned. "If Pete isn't responding to these, something is definitely going down. I'm calling my dad."

"I've got your pops on speed dial," Cammie said. She punched a number and handed the phone to Mia. It rang a handful of times, then went to the factory default voice mail message. Mia tapped her foot impatiently as she waited for it to end. "Dad, hi, call me, I think we may have a problem."

Mia ended the call. Her own cell phone began to ring—in her office, where she'd left it. She dashed down the hallway with Cammie and caught the call just in time. "Yes, hello."

"Hi, this is Teri Fuoco from—"

Mia disconnected the call. "It's that stupid reporter from the *Triborough Trib*." Her cell rang again. Mia ignored it. "How did she even get my cell number?"

Cammie held up a hand and rubbed her middle and index finger with her thumb. "Money. Cashola. Probably paid one of your Florida 'friends' or co-workers for it."

Mia scowled. "Probably. They couldn't talk to the cops or reporters fast enough when I was a suspect in Adam's disappearance. My 'bestie' down there told the TV news that she was only friends with me because she was afraid she'd get 'whacked' if she wasn't. She's lucky I didn't whack her for saying that." Her cell rang again. "Shut *up!*"

"Little advice? Take the call, say 'No comment,' and repeat it until she gets the message."

"Fine." Mia, disgruntled, answered the call. "*What?*"

"Ms. Carina, this is Teri Fuoco."

"How about telling me something I don't know?"

"Your father's been arrested and charged with the murder of Giorgio Bouras."

Chapter Seventeen

Mia dropped the phone and leaned against the office door frame. She closed her eyes and muttered a prayer. Cammie tugged at her sleeve. "What happened, what's wrong?"

"Dad's been arrested for Giorgio's murder."

Cammie gasped. "What? *Nooooo*." She clenched her fists in anger. "That's it. Pete just got his last hot picture of me in a thong."

"Hello?" Teri's voice, coming from the floor where the phone lay, sounded faint.

Mia bent down and picked up the phone. "No comment."

"I haven't asked you anything."

"Doesn't matter; whatever you ask, the answer is no comment. And I'm blocking your number. I just remembered I can do that. Buh-bye."

Mia ended the call and blocked the reporter's phone number. She stared at her cell, paralyzed for a moment. Then she put in a call to a number on her speed dial list.

"Hey, Mia." Mickey Bauer, the family's defense

attorney, sounded beleaguered. "I was just about to call you."

"Is it true? Did they arrest Dad?"

"Yes." The word came out as a long sigh.

"Figlio di puttana!" Mia cursed. "Why was he arrested? What evidence do the police have?"

"Nothing, if you ask me. But with his record, it wasn't hard to get a judge to sign off on an arrest warrant."

"Still, the police must have something on him."

"Security camera footage showing him throwing out garbage in the dumpster not that long before Giorgio was discovered, which means he was already in there. The garbage bag was full of some rotting flower arrangement. The police are saying he was trying to use the garbage and the stench of it to cover up the body."

Mia let out a groan. "Are you kidding me? I'm the one who told him to throw out those flowers. They were stinking up his office."

"You did?" Mickey's voice brightened. "That's good. I can use it."

"Where are they holding him? Rikers?"

"Where else? I'm working on getting him arraigned tomorrow. I'll be in touch."

"Great, thank you." Mia was about to end the call when a new thought filled her with fear. "Mickey . . . you didn't tell my grandmother about Dad's arrest, did you?"

"Yeah, I couldn't find your cell number, so I called her to get it. Why?"

Mia ended the call and began running down the hall to the front door. Cammie ran alongside her. "Where are you going?"

"Where are *we* going. I need you to give me a lift to Rikers Island."

Cammie dropped Mia off in the Rikers parking lot, where visitors picked up shuttles that took them over a bridge to the island that housed the massive prison complex. Mia shuttled to the visitor center and passed through a scanner. A guard searched her purse, then directed her to a shuttle that would take her to where Ravello was being held. *Triborough Correctional is like a spa compared to this place,* she thought as she endured a second search outside the visitor's floor. After securing her purse in a locker, a guard recited the rules of a visit to her. "You must remain seated with your hands above the table," he said. A woman yelled in Italian from inside the visitor's room. "You are not allowed to exchange any items with the person you are visiting or anyone else." There was the sound of more yelling. "Sorry, there's an old lady in there making a scene."

"That would be my grandmother. And I know the drill. My brother and my dad have both been here before."

"Good. Go on in."

Mia entered the barren room. Ravello, clad in a prison-issue jumpsuit, hands cuffed, sat across from Elisabetta. Or at least he would have been if Elisabetta wasn't yelling at a guard in Italian. "Mama, please, leave him alone," Ravello pleaded with her. "It's not his fault I'm here."

"Then who should I be yelling at?"

"Anyone but me, lady," the guard said, "unless you want to end up in a cell yourself."

Elisabetta launched into another tirade. "Nonna, *stai zitto*," Mia commanded her grandmother sternly. "That's enough."

"Mia," Ravello said with relief. "Maybe you can talk her down."

"Madonna mia, quest'è pazzo." Elisabetta, overwhelmed with frustration, thrust her fists in the air as if appealing to the heavens.

"Yes, it's crazy-making," Mia said. "But yelling at this poor man won't help. Apologize to him."

Defeated, Elisabetta lowered her fists. *"Mi dispiace,"* she said to the guard. "I'm sorry. I was upset. I know my son didn't kill anyone."

The guard gave a slight nod to acknowledge the apology. Mia put her hands on Elisabetta's shoulders and gently steered her toward the door. "Wait outside. I'm going to talk to Dad."

Elisabetta blew Ravello kiss. *"Ti amo, bambino.* Stay strong."

Ravello gave his mother a weary smile. "I will. Love you too, Mama."

Elisabetta left and Mia sat down across from her father. "I feel terrible, Dad. The only reason you're here is because I told you to throw out those stupid flowers."

"Don't blame yourself, sweetie. They would have found some other way to bring me in for this." Ravello's shoulders sagged. "Running Belle View was a pipe dream. It was bound to go down one way or another and take me down with it."

Mia's heart broke for her father. "No, don't even

think that." Mia, remembering the rules for visitors, suppressed the urge to take his hands in hers. "I talked to Mickey. He thinks the case against you is weak. We're gonna get you out, find out who killed Angie and Giorgio, and make Belle View the best catering hall in the city, and I mean the *whole* city." A voice came over the loudspeaker announcing the end of visiting hours. Mia stood up. "I'll see you at the arraignment. Right now, I better get Nonna out of here before she tries to arrange a prison break for you."

Elisabetta was uncharacteristically quiet on the cab ride home from Rikers. As soon as they got inside the house, she motioned for her granddaughter to come into the kitchen, where she filled two wineglasses from a bottle of Boldano Montepulciano. She handed a glass to Mia. "*Che giornata.* What a day."

Mia raised an eyebrow. "Ain't that the truth." She took a big gulp of wine. A blinking light on her grandmother's ancient answering machine drew her attention. "You have messages."

Elisabetta made a face. "Doctor appointments or telemarketers. Those are the only calls I get on the home phone anymore."

"Or . . ."

Mia pressed "Play" to hear the message. "Hi, this is Dylan Schreiber from the *New York Post.* I'd like to talk to you about Ravello Carina's arrest. You can reach me at—" Mia fast-forwarded through this message, the next, and the five that followed. Her worst fear was realized—every call was from a news organization looking to build a story around her father's arrest.

She pressed "Erase" and wiped the machine clean of them. "This is terrible. The last thing we need is more bad publicity." The phone rang and Elisabetta reached for it, but Mia stopped her. "No! No talking to the press. Let it go to voice mail."

The women waited, frozen in anticipation as the machine picked up. "Hello, did you know you can cut your energy bill in half by installing solar panels?" a voice chirped. Mia disconnected the call and the women relaxed.

"Who knew there'd be a day when I'd be grateful for some telemarketer?" Elisabetta said.

Doleful, she shook her head and took a seat at the kitchen table. Mia followed suit. She took another swig of wine to steel herself for what had to come next—an Internet search. Mia typed her father's name into a task bar on her cell. The first post linked to the lead story on the *Triborough Tribune* website: "Made Man a Murderer?" featuring the loathsome Teri Fuoco's byline. Page after page of links to Ravello Carina followed. Too many pages. Mia closed the app and knocked back the rest of her wine, then grabbed the bottle and emptied it into her glass.

Hero raised himself on his hind legs and put his front paws on Elisabetta's lap. The old woman picked him up and held him close to her heart. "*Chi è mamma piccolo bambino?*" she cooed to him in a squeaky voice. "Who's Mama's little baby? I read they like it when you talk baby talk to them."

"Uh-huh." Mia's response was pro forma. Her focus was elsewhere. It was time to put a question to Elisabetta. A question she'd been wanting to ask for most of her life. "Nonna . . . why did Dad make the choice he did? He's smart and such a good man in his heart. Why did he . . ."

"Join the Family?"

"Yes. All my life, I've wondered. Now I'm finally asking."

Nonna glanced at her wineglass. "A piece of cork." She took a paper napkin and dabbed it into the glass to remove the errant scrap.

"Stop stalling."

Nonna swirled her wine. "I'm stalling because I blame myself. Ravello was such a good boy, but all over the place, especially after his papa, your *nonno*, died. Ravello was only ten when that happened. He was very bright but had trouble with his studies. He couldn't focus. He was fidgety, always moving."

This was a revelation. "Dad had ADHD?"

"See, nowadays there's a name for that kind of behavior. Back then, a kid was just considered a problem. You get treated that way enough, by teachers, principals, even your own mother, you begin to act like a problem. For your father, that led to him getting in trouble. And eventually connecting with the Family."

Mia mulled this new insight into her father. He'd always seemed so measured, so focused. She pictured him as a young boy, struggling to do what came easier for others, judged by his peers and teachers. "Now it's hard to imagine Dad as someone with attention deficit disorder. But I guess as you grow older, you learn to manage it."

"That's what he's done. When he was a kid, it controlled him. Now he controls it." Elisabetta sighed. "I wish I could go back in time with what I know now.

Instead, we can only push forward." Tears rolled down the old woman's cheeks. "That's why I'm so glad you're here now, *bella*. With you helping him at Belle View, he finally has a chance to go straight. But not if he's jailed for a murder we know he didn't commit."

Mia, her own cheeks wet with tears, embraced her grandmother and the two women clung to each other. Mia loved the familiar comfort of her *nonna*'s arms. When she was a kid and her parents engaged in one of their histrionic arguments, she'd sneak out of the house and seek refuge with Elisabetta, who could be counted on for sympathy, a plate of homemade pasta, and an illicit glass of wine.

Mia's cell pinged a text. She picked up the phone and read the message. "It's from Mickey Bauer. Dad's arraignment just got switched from two P.M. to nine A.M. Here's hoping the press doesn't find out about the time change or oversleeps." She wagged a finger at Elisabetta. "You can only come with me if you promise not to go ballistic on the prosecutor."

"I can't promise that, so go without me."

"*Va bene.* I'm going to bed early so I'm in good shape in the morning. Here's hoping Dad will be released and the story will blow over." Mia got up from the table. "And you've got nothing to blame yourself for, Nonna. You were a widow dealing with your own grief, raising a kid by yourself in a time before anyone defined kids' issues. You obviously did something right because Dad adores you." She hugged her grandmother again. "And so do I."

* * *

Mia sat in the ornately paneled courtroom with her hands clasped together tightly to prevent them from shaking. Her heart hammered as Mickey Bauer pleaded her father's case in front of a grim-looking judge. "A man threw out rotting flowers, Your Honor. That's it. He threw them out because his daughter, who happens to work with him, complained that the smell was distracting and probably a detriment to wooing customers to their catering hall business."

The prosecutor, a man whose intensity screamed Type A personality, cast a baleful glance at Ravello. "The man Mr. Bauer is referring to also happens to be known to law enforcement as a member of the Boldano crime family."

"If that's the case," the judge said, "you'd think Mr. Carina would know better than to dispose of a body in his own dumpster."

"Especially one not set to be picked up for another two days," Mickey threw in. "My client would've needed a lot more rotting flowers to cover up *that* smell."

The judge used his index finger to push his wire-rim glasses against the bridge of his nose. "I'm dismissing this case without prejudice in light of the fact I don't see adequate evidence on the part of the prosecution to bring a second-degree murder charge against Mr. Ravello." He addressed the prosecutor. "Come back when you have some solid evidence, Mr. Robbins."

Mia released the breath she was holding. She followed her father and Mickey Bauer up the aisle and out of the courtroom.

"Nice job, Mickey," Ravello said. He was more

relaxed than Mia had seen him in days, although not by much.

"Yes, we can't thank you enough," Mia said, echoing her father's gratitude. But the lawyer seemed distracted.

"You might want to hold back on the thanks," Bauer said. He made a slight gesture with his head toward the prosecutor, who was glaring at them. "Robbins is the most ambitious prosecutor in the office, and that's saying something with those sharks. He could get a ton of publicity off a case with your father. This thing won't be over until the real killers are caught." He checked his smart watch. "I gotta go. My kid's playing Chester Arthur in a school play about the presidents. Whoever the heck Chester Arthur was."

Bauer took off, leaving Mia and Ravello. "I know Mickey's right," Mia said, "but we can still celebrate that you don't have to go back to Rikers today. Lunch?"

"I'd love to, but I think I need a little time to myself," Ravello said. "You don't mind?"

"No, of course not. I'll go back to Belle View and tell everyone the semi-good news."

Mia headed down the long hallway toward the building's elevator. She noticed a woman standing in an alcove—it was Lin Yeung. Their eyes met, and they acknowledged each other with discreet smiles. Mia didn't understand why her father felt compelled to hide his relationship. Everyone in the family—and the Family—agreed that he and her mother had stayed married far longer than they should have. Maybe this led to Ravello, like his daughter, doubting his instincts when it came to relationships and wanting to be a hundred percent sure Lin was the woman for him before he brought her into his world. Whatever the reason for his hesitation, Mia respected him too much to press the issue.

The elevator door opened, and a frazzled Teri Fuoco jumped out. Her hair was unkempt, her shirt buttoned wrong. "Hey, hi," she said, greeting Mia like they were old friends. The reporter panted as she spoke. "My court connections let me know about the time change for your father's appearance, but I accidentally set my phone alarm for six P.M., not A.M., so I woke up late. Which courtroom are we in?"

Mia stepped into the elevator and pressed the open button. "'*We*' aren't in any courtroom because case was dis-*missed*." She punctuated this with a triumphant finger snap, reveling in the aggrieved look on the reporter's face as the elevator doors closed.

Rather than take the subway, Mia treated herself to a cab ride to Belle View. She texted her grandmother the arraignment outcome and was rewarded with a screenful of happy emojis. When she got to Belle View, she discovered Guadalupe and Evans were on lunch break and Cammie had never come in at all, so she had the place to herself. Mia welcomed the solitude. She fixed herself a sandwich with cold cuts she found in the catering hall refrigerator, then settled down in her office to eat and scroll through almost two days of e-mails. There was a knock on her door. She opened it and was more pleased than she'd ever admit to see Jamie Boldano standing there.

"Hi. This is a nice surprise. Did I butt-dial a Pick-U-Up ride?" Jamie didn't crack a smile at her small joke. "I've been meaning to call you. It's been an insane couple of days." Jamie looked uncomfortable, which made her nervous. "Jamie, why exactly are you here?"

He stepped into the office and closed the door, then stood against it. "You have a problem. A big one."

Mia paled. "Your father."

Jamie gave a grave nod. "I came by to give you a heads-up that my dad's not happy about what's going on here."

"How not happy is he?" Mia asked. Jamie stretched his hand high above his head. *"Marone."*

"I thought you should know."

"I appreciate that."

"I better go," Jamie said. He turned to leave.

"No," Mia said. "Don't. Take me to your father."

Chapter Eighteen

Mia and Jamie were quickly on their way to Stony Harbor, an affluent community on Long Island's South Shore. "I really appreciate this," she said. "You didn't cut any classes to take me, did you?"

"No, I only had morning classes today. You'll be making my mom happy. She's been bugging me to visit for weeks. Between school and driving, I haven't had time."

Mia glanced out the window as they drove through Alley Pond Park on the Grand Central Parkway. Jamie dropped down to the Cross Island Parkway, and Queens morphed into Long Island. "You're such a good person to do this for me."

"Driving you to a place I need to go anyway doesn't make me a good person. It's no big deal."

"Yeah, it is. You do stuff for other people all the time."

"You do, too." Mia gave a derisive snort. "Really, Mia. Look at right now. You're so willing to help your dad that you're not afraid to talk to *my* dad. I would be. You're way braver than me."

"He doesn't scare me. Okay, maybe a little. But we always got along."

"He loves you. He was so mad about Adam cheating on you like that. He wanted to kill him. Not that he did," Jamie hastened to add.

"Are you sure?"

"Yes. Of course. Kind of."

The two lapsed into silence for the rest of the ride. Mia had lied to Jamie. While she generally wasn't scared of Donny Boldano, given the current circumstances, having a heart-to-heart with the mob boss terrified her. For a panicky moment, Mia considered backing out. But she reminded herself of the peril her father faced and summoned up the courage Jamie assumed she had.

Twenty minutes later, Jamie pulled up and parked in front of a nice but not ostentatious white-columned, two-story house on a leafy side street. The only difference between the house and its neighbors was the high brick wall, also painted white, that surrounded the property, and a preponderance of security cameras. Jamie punched a code into the front gate. "Hopefully my dad hasn't changed it since I was home last. He does that on a pretty regular basis." The gate swung open, and Mia gave him a thumbs-up.

They entered the property and the gate automatically closed behind them. The front door opened as Mia and Jamie approached. An immaculately dressed woman in her late fifties with strong Roman features stood in the door frame. "*Finalemente.*"

"Hi, Mom," Jamie said with an embarrassed grin.

Aurora Boldano came down the front steps and enveloped her son in a hug. "I thought the only way to get a visit out of you was to pretend I died so you'd

be forced to come to a visitation." Aurora let go of
Jamie. "And you brought our favorite girl." She threw
her arms around Mia.

"It's great to see you, Mrs. B," Mia said.

"Stop that, we're adults now, it's Aurora."

"I'm not good at calling my friends' parents by
their given names."

"So polite you are." Aurora let go of Mia and addressed them both. "Are you hungry?"

Mia wondered if there was an Italian household
anywhere in the world where that wasn't the first
question out of someone's mouth. "Not right now,
but thank you."

"She's here to talk to Dad," Jamie said. "But I
could eat."

Aurora gave her son an affectionate squeeze.
"That's my baby boy. The mister is out in the gym,
Mia."

Jamie went inside with his mother. Mia, feeling
tense, followed a stone path that looped around the
side of the house to the backyard. While she trusted
Donny wouldn't harm her father—at least she hoped
not—Mia feared he'd wrest Belle View away from
him . . . and her, if she was being totally honest. She
reached Donny's gym, which was housed in a pavil-
ion at one end of the Boldano's Olympic-sized pool.
A few wiseguy wannabes, including Jamie's older
brother Donny Junior, were huddled around a table,
smoking and checking their cell phones. Mia knew
their type all too well; she'd been married to one
of them. They were guys who looked like off-brand
versions of their Wall Street counterparts, with clothes
a little too flashy and hair a little too slick.

Donny Junior waved to her. "Mia, hey."

"Hi, Donny."

His companions tore themselves away from their phones to check her out. A couple of them tossed suggestive smiles her way; one even wiggled his eyebrows up and down lasciviously. That was something else she'd learned about the wannabes—they flirted like hoods from a 1950s B movie. The #metoo movement had sailed right over their expensively-coifed heads. "Come join us," one called out, waving her over. "We could use a little eye candy."

Donny Junior slapped his hand down. "Eh, shut up. That's my brother Jamie's girl."

"I'm not Jamie's girl, I'm not anybody's girl," Mia threw back at them. "And I know how to shoot."

This earned a few *whoa*s, followed by laughter. "Burn," the flirtatious guy teased Donny Junior, who glared at him.

Mia escaped into the gym, where she found Donny Boldano Senior on a treadmill, wearing a track suit that looked a lot like one of Elisabetta's. He was watching a real estate show on a small TV embedded into the treadmill. "Mia, *ciao*," the mob boss said without losing stride. "It's good to see you."

"You too, Mr. B. Can we talk?"

He motioned to the treadmill next to him. "Hop on."

Mia kicked off her heels and got on the treadmill. She began a brisk walk, matching Boldano's pace. "What are you watching?"

"One of those shows where people buy houses on tropical islands."

"I love those shows," Mia said. "They're all, like, 'Our budget is four million dollars and we can live in Tahiti because I can run my business from my phone.'"

Donny barked a laugh. "I don't know what that

business is, the one you can run from a phone in Tahiti, but I want in on it."

"I'm with you on that."

"How's your grandma?"

"Good."

"She's a pistol, that one. What do you all call her?"

"Little Mussolini."

Boldano chortled. "Little Mussolini," he repeated. "Little *Il Duce*. I like that. And your mother? How is she?"

Mia got that this question, while framed casually, was a quest for information. Donny Boldano never liked Gia and had helped Ravello get the couple's marriage annulled. Mia knew Donny, who believed in maintaining a low profile, wouldn't like what he was about to hear. "The last time we spoke, she told me she was up for a role on a reality show about Italian housewives."

Boldano pursed his lips. "I'll have someone talk to her."

Mia knew the Family had strict rules about applying muscle to women and children, but to be sure, she asked, "Just talk, right?"

"*Ma, certo.* Now, let's talk about why you're here."

Beads of perspiration formed on Mia's forehead. She didn't know whether they were the result of nerves or the mile she'd already tread on the treadmill. She wiped them away with the back of her hand. "You heard what happened at Belle View. And with my dad." Boldano gave a slight nod but said nothing. "It's bad luck. Nothing more than that. Yeah, it's a lot of bad luck, but the judge threw out the case against Dad, so now the press will go away because there's no story anymore, at least with my dad. I know in my heart the murders will be solved soon and when they are, it'll be like none of this ever happened."

Mia grew impassioned as she spoke. "Belle View has so much to offer, Mr. B. It's got a 'bella view' for one thing. The banquet rooms are terrific spaces that can be dressed up for big, fancy affairs, or down for smaller ones. Guadalupe, our chef, can do anything, plus she's a vet." Mia threw that in knowing that Boldano, who'd tried to enlist in the Armed Forces as a teenager but was rejected due to a heart murmur, had a soft spot for veterans. "I don't see Belle View as only a business, though. I see it as a place where we can host Family functions. Weddings, christenings, first Communions, birthdays, anniversaries. All of us coming together to celebrate the most important events in our lives at our very own Family venue."

She glanced over at Boldano. He had an impassive look on his face. Mia plunged ahead. "Please don't blame my father for what's going on."

"There was a lot of publicity about his arrest. You know I don't like publicity."

Mia couldn't ignore the hint of a threat underlying Boldano's measured tone. Uneasy, she stepped up her pace on the treadmill, breaking into a full sweat. "Dad is a victim of terrible circumstances. You should see him with potential clients, Mr. B. He's warm and kind and generous. They love him. All I'm asking is that you give him—us—a chance to make Belle View a place where party dreams come true."

"Agh," Boldano said, slapping his forehead.

"What?"

He pointed to the TV. "They picked house number

three. It'll go in the first hurricane. It's too close to the ocean."

"That's a high-class problem I wouldn't mind having," Mia said.

Boldano got off the treadmill, which slowed and came to a stop. Mia followed his lead. He picked up two towels and handed one to her. "My sources tell me Belle View needs a lot of work."

"Not a lot, necessarily. The bones are good. Equipment's good. I'm not gonna lie; it needs sprucing up. But that's cosmetic."

Boldano wiped his face and his armpits. He sat down on a stationary bike and began pedaling. Mia did the same on the bike next to him. "I've always been fond of you."

"And I you, sir."

"I was very unhappy about that piece of trash you married. I wasn't sorry to see him disappear. And no, I had nothing to do with that."

"I wasn't thinking—"

"Yes, you were."

"Okay, I was."

Boldano ruminated as he pedaled. "So, you really think this Belle View place has potential."

"*So* much potential."

The gangster turned up the dial on his bike. Mia did the same, matching his rhythm as sweat dripped into her eyes and stung them. Her heart pounded so loudly she was afraid Donny would hear it and know how jittery she really felt. She swallowed her fear and fought to project strength.

The don dialed down the speed on his bike. "All right then," he said. "I'll back off. Which means handling all of this is on you. No more murders, or at least no publicity about them or anyone involved with the place."

"I am all over it," Mia said, euphoric about the reprieve.

Boldano cracked a smile. "I bet you are. You got your mother's looks, your father's big heart, and your *nonna*'s moxie. It's a winner's combination."

"God, I hope so."

The fervent tone in Mia's voice elicited a loud laugh from Boldano. "Here's the deal. Once everything's back to normal, I'll see if I can find some money to fund upgrades. If we're gonna hold on to Belle View, it has to be a place I'm proud of. But any money going in or coming out *has* to be legit. The minute there's a stink on the place—not counting the current one, which at least isn't financial, that's where the feds are breathing down my neck—it's useless to me. *Capisce?*"

"*Capisco. Grazie*, Mr. B. Thank you."

The mob boss dismounted and stood in front of Mia. "There is one thing I want you to do for me."

Mia stopped pedaling. "*Naturalemente*. What?"

"Marry Jamie."

Chapter Nineteen

Mia stared at Boldano, thrown by his request—no, his order. Then she found her voice. "Mr. B, you know Jamie and I are very close. He's one of my best friends, if not my best."

"Which is perfect. Isn't that what your generation wants these days? Everyone to be their best friend? Parents, lovers, you should pardon the expression."

"Yes." Mia stretched out the small word as she searched for the proper response. "I think it's crucial for a relationship to be based on friendship first. That's what doomed me and Adam. We were all about attraction, but at the end of the day, didn't have much to say to each other."

"That's why you and Jamie should be together. You got both things going on, the talking and the attraction. Any dummy can see that, which includes Donny Junior."

Mia dismounted and paced the gym floor. "A relationship has to be a mutual decision. I can't exactly hurl myself at Jamie."

"Yes, you can. Hurl! Hurl away."

Mia clasped her hands to her head. She took a breath. "Mr. B, there's this thing called the friend zone. It's where you pass through an attraction and land on friendship. And there's no going back."

"Bull crap," Boldano said, only he didn't use the word *crap*. "Mia, *bambina*, sit." He took her hand and pulled her down next to him on a bench in front of lockers. "I know Jamie cares about you deeply. I want him to have a happy life. And I don't think that's going to happen with his girlfriend."

Mia suddenly felt like someone had taken a fist to her stomach. "Jamie has a girlfriend?" she asked, aiming for nonchalance.

"You didn't know?"

"No, but I'm happy for him."

Donny Boldano glowered. "Don't be. I don't like her. She's not right for him. A city girl."

"Queens is the city," Mia said, her voice weaker than she wished. She forced herself to summon up inner strength. "I'm sorry, Mr. B, but Jamie and I can't be forced into a relationship. I'm still recovering from my horror of a marriage. Jamie already has someone special in his life. It wouldn't be fair of me to interfere with that."

"I don't hear you ruling it out." Boldano spoke in a low voice, his tone conspiratorial.

Mia stood up. "I better go. Nonna took what happened with my dad hard and I want to make sure she's okay."

"There, right there." Boldano stood up and pointed at Mia's heart. "A girl whose heart's in the right place. A girl with family values. That's what I want for my son."

"*Addio*, Mr. B. Thank you for believing in my dad and me. And Belle View."

Mia kissed the mobster on both cheeks and left the

gym. She made sure she was out of Boldano's sight line, then bent over, put her hands on her thighs, and gasped for air. She straightened up but was overcome with a wave of dizziness and clutched the side of the house for support. "*Jamie has a girlfriend, big deal,*" she thought. "*Why am I taking this so hard? There's nothing going on between us. I'm just upset about this day, this week, this freaking year.*"

"Mia?"

She heard Jamie calling and pulled herself together. "Yeah, coming."

She started for the front of the house. He met her halfway. "There you are," he said with his dimpled smile. "I was afraid you ran off on me."

"No, no running," Mia said. She stared past him, afraid eye contact would set her off emotionally. "Just treadmilling with your dad."

"How'd it go?"

"I'm still here. And he's giving us more time."

"Yes!" Jamie fist-pumped and hugged Mia. She stood stiff in his embrace, and he let go. "Mom wants you to stay for dinner. It's one of her best. Bracciole, homemade manicotti, tiramisu for dessert."

The thought of food made Mia queasy. Her stomach hadn't settled from its reaction to Boldano's revelation about Jamie's love life. "I'd love to, but I really need to get home. I'm pretty burnt out from the day. But you stay. Have dinner with your family." *And not your girlfriend*, a little voice said inside her head, to which another voice responded, *Shut up, Mia.*

"I'll drive you home. I'll get Mom to make us doggy bags."

"No." The word came out more forcefully than Mia

planned. Jamie looked puzzled and a little hurt. "I already called for a ride," she lied.

"From here? That'll cost a fortune."

"I know how much your mom wants you to stay. I'll take a rain check."

Jamie shrugged. "Whatever. I'll wait with you."

"I have calls to make, e-mails to send. I mean, after the last couple of days . . ." Mia made a bomb noise and gestured to her head as if it were exploding. "Go. Eat. Spend time with your mom."

She pushed Jamie toward the front door. He quirked his mouth in a half smile. "Talk to you later."

Mia watched him go inside. When she was confident he was gone, she opened the Pick-U-Up app and requested a driver for a long and very expensive ride. Then she began to cry.

"I'm the worst brother in the world."

"Stop it. You're a great brother." Instead of going home, Mia had opted to visit Posi. The room, dreary to begin with, was made drearier by a gray drizzle falling outside and staining the windows.

"No, I'm terrible," Posi said, his expression glum. "I should be out of the place, helping you and Dad with Belle View. Instead, it's all landed on you."

"I'm handling it."

"You're doing way more than that. Give yourself a little credit. The place hasn't folded, Dad's not in jail for murder, and you talked Donny Boldano off the ledge. That's yuge."

Mia shrugged. "Dumb luck. Mr. B always liked me."

Posi eyed her. "There's something else going on."

"No, there's not."

"Yes, there is. I know you, Sis." He pointed at her eyes. "Red lids. You've been crying."

"No, I haven't. It's allergies."

Posi shook his head. "Allergies don't give you blotchy skin. Nothing personal, but you're not a pretty cry-er."

Mia glowered at her brother. "Thanks for that. Just what a gal feelin' blue needs to hear."

"Stop talking like an old-timey movie and tell me what's going on."

"It's stupid." Mia hesitated. "Jamie has a girlfriend."

"Ah." Posi sat back. "There it is." He shook a finger at her. "Hasn't our life together shown it's a waste of time trying to keep stuff from me?"

Mia, annoyed, swatted at his finger. "Stop making this a thing. It's not. I don't know why it's pushing my buttons. It shouldn't."

"Of course it's gonna bother you. You're totally in love with him."

"I am not! As a matter of fact, I got invited to a hot club tonight by a hot guy."

"What club?"

"The Union."

Posi raised his eyebrows. "Nice. I heard that place is awesome. You gotta tell me all about it. And about the guy. See if he's worthy of the Positano Carina Seal of Approval."

"Oh, I'm not going."

"*What?* Why not?"

"I'm just . . . I'm not in the mood. Not after what happened with the murders and Dad and every-thing."

Posi leaned forward and put his hands on Mia's

shoulders. Henry Marcus, the guard on duty, took a step toward him. "No contact, Posi." He sounded apologetic, and added sotto voce, "I gotta at least look like I'm doing my job."

"My bad." Posi let go of Mia. He crossed his arms in front of his chest and stared her down. "Messina Florence Carina, stop being a martyr."

Mia gaped at her brother, then responded with anger, "You've got a lot of nerve saying that to me, Mister Worst Brother in the World."

"If not me, who? And I'm not talking about all you're doing for Dad and for Belle View. I'm talking about you hiding behind your messed-up personal life. You were in a bad marriage. So what? I've been in two already, and you know there's a third in my future."

"I'm not being a martyr, Posi." Mia tried to keep her voice from quavering. "At least you're divorced. I'm not a divorcee, I'm not a widow. I don't know what I am. And I haven't been to a club since forever. I don't even know if I remember how to dance. Plus, the guy who invited me is the DJ. What do I do, stand there and go like this?" Mia snapped her fingers and mimed dancing in place. "I'll look ridiculous. I'll *feel* ridiculous."

The expression on Jamie's face wasn't devoid of compassion. "Look, you want to keep pretending you don't have a thing for Jamie, it's your call. But when a hot guy asks you to a hot club . . . you go."

"I'll think about it."

"Don't think, Mia. *Do.*"

Henry tapped his watch. "Time's up, you guys."

Mia rose from her chair. "I'll let you know if there's anything new with the murders."

"Go to the club tonight, Mia."

"Stop bugging me. I said I'll think about it. Love you."

"Love you, too. Go to the club."

"Argh!"

Henry opened the door for Mia. "I'm with your brother on this. Go to the club."

Rankled, Mia uttered a profanity and tromped out of the visiting room.

It was still drizzling when she got outside. Mia pulled out the portable umbrella and pair of folded-up plastic booties Elisabetta insisted she always carry in her tote bag. She slipped on the boots and opened the umbrella. Her empty stomach growled. Salambini's Pizza and Pasta—home of the infamous prom invitation pizzas from Mia's past—loomed on the corner of Thirty-First Street. She stopped at the restaurant's to-go window and ordered a slice she instantly wolfed down. A teen about the age her prom suitors had been stepped up to the window. "Pepperoni pizza, please."

"Prom, huh?" Mia said with a conspiratorial wink.

The teen looked at her like she'd lost her mind. "No, ma'am. I'm hungry."

He paid for his food and moved away from Mia. *Great, now I'm a crazy lady* and a *'ma'am.' Could today get any worse?*

Depressed, she started for home. Then on impulse, she detoured to the cell phone store where Chris Tinker worked. She looked through the front window and saw a girl arranging a display of phone accessories. The employee wore the same light blue, logo-ed polo shirt that Tinker was wearing the day Mia spied on him. The girl finished what she was doing and retreated behind the counter. Mia entered the store.

"Hi, can I help you?" the clerk asked.

"I was looking for the assistant manager. Chris Tinker." Mia took out her cell phone but held it at a distance so the girl couldn't see how old it was. "He sold me a phone and I have a few questions about it."

"He doesn't work here anymore."

This was an unexpected development. "Really? I just bought the phone last week."

"That's about when he disappeared."

Mia's heart raced. The situation was growing more interesting by the minute. "What do you mean, 'disappeared'?"

"Well, maybe not disappeared," the girl backtracked. "He never showed up to work. We left messages on his phone, but he never got back to us. I still have his last paycheck."

"Wow. That's so strange."

"Tell me about it. Anyway, I can help you with your phone."

Mia feigned checking the time on her phone. "You know, I didn't realize how late it is. I'll have to come back. Thanks anyway."

She made a fast exit and hurried down the block, finally stopping under a store awning, where she put a call in to Cammie.

"Hey, what's up?" Cammie yelled into the phone over the noise of a subway.

"Where are you?"

"On the way to Manhattan. I'm seeing a show."

"Can you find out from Pete if he knows that Chris Tinker is missing? He was one of the guests at the bachelor party and he knew Angie, the first murder victim. I can't believe I'm saying 'first.' What a world."

"Pete's right here. He bought the theater tickets. I let him come with me, but I'm making him sit across from me on the subway. Hey, Pete, did you know someone named Chris Tinker is missing? . . . He didn't know. What? . . . He was a bachelor party guest, Peter, knew the dead stripper or call girl or whatever she was. I swear, Mia, sometimes I don't know how he keeps his job . . . What? I can't hear you because of the express train on the other track. Speak up! He said thanks, he'll have Hinkle look into it. Gotta go, we're going into a tunn—"

The call failed. Mia parked her phone back in her tote bag. Then she traipsed toward 46th Place, dodging the occasional puddle.

Darkness had fallen by the time Mia reached home. "That you, *cara bambina*?" Elisabetta called from her kitchen.

"*Sì.*" Mia took off her booties, then her shoes, and padded down the narrow first-floor hallway. Nonna and her friends Phyllis, Lucy, and Joan were in the living room, seated around a card table playing canasta.

"Joan brought over a tray of tricolore cookies," Elisabetta said. "They're in the kitchen. Help yourself."

Mia went into the kitchen, where she poured a cup of coffee to go with the handful of three-color cookies she grabbed. "I got my electric bill from the Easter display," she heard Joan say. "It was the highest ever."

There were muttered reactions from the others.

"You think that's bad," Lucy said. "Mine was so high I can't pay it off all at once. I have to pay in installments." Heightened mutters followed this revelation.

"That's nothing," Phyllis scoffed. "You know what I have to do to pay off mine? *Borrow money from my children.*"

This elicited gasps and even a *"Madonna mia."* "Can't top that," Elisabetta said, her voice flat.

Mia stopped eating midbite, her appetite gone. She'd never heard her grandmother pass up a chance to one-up her friends on a holiday electric bill. The stress of the events at Belle View were wearing on the poor woman. Mia had to help her. She put down her coffee cup and strode into the living room. "Nonna, I saw your credit card bill in the junk drawer," she scolded. "No wonder you're hiding it. I can't believe how much money you already spent on Memorial Day decorations, and it's not even happening for a month. It's Memorial Day, not the Fourth of July, for goodness' sake."

The other women exchanged glances. "How much did she spend?" Phyllis asked. "I only ask cuz I'm curious."

Mia shook her head. "No. I can't even tell you how much, it's so embarrassing." She scowled at Elisabetta. "We'll talk about this later. But no more spending on decorations, you got it? You'll have to take out a second mortgage on the house to pay off the bills."

"Second mortgage," Phyllis muttered, looking pale.

Elisabetta tried to look stricken but held her hand of cards over her mouth to cover a smile. *"Si, bella.* I'll try to be more careful. But no promises."

Mia pretended to storm out of the room, then

took the stairs up to her apartment two at a time, rejuvenated by her good deed. It was a nice alternative to a murder investigation that was starting to feel like an exercise in futility. Pete didn't seem all that excited about her Chris Tinker revelation. Maybe he was right, and it was a dead end. The cell phone salesman had a major drinking problem. For all she knew, "Tinker the Drinker" might be somewhere drying out.

She stepped over Doorstop, who was splayed out across the entry, per usual. After feeding him, she cleaned out his litter box, refilling it with a combination of litter and her shredded wedding photos. Mia flashed on what Posi said to her: "Don't think. Do." It reminded her of an old Italian saying she'd grown up with: *Gli uomini facciare le donna parlare,* which translated to "Men act, women talk." She'd always hated how sexist and dismissive the expression was, especially since the Family's wives, mothers, and daughters couldn't talk about the one thing they really wanted to: what their husbands, sons, and brothers did for a living. This lack of communication drove Gia Carina crazy and led to some of her biggest fights with Ravello. Mia sympathized with her mother on this issue.

Her mind wandered to the news Donny broke about Jamie having a girlfriend. A "city" girl. Probably a college girl, educated and sophisticated. Everything Mia wasn't. She finished cleaning out Doorstop's litter box. Then she went into her bedroom and pulled a pair of pleather jeggings out of a rococo drawer. She dug through another drawer and found a stretchy purple top with a hint of sparkle.

Mia held the top and jeggings up to her in front of the full-length mirror attached to the back of the bedroom door. All she needed was her black leather ankle booties, and she'd have a great outfit.

The hell with murders and fancy Manhattan girl-friends. Mia was going clubbing.

Chapter Twenty

Mia showed up at The Union around eleven P.M., fortified by four espressos. The club, housed in a deconsecrated Methodist church near Manhattan's Union Square, was painted a shade of pink usually found in the Caribbean islands. Even though it was early for the nighttime scene, a line of would-be patrons stretched halfway down the block.

Mia approached the bouncer guarding the club's entrance. He scanned her from head to toe, not in a sexual way but in an "are you cool enough to get in?" way. "I'm on the list," she said. "Mia Carina. I'm a friend of Dee's," she added, feeling smug about being gifted with the privilege of using DJ DJ's nickname.

The bouncer scrolled through a list on his iPad, then waved her past him, into the hallowed halls of the currently coolest club in New York City.

The Union's interior was so dark Mia bumped into half a dozen people as she wended her way to the DJ booth. Red and blue lights swooped around the nave-turned-dance-floor, making her feel like she'd been caught up in a drug bust. Electronic dance music blasted from every orifice in the old building. Mia, sticking to the room's perimeter to avoid a sea of dancing humans, couldn't resist resting a hand on one of the church's walls. It literally vibrated with each bass note. She surveyed the crowd and suffered an attack of insecurity about her outfit, which suddenly felt more Florida than Manhattan. Mia hoped the darkness and whatever drugs the club-goers were on would distract from her fashion faux pas.

She arrived at the DJ booth, which had commandeered the altar and was an open setup more akin to a stage set. Another DJ was working alongside Dee, who was a study in concentration as he deftly manipulated a complicated array of equipment that looked like it could launch a spaceship. He glanced out at the crowd to take their dance temperature, and Mia waved to him. He responded with a wide smile that dispelled her self-doubt and waved her onto the altar to join him. She did so.

"I wanted to thank you for the Koller gig." Dee yelled to be heard over the eardrum-shattering music. "I already got calls from some of their friends and frenemies. They're the best kind of clients because they'll spend a ton of money to one-up everybody in their social circle."

"I'm working with one of those now," Mia yelled back. "Except she's trying to one-up her own twin sister."

Dee whistled. "Cold."

"But great for business."

"You know it." He winked and fist-bumped Mia.

"Dee, I'm going out for a smoke." The other DJ, a tattooed guy in his early twenties who had a bass clef note shaved into the back of his hair, took a pack of cigarettes off his console.

"No worries, man. Mia, this is Ty, my assistant. I'm

training him so that we can do two gigs a night. If we work the same gig, he covers when I need a break and vice versa."

Mia and Ty exchanged greetings, then he took off with his pack of cigarettes. "Take his seat 'til he comes back," Dee said. He handed her headphones. "These'll help you hear the music without going deaf. Hey, Sarah!" He flagged down a cocktail waitress dressed in a black unitard who so blended in with the dark interior, she looked like a floating head. "Mia, what do you want?"

"This looks like a beer and whiskey crowd. Would I sound ridiculous ordering a glass of chardonnay?"

Dee chortled. "Yes, but it doesn't matter because no one can hear you."

"Or see me." Mia squinted. Her eyes still hadn't adjusted to the schizoid lighting system that ranged from nonexistent to blinding flashes akin to an emergency alert.

Sarah's head floated off. Mia settled back into Ty's leather chair, which proved comfortable. She bopped along to the music, a fun mix of EDM, current pop hits, and retro dance tunes updated with new beats. Despite the frenetic energy of the club, Mia felt more relaxed than she had since starting at Belle View.

Sarah returned with drinks. She passed an IPA beer to Dee and handed Mia her wine. Mia reached into her purse for her wallet, but by the time she'd pulled it out, the waitress had disappeared. "Put that away," Dee said. "Drinks are on the house for me and my guests, but no way I'd let you pay even if they weren't."

"Then thanks to both The Union and you."

Mia sipped her wine and evaluated the timbre of

the night. *Is this a date?* she wondered. *It kind of feels like one.* She noticed the area of the dance floor closest to the DJ booth was occupied by single women and a few gay men. They danced suggestively, trying to get Dee's attention. The club was pulsating with sexual tension as well as music, and for a minute, Mia felt overcome with it herself. *Down, girl,* she warned herself, then drank a big gulp of wine.

"What's your favorite dance song?" she heard Dee ask, and then realized he was talking to her.

"Oh. Honestly? Like, not trying to pretend I'm hip or anything?"

"I want total honesty."

"My parents were disco royalty in the seventies. They won contests. You could call KC and the Sunshine Band our house band."

Dee grinned. "I love me some KC. Pick one."

"Easy peasy. 'Get Down Tonight.'"

"Nicholas," the DJ called to a dancer near the booth. "Help my friend Mia down and dance with her to the next song."

Nicholas gave Dee a thumbs-up. He said something to his male partner, who drifted away, then Nicholas held out his hand to Mia. She came around to the front of the DJ booth and let him help her onto the dance floor. A second later, the sound system blasted the familiar double-speed guitar solo that launched the sexy song.

Nicholas was a fantastic dancer. He spun her around, then did the Bump and Double-Bump. Mia responded with the Hustle, he followed her lead, and soon half the dance floor joined in. She danced with total abandon, letting the music overtake her inhibitions. The song segued into a medley of disco tunes, and Mia kept dancing. She couldn't remember the last time she'd felt so free. There was no thought of her adulterous ex or murder victims or Jamie Boldano. The night felt like the fresh start she so desperately craved. *Maybe, just maybe,* she thought, *I'm finally moving on with my life.*

Mia got home at five in the morning. After the club closed, she'd gone to an all-night diner with Dee, Ty, Nicholas, and a few more of their friends. She had so much fun laughing and joking around with the group that for the first time in her life she could envision herself not as an Outer Boroughs girl, but as a cool denizen of the Big Apple.

She snuck into the house and tiptoed up the stairs so she didn't wake up Elisabetta, who would respond with a lecture about what awaited girls who partied all night in the Gomorrah that was Manhattan. Mia made it to her room and collapsed onto the bed. Doorstop, who had stretched out to take up most of it, responded with an annoyed meow, but moved over to make room for her. Mia put an arm around him. He forgave her and snuggled under it. "I had a blast tonight, bud," she said, stroking his ginger fur. "I'm still totally wired from it." Then she passed out wearing her club outfit.

Mia woke up two hours later. After spending a half hour trying to go back to sleep, she gave up. "I think I'll go to Belle View," she told Doorstop. "No one will be there yet. I can get things done without interruptions." The cat responded with a sleepy meow.

Mia put up a pot of coffee, which she'd need with only two hours of sleep, and got ready for work. She stuck her hand out the kitchen window to gauge the morning temperature. Despite the bright sun and clear sky, there was a chill in the air, so she threw on an emerald sweater and skinny jeans. She put on ballet flats and tiptoed down the stairs, again trying to escape without alerting her grandmother. This time, she failed.

"Eh, Mia, *vieni qui*," Elisabetta called from the kitchen as Mia's hand touched the front doorknob.

Mia let go of the knob. "Coming," she said, and dragged herself toward the kitchen for the expected tongue-lashing.

Elisabetta, wearing a baby-blue track suit with dark blue racing stripes down the side of the legs, was at the stove frying up eggs and potatoes. Hero stood beside her, on the alert for any scraps that fell to the floor. "I didn't hear the stove or microwave going upstairs. You shouldn't go out without eating breakfast. *Siediti*. Sit." Mia sat and Elisabetta placed a plate piled high with eggs, peppers, and potatoes in front of her. "*Mangia*. And tell me about the boy."

The scent wafting up from the plate was too delicious to ignore and Mia dug in. "What boy?" she said, her mouth full.

"The one who kept you out to all hours doing I don't wanna know what last night."

"It was nothing, Nonna. Someone invited me to a club; we all hung out after. No romance."

"I'm sorry to hear that."

Mia stopped midbite, surprised at her grandmother's reaction. "You are?"

"*Ma certo*, of course. You're a woman, Mia. Special and beautiful. Don't let one bad choice ruin your life.

Let another man, a good one, love you. And give me a great-grandbaby."

"*And* there it is. . . ." Mia shook her head, amused by her grandmother's blatant agenda. "I will, Nonna. Eventually. I'm even supposed to see this guy Dee again. We're working a party Saturday night and he said something about hanging out afterward. But for now, last night was only a nice break from worrying about Belle View and Dad and mysterious deaths."

Elisabetta mimed spitting. "Feh. That Pete Dianopolis couldn't solve a case if the killer came up to him and screamed 'I did it!' in his face and handed over a murder weapon covered with his fingerprints. You got any suspects?"

"Maybe. A guy who was at the bachelor party disappeared. He didn't pick up his paycheck and no one at the store can reach him."

"Can his friends?"

Mia put down her fork. "I hadn't thought of that."

"Your generation doesn't give a job the respect it deserves. But God help them if they can't send one of those text messages they love so much to a friend."

"Excellent idea, Nonna. He's a good friend of the groom's, John Grazio. I'll see if I can manipulate some info out of John when I get to work." Mia kissed her grandmother on the cheek, got up, and deposited her plate in the sink. She patted her stomach. "And that breakfast just earned me a bike ride instead of a cab ride."

"*Si*, but first you're coming with me to welcome the new neighbors."

"They moved in?"

"A van unloaded all day yesterday while you were

gone. I'm gonna do like you said, make nice, then bring up Rose's Virgin Mary. I baked a welcome-to-the-neighborhood lasagna." Elisabetta lifted a to-go container double-wrapped in tin foil off the top of the stove. *"Andiamo."*

Elisabetta marched out of the house, lasagna in hand. Mia tagged along behind her toward Rose Caniglia's former home. They scurried up the front steps, which were lined with empty boxes. It was early, so Mia listened for sounds of life coming from the home. She heard a baby cheerfully babbling, followed by the murmur of a male voice. Mia nodded to her grandmother, and Elisabetta rang the bell. The front door opened. They were greeted by a handsome man with salt-and-pepper hair who appeared to be in his early forties.

"Ciao, I'm Elisabetta Carina and this is my granddaughter, Mia. We wanted to welcome you to the block."

Elisabetta handed him the lasagna. "Thank you so much," he said. "Come in, please. Forgive the mess. Between unpacking and keeping the babies happy, things are a little crazy right now."

"Of course, we totally understand," Mia said.

"Come meet the kiddles."

They followed the man into Rose's old living room. Her decades-old carpet had been pulled up, revealing lovely hardwood floors that would mate well with the new owners' impressive collection of mid-century furniture. An infant boy and a baby girl about a year older prattled from their bouncers. "You're lucky. They just ate so they're in good moods. I'm Philip, by the way. Let me get my better half down here to meet you." Philip went to the second-floor staircase and called, "Finn, we have guests, come downstairs."

Mia and Elisabetta cooed over the babies while they waited for Finn. A minute later, another handsome man roughly the same age as Philip appeared. "This is my husband, Finn. Finn, these are two of our new neighbors, Elisabetta and Mia."

Elisabetta was silent. "So nice to meet you," Mia said. She suppressed the urge to elbow her grandmother in the ribs to prompt a polite response.

"The pleasure is all ours," Finn said.

Philip held up Nonna's lasagna. "Look what they brought us."

"Lasagna? Che deliciozo. Grazie."

Philip rolled his eyes. "Don't mind him. He doesn't really speak Italian; he just took an immersion course before our honeymoon in Tuscany."

Finn made a face at Philip, then smiled at the women. "You know what they say, use it or lose it. Anyway, we're so happy to meet you. We're very excited about our new neighborhood. Please tell us anything we need to know about it. We want to fit in."

Mia made a choking sound. She cast a sideways glance at her grandmother, not sure how the elderly woman would react. There was a brief pause, then Elisabetta said, "The first thing you need to know is that the Virgin Mary statues and grottos in everyone's yard are an important part of 46th Place and mean a lot to everyone who lives here, no matter what their race or religion or . . . sex."

"We thought so," Philip said. "That's why we sent ours out to be cleaned and restored. We discovered she's marble, not plaster. She'll be gorgeous after her makeover."

This was a surprise to Elisabetta, as well as Mia. "You didn't get rid of her?"

Finn looked horrified. "No. We were both raised Catholic. We would never do that."

"Although our interior designer wanted us to," Philip said. "That's one of the reasons we fired her."

"That nasty blond lady?" Elisabetta asked, not bothering to hide her relief. "She's gone?"

"Yes," Finn said. "If she had her way, she would've put a match to this whole place. Fair warning, we will be re-doing the interior, but that's to make it more kid-friendly. We're not touching the outside. Like I said, we want to fit in."

Mia picked up a plaintive note in Finn's voice, and felt for the couple. "You already do. Right, Nonna?"

"*Si,* yes. I just have one question. Do you want to be called gays or homosexuals? I can't keep up with what's right these days."

The men exchanged a look, then Philip said, "Um . . . how about just calling us Philip and Finn?"

"Philip and Finn, it is," Mia quickly said. "Welcome to 46th Place. We're thrilled you're here. Let us know if you need anything. We're in the corner house on the other side of the street. I'll leave our phone numbers in your mailbox."

The four said good-byes as Mia ushered her grandmother out the door and down the front steps. "Wait until I tell the Army about this," Elisabetta said.

"Nonna, you're not going to make a big deal about the fact they're gay, are you?"

"Meh, who do you think I am?" Elisabetta said, affronted. "I was talking about Rose's Virgin Mary being marble. But I better tell the Army about the gay thing, too. Just so they don't open their mouths and something stupid comes out."

"We wouldn't want *that* to happen."

Elisabetta cast an acerbic look at her granddaughter. "Isn't it time for you and your sarcasm to go to work?" They reached home and Elisabetta pointed at Mia's bicycle chained inside the front yard. *"Arriverderci, bella."*

With the wind at Mia's back, the ride was cold but shorter than usual. She dismounted the bike and reached down to retrieve the sturdy lock she'd treated herself to. She stood up, lock in hand, and gave a shriek when she found herself face-to-face with Teri Fuoco.

"My sources tell me your father is still the only person of interest in both murders," the *Trib* reporter said.

"What are you, a ghost? How do you suddenly appear like that? And not even a hello?" Mia glowered at the other woman, then brushed past her, pushing her bicycle toward Belle View.

"I'm not gonna stop," Teri said, following behind her.

"You're on private property," Mia said. "Don't make me call the police and report you."

Teri jumped off the curb. "I'm on public property now. Marina parking."

"I recommend you park yourself somewhere else, and fast."

Mia pulled open the heavy glass door and was

about to go in when Teri called to her, "I'm doing this for my father. Just like you."

There was a note of anguish in the reporter's voice. Mia let go of the door. "What do you mean, you're doing this for your father?"

Teri rubbed her eyes. She cleared her throat, but when she spoke, her voice quavered. "Dad was a reporter for the *Trib*. He spent years tracking the Boldano family. He was obsessed with doing an exposé on Donny. For a while, Donny kept one step ahead of him. But Dad wouldn't give up. He finally had the material for a great story and took it to the publisher—who killed it. Maybe because he was afraid of being killed himself. I don't know what happened. All I know is Dad got demoted to covering local politics. He had a heart attack during a meeting on adding a composting component to the city's recycling stations. I think he died of boredom. But"—the quaver disappeared from Teri's voice and she stood taller—"there's a new publisher at the *Trib*. New publisher, new rules. He's hungry for content and loves that I want to finish what my dad started."

Mia was silent. Teri's story about her late father hadn't set off any B.S. alarms, which was too bad. Duking it out with a con artist would have been much easier. "I'm sorry about your dad."

"Thank you." Teri said this with sincerity.

"But there's no story here. Belle View is a legit business. My dad is its legit owner and manager. You're gonna have to take your shovel and dig up dirt somewhere else because I can guarantee you will find nothing, repeat *nothing*, here. *Capisce?*"

"*Ho capito.*" Teri's accent was flawless, but with a last name like Fuoco, it would be.

Mia sagged. The confrontation, coming on top of the last few days' tidal wave of events, was wearing her out. "I know I can't stop you from writing what you wanna write. Just make it the truth. Please."

"I always do," the reporter said with pride. "But *capisce* this: if you ever try to bribe me or threaten me or strong-arm my boss, I will definitely be writing *that* truth."

Teri strode over to a tiny Smart car. She got in and slammed the door shut, then backed out of her parking space and puttered out of the lot. As Mia watched her go, she thought to herself, *That thing looks dangerous. I hope she's not taking it on the highway.*

Having rid herself of the irritating reporter, Mia was ready for the respite of an empty Belle View. She wheeled her bike into the building, parked it in the hallway, and then went to her office. She tapped John Grazio's cell number into her phone. It was 8:15 A.M., a perfectly respectable time to call the Koller Properties security employee, whom she figured was either at work or on his way there. "John Grazio here," he answered. He sounded slightly out of breath.

"It's Mia Carina. Are you on your way to work?"

"Yeah, and I'm running late. I had to spend the morning listening to Alice gripe about her obnoxious twin's giant baby shower. You'd think Annamaria was delivering the next Lion King."

"I'll keep this short. Have you talked to Chris Tinker lately? I bought a phone from him and have a question, but they told me at his store that he quit."

There was a pause. "No, haven't heard from him," John said. "I wouldn't worry about Chris. See if they can help you at the store."

"Between us, he sort of gave me the phone, so I

can't let the store know I have it. Can you give me his number?"

"What? I couldn't hear. You're breaking up—"

The call abruptly ended. "Seriously?" Mia said to her phone. "The old 'you're breaking up' is the best you can do, liar?" She may not have gotten a lead on the errant cell phone salesman but Grazio's lame response made it obvious that Drinker was up to something and the groom-to-be knew what it was.

A notification popped up on her computer. She checked her in-box and saw a daunting number of unread messages, the overall bulk of them alerting her to the fact that it was time to stop sleuthing and start working. The first order of business was sending an unhappy bride-to-be some potentially good news. Rather than re-order the pasta forks that Mia was forced to give out to placate the fiftieth anniversary party guests on the night of Angie's murder, she was going to ratchet up the Paluski-Grazio favors. She pulled up the file for Annamaria Paluski's wedding to see what Alice was competing against. Her twin had given out ceramic candy dishes. "Oh, we can beat that big-time," Mia murmured as she searched the site. "Aha, got it."

She bookmarked a page, then composed an e-mail to Alice Paluski: "For favors, instead of the pasta forks, which were ordered before I came on board, and I have to admit I've seen before, what about giving every guest a wine bottle with a label that has your names and wedding date on it, along with a wine-stopper that has a crystal heart on the top and comes in a black-and-gold box, which can also have your names and wedding date on it?" Alice's response was instantaneous. "YES!!!!!!!! I LOVE IT SO

MUCH!!!!!!!!! EFF YOU, STUPID PASTA FORKS
AND ANNAMARIA'S CANDY DISH!!!!!!"

Mia did a triumphant fist pump. "Mia Carina for
the win," she trumpeted to the air. Then an idea occurred to her. She typed another e-mail to Alice.
"Does your vet clinic ever get rescues to adopt out?"

"All the time," Alice wrote back. "We have a
non-profit thing where we give free first exams and
treatments to them, so a lot of rescue groups come to
us. We even have a spaymobile we take to poor places
where we do free spaying. Why?"

Mia thought of her new friends in the pet bereavement group. "I have some friends I want to connect
with you. Will be in touch."

Pleased with herself, Mia put her hands behind
her head, her feet on the desk, and leaned back in
her office chair, careful not to tip over. She was about
to begin cleaning out her in-box when she heard
what sounded like water running. Mia sat up and listened closely. Water ran and then stopped. She heard
footsteps on the floor above. Her heart thumped.

She wasn't alone in Belle View after all.

Chapter Twenty-One

Mia rose to her feet. She kicked off her shoes to make her footsteps silent, then took a quiet walk from her office into the hallway. Fighting to control her fear, she crept along the wall, now grateful for the linoleum floor she'd hated on sight. At least it didn't squeak the way a wood floor might. She reached the end of the hallway and peered around the corner, taking care not to be seen. The foyer was empty. She heard footsteps again, this time starting down the facility's stairs. Mia ducked out of sight. She heard someone open and close the front door. Then she heard a motorcycle engine revving. She dropped to the ground and crawled along combat-style, so no one could see her through Belle View's large glass windows. Mia reached the window nearest her, which was half-hidden by an overgrown bush outside. She raised herself up enough to see over the bush and caught the back of Evans as he sped off on his motorcycle.

When Mia was sure he was completely out of sight, she stood up and scurried to her office. While she'd looked up Evans's former employers, she hadn't done a full-on Internet search for anything related to him.

She put her shoes back on, plopped down in her office chair, and typed in the sous chef's name. It only came up in connection with the shuttered restaurants he once worked at. Aside from that, it was as if he didn't exist. Did he? Mia wondered. Maybe Evans Tucker was a false identity. If so, then who exactly was this strange Belle View employee?

"Morning." Cammie sauntered by, holding a large coffee.

"Cammie, what do you know about Evans?"

"Is this gonna be a long conversation because I have to leave in twenty minutes for a belly dance class." She pulled a hot-pink belly dance scarf out of her purse and shook it, making the small silver coins jingle. "My personal trainer says nothing works the abs like belly dancing. It's sexy too, so it's another thing to torture Pete with." She put the scarf back in her purse. "Why are you asking about Evans?"

"Because," she said, leaning forward, "I know why he discovered the fire. He's been crashing here at night. Evans has been sleeping at Belle View."

"Really? Here?" Cammie looked stunned, then skeptical. "That's kind of hard to buy."

"It's a perfect location. Think about it. There's always some kind of food in the fridges. We've got showers and big comfy couches in the bridal lounges." Cammie still looked dubious. "I bet I can prove it. Come with me."

Mia led Cammie up the stairs to the second-floor bridal lounge. The room looked pristine. "I don't know, Mia," Cammie said. "I don't see anything telling me someone was here."

"Let's look in the bathroom."

The women stepped inside. "There!" Mia pointed

inside the shower. Drops of water clung to the drain, others to the shower door. "Someone used this shower very recently."

"It is a little steamy in here," Cammie had to admit. "Wait, are you thinking that Evans is the murderer?"

"Maybe."

"He can't be. He's such a good cook."

"What does that have to with anything?" Mia asked. "Especially being a killer. It makes him more of a suspect because he's good with knives."

Cammie wrinkled her nose with distaste. "Yuck."

"You have to admit, Evans is nice but he's a strange guy. We uncovered a secret. Maybe there are others we haven't sussed out yet."

"Or maybe he's homeless and doesn't want us to know."

"Oh," Mia said, deflated. "I didn't even think about that."

"I've known him longer than you. He's got a lot of pride. Still . . ." Cammie looked around. "I have to admit, I'm a little creeped out. I'm not sorry I have to leave. I'll be back later. Maybe."

Cammie turned to go. Mia grabbed her arm. "I need you to help me spy on Evans. He's working the Koller party next Saturday night, so it'll be a different environment, not a place he's used to. He won't be as comfortable, and he might let a clue leak. Come to the party. Follow him around and see if you pick up anything hinky. I'll be too busy doing party stuff."

Cammie considered this. "Hmm . . . Pete would hate the thought of me putting myself in a potentially dangerous situation. I'll do it!"

"Great. There'll be a lot of suspects at the party. The Koller brothers, probably Sofeea Sloan, the sketchy madam, John Grazio—who, even if he's not the killer, knows more about his pal Chris than he's letting on—even Dee, and now Evans. If the murders were about real estate, there could be suspects there I haven't even mentioned."

Cammie held up a perfectly manicured index finger—peach with a tiny white rosebud painted over the primary color. "Back up. Who's Dee?"

"The DJ for the party. He did the bachelor party and is kind of famous, but since he was at Belle View the night of Angie's murder, I don't want to rule him out just because he's really good-looking and I had the best time hanging out with him and his friends last night."

Cammie grabbed Mia by her upper arms and shook her. "Listen to you! Listen! You are so terrified of getting into another relationship that you'd rather have a hot guy being a murder suspect than a possible new boyfriend."

The truth of Cammie's blunt statement so shook Mia that she burst into tears. Cammie replaced shaking with a hug. "I know," Mia sobbed. "I'm a total headcase. It was one thing when Jamie and I were kind of flirting, but then I heard he had a girlfriend and I got upset in a way I didn't expect. Then Dee seemed interested, and he's being really cool and taking it slow, and last night felt so different and good, like I was getting my personal life back. But I'm scared. What if I mess it up again? Like I did with Adam?"

Cammie looked upward, held a fist in the air, and let fly a string of Greek four-letter words. "I curse you, Adam Grosso! I curse you to the grave and beyond!"

She lowered her fist. "You think the Boldano Family would have made itself useful and taken him out."

"We don't know that they didn't."

"True. Mia, sweetie, you're not the first person to have a starter marriage." Cammie said this with affection. "And God knows you won't be the last. There's probably a divorce in America every five minutes. Look at me and Pete."

"But you know you're getting back together."

"Probably, but do *not* tell him that. He'll cut off all the perks I get from making him try to woo me back. Forget about me and Pete. My point is, stop beating yourself up for making a bad choice and start focusing on making a good one."

"Posi said the same thing. I hear you both here." Mia tapped her head. "It's just not coming through here." She sniffled and tapped her heart.

"It will, *agapiménos*. My little sweetheart." Cammie gave Mia a kiss on the cheek. "Now, let's talk about that spying thing. Do I get to wear a disguise? I'm down with that. Except for a wig or a hat. Nothing to mess up the 'do." Cammie patted her 1980s coif.

Mia dabbed her eyes with the bottom of her sweater and managed a smile. "No costume. We need to look like we're there for only one reason: to throw a party that will make all of Cimmanin's friends incredibly jealous and want to hire us to throw even better parties."

"Cimmanin? Funny, that's how I say cimm-cimm—the brown spice. See? I can never say it right."

Mia thought the days preceding Cimmanin's party would drag on slowly, but instead they rocketed by.

She took the subway into Manhattan to meet up with Cimmanin, who gave her a tour of the Koller penthouse where the birthday party would take place. It was a sleek, all-white space with breathtaking views from three walls of floor-to-ceiling glass. Bathrooms, elevators, service rooms, and a kitchen off a long hallway made up the fourth wall, but a double glass door at the east end of the hall led to a glass-walled outdoor terrace with another spectacular view. There was no salmon-colored marble to be found anywhere in the penthouse. Mia assumed the contractor ran out by the time he reached the top of the building.

Mia also managed to rein in the groom's-mother-zilla. Lin sent a sample blue rose that was breathtaking enough to make Mother Nature jealous and Barbara Grazio almost happy. "It's close," the curmudgeonly woman said. "If that's the best you can do, I guess I'll have to live with it." Mia got her secret revenge by pitching the shade of "Barbara Grazio Blue," as she now called it, to Cimmanin as her party's color scheme.

Throughout the week, Jamie Boldano called and texted to check in with her. She put him off by blaming a heavy workload, which wasn't a full-on lie. Between booking new events and working on upcoming ones, she was almost as busy as she claimed to be. Jamie got the hint and left her alone, which Mia forced herself to accept as for the best. She hired staff for Cimmanin's party and went over the menu with Guadalupe, making any adjustments necessitated by the fact they weren't cooking on site. "If I can feed a tent of soldiers with chafing dishes and Sterno cans during a rocket attack and not hear any complaints,

I think I can take care of a group of skinny white girls and boys," the Dominican chef said. "Right, Evans?"

"Don't talk to me, I'm trying to get these cookie cups right." In addition to asking him to come up with a special dessert for the party, Mia had put Evans in charge of liquor for the event's several bars. He'd chosen to combine the two tasks by making chocolate chip, snickerdoodle, and oatmeal cookie "cups" that would be filled with the booze of a guest's choice at the party.

Mia watched as Evans, brow furrowed, placed balls of dough into a pan for mini muffins, then used a muddler to press down and create a small crater. She knew he was still spending his nights at Belle View. Mia had shared this disconcerting discovery with Ravello. She also told her father something Guadalupe had told her in confidence. The chef was missing one of her favorite knives—a carving knife, exactly like the one found in Angie. "We'll keep an eye on Evans," Ravello said. "Be vigilant, *cara mia*. *Chi dorme non piglia pesci*. Those who sleep don't catch any fish." It wasn't one of her father's best Italian sayings, but it sort of made sense.

The day of Cimmanin's party finally arrived. The staff, full-time and part-time, showed up at Belle View hours before the event to load up a van with food and supplies. Ravello was already in Manhattan; he'd taken on the task of managing the centerpieces, which Mia knew was an excuse to spend time wooing Lin Yeung.

Guadalupe and Evans drove the van while the others rode on the minibus Mia rented to shuttle them to and from the party. "I have to admit," she said to Cammie as they strapped themselves in, "it's nice working a party where someone says, 'I don't care what it costs, make it happen.'"

"You learn to love the clients with deep pockets," Cammie said. "Any updates on Evans?"

Mia twirled a lock of hair around her finger and shook her head. "No. Nothing new." Mia's anxiety level soared as the minibus drove over the Queensboro Bridge. She was battling a bad case of nerves, brought on by the stress of pulling off Cimmanin's party while also spying on the various suspects who'd be attending.

"Well," Cammie said, "maybe we'll get lucky and find a clue that points to someone besides him tonight."

"I hope so. I love his cookie cups. I sampled an oatmeal filled with a shot of rum, and it was to die for."

Without weekday traffic to slow it down, the Belle View caravan made good time. The van pulled into the Koller Properties loading dock and the minibus parked on the street in front of the company's building. The bus passengers disembarked. "I'm in the city, I'm in the city," Missy, hired to cater-waiter the party, squealed, jumping up and down. "And don't tell me Queens is the city, Mia. This is the *real* city."

"No time to argue," Mia said.

She noticed John Grazio talking to a security detail. All wore gray turtlenecks and blazers featuring the Koller Properties logo, as well as headsets. Grazio saw her and excused himself from the group. He walked over to Mia and after they exchanged greetings, said, "I have to confirm everyone in your group is approved and then distribute badges."

Mia produced a paper from her jeans pocket. "I

printed out my list of who's working tonight. You can match it up against yours."

Grazio walked off with her list. A knot of paparazzi and reporters had gathered on the sidewalk behind a temporary barrier. Mia noticed Teri Fuoco among them. She looked away, but it was too late—they'd already made eye contact. Mia marched over to her adversary. "I hate to disappoint you but all that's going on here is Belle View is catering a party. There's no story."

"I'm on a break from all things Boldano," Teri retorted. "My boss wanted me to cover the party. With a bunch of obnoxious rich jerks getting wasted, odds are pretty good someone will do something stupid I can write about. And I don't mind getting out of Queens and into Manhattan for a change."

Mia stared at her. "You didn't say 'into the city.'"

"Huh?" Teri said, confused.

"You said 'into Manhattan,' not 'into the city.'"

"Well, duh," Teri said. "Queens *is* the city. Jeez, show our borough a little respect."

A photographer nudged Teri. "Is she anyone?"

"Depends on your definition of anyone," Teri said with a shrug. "She's Ravello Carina's daughter."

"That counts."

"Oh, so not happening," Mia said. The photographer tried to take her picture, but she thwarted him by covering her face with my hand while using the other to shoot the bird at both him and Teri.

John Grazio approached Mia. He held up her list. "Your gang checks out. You're good to go."

Her group approved and vetted, Mia put the Belle View employees to work, instructing them to help Guadalupe and Evans unload everything from the van onto a freight elevator. The crew formed an assembly line, passing food, beverages, and serving equipment onto a capacious elevator. Then they all squeezed into a second elevator and traveled up to the Koller penthouse.

"Whoa," Missy said when the elevator door opened, and she stepped into the penthouse. Her fellow cater-waiters, all "bridge and tunnel" kids who rarely got into Manhattan, if ever, were equally awestruck. They ran to the various windows and gaped at the view. "I can see the Empire State Building," Missy called out, excited. "And the Statue of Liberty."

"I can see Queens from this window," said Jeremy, a lunchtime waiter at Roberto's who Mia had brought on to replace the late Giorgio. "Almost to my house."

"I got a great view of Central Park and all the buildings I wanna live in someday." This came from Elena, a sultry aspiring singer in her mid-twenties. "Who do I have to sleep with to get a place like this?"

Kevin Koller emerged from a passenger elevator in time to hear Elena's question, which Mia knew to be a genuine inquiry and not a joke. "That would be me or my brother, but we're taken," Kevin quipped. Mia was struck by this flash of humor. Relieved of the shadow cast by his domineering older brother, the younger Koller seemed relaxed and almost jovial. He crooked a finger at her. "I want to show you something."

Mia followed him to a utility room next to the service elevators. A pop-out cake took up half of it. She shuddered at the sight, which brought back unpleasant memories of finding Angie's lifeless body.

"What's the cake for? Cimmanin and I never talked about renting one. Is it from another party?"

"Nope." Koller looked pleased with himself. "I've got a big surprise for Cimmanin. I hired Brianna to sing 'Happy Birthday' to her."

Mia's eyes widened. "Brianna?" she repeated. "*The* Brianna?"

"Uh, yeah. What, you think I'd hire some celebrity impersonator?"

"No, it's just . . ." There was no singer in the world more famous than Brianna, at least that week. Mia didn't have time to keep up with pop culture, so for her to know that the multitalented performer currently had four songs on *Billboard*'s Top Ten list verified Brianna's superstar status. "I can't believe you were able to book her."

Koller waved a hand to indicate it was nothing to land the celebrity. "That's what a couple of safety deposit boxes of gold bricks are for. Everyone has a price. Even Brianna. Back to the party: after everyone eats, she'll jump out of the cake and sing 'Happy Birthday.' Then she'll sing a couple of her biggest hits to a background track. I didn't hire her band. Too expensive."

Koller strolled off, leaving Mia to marvel at the gall of a gazillionaire who'd shown himself to be both profligate and a cheapskate. Then she evaluated the ramifications of this new twist to the party. Brianna would surely come with her own security team. Coupled with Koller's, that meant a lot of eyes on the crowd, who'd be on their best behavior until they were too drunk to care. The double dose of security was a setback to Mia's plans. When it came to her list of murder suspects, the best she could hope for was either her, Cammie, or Ravello picking up an overheard conversational clue they could parse.

She returned to the main room of the penthouse, where the waitstaff was draping white tablecloths over the rented ten-top party tables, then setting them with the rental company's best china and flatware. Having finished setting up several long tables as buffet stations, Guadalupe and Evans had relocated to the facility's small kitchen to prep the passed hors d'oeuvres. Mia clapped her hands to get everyone's attention. She shared the breaking news about Brianna, which was met with screams and more jumping up and down from Missy, whose general excitement was turning her into a human pogo stick. "No photos, no autographs," Mia cautioned. "Maintain distance from the celebrity at all times. And absolutely no dancing." Kevin Koller hadn't mentioned any of this, but he didn't seem the type to let the hired help in on the fun. The staff was disappointed but understood. Mia had a feeling they'd be way more well-behaved than Koller's party guests.

She heard the thud of the freight elevator doors opening. A minute later, Lin appeared pushing a service cart loaded with the most exquisite centerpieces Mia had ever seen. Ravello was behind Lin, pushing a cart that held a more elaborate floral display destined for the birthday girl's table. All centerpieces featured an array of white orchids and hand-tinted bright blue roses arranged in plain white bowls. The arrangements were simple, yet breathtaking.

"*Ciao, bambina.*" Ravello kissed his daughter on both cheeks. "I want you to meet a friend of mine.

Lin Yeung. She's the florist I met on that cruise I went on. She's pretty good, huh?"

"Amazing. So nice to meet you, Lin."

Mia extended her hand and Lin gave it a light shake. "And wonderful to meet you." A look passed between the women, tacit agreement that their previous meeting would never be shared with Ravello.

"I'll put you two in charge of putting out the arrangements. After that, Dad, I need to talk to you and Cammie."

"You go ahead," Ravello told Lin. "I'll catch up." The floral designer pushed her cart away. When she was out of earshot, Ravello turned to his daughter. "I wanted to tell you that I'm thinking of asking Lin out on a date."

"Really?" Mia said, playing dumb. "She seems super nice and I wouldn't mind having a florist in the family. Go for it."

Ravello, beaming, took off after Lin. Mia, happy for her father, tried to ignore the anxiety that was making her stomach roil.

The remaining hours of party prep went smoothly. Dee and Ty arrived with their equipment. Being party pros, they set up the DJ booth quickly and with ease. Mia was relieved to learn that Dee already had the tracks to all of Brianna's hits, having worked a corporate gig where she was the expensive entertainment. Cimmanin, in a bathrobe and hair rollers, stopped by to check on the staff's progress and her screams of joy served as a seal of approval. "I love everything, especially the centerpieces," she declared. "Kevvie, if we get that summer place in the Hamptons, we gotta plant blue roses." Mia figured she'd let "Kevvie" break the news that blue roses didn't exist in the real world.

Minutes before the guests began arriving, Mia pulled Cammie and Ravello into a huddle. Lin, who had stayed per Ravello's request, joined them. "The one thing we can do tonight is circulate. The Kollers and guests will think we're just doing our job. But what we're really doing is listening in to conversations and seeing if we can pick up any clues that would help suss out Angie's and Giorgio's killers and get the police off our backs. *Capisce?*"

"*Capisco.*"

"*Katalavaíno.*"

"*Tôi hiểu.*"

"Excellent." Mia clapped her hands like a quarterback. "Let's do this."

Ravello pointed to his eyes with both index fingers, and then patted the back of his head. Mia nodded. When she was little, her father liked to tease her by asking, "Who's got eyes in the back of her head?" He'd turn her around and announce to the back of her head, "There they are, I see them!" while she giggled. Eventually, Mia realized this wasn't a game. Her father was training her. He was sending a message: Always be aware of your surroundings. Have eyes in the back of your head.

A half hour into the party, Mia knew it was a hit. The room was packed with an un-diverse selection of the Big Apple's wealthiest Caucasians. Some were kitted out in designer finery, others—mostly the younger guys—were in jeans and T-shirts. A table set up for gifts creaked under its load. John Grazio patrolled the room, his strained expression a contrast to

the festive atmosphere. Sofeea Sloan, dressed in a
low-cut clingy black gown, glided into the room holding hands with Bradley Koller. Mia noticed a few of
the older male guests looked nervous at the sight of
her. Dee and Ty spun what she considered warm-up
tracks, songs that brought life to the event without
pulling people onto the dance floor too soon and
burning them out. Forty-five minutes into the shindig,
Cimmanin made a grand entrance on Kevin Koller's
arm. Mia had no idea how the birthday girl pulled
it off, but she managed to find a body-hugging
mini dress in the same shade of blue as the centerpieces. She threw open her arms as if to embrace the
crowd. "Welcome to my party, everyone. Eat a lot,
dance a lot, and drink until you're totally effed up.
Whoo-hoo!"

The guests took Cimmanin at her word, devouring
the hors d'oeuvres and lining up at the bars. Mia alternated between event duties and eavesdropping on
conversations. The latter task was made difficult by
the party's high decibel level, courtesy of the thump-
ing music and a hundred different conversations
happening at once. The room, lit only by votive
candles and the ambient light of the surrounding
skyscrapers, was dark as pitch. Dee blasted a popular
song and people took to the dance floor. As Mia negotiated her way around them, her attention was
drawn to a male guest hovering on the sidelines. He
was dressed in jeans and a hoodie with the hood
pulled over his head, giving him the appearance of a
young Unabomber. Mia switched course. She positioned herself behind a knot of guests chatting and
peeked around them at the mysterious guest. *Could it
be?* she wondered. A shock of unnaturally blond hair

slipped out from under the guest's hoodie. He tucked it back, then turned and walked away from the dance floor to the bar. His duck-footed gait confirmed Mia's suspicions.

The guest was missing cell phone salesman Chris Tinker.

Chapter Twenty-Two

Mia started to follow Chris, but she was waylaid by Missy. "We've burned through all the hors d'oeuvres," the young waitress said. "I thought rich people didn't ever eat because they're always trying to be thin."

"They're drinking like they just docked from a year at sea in a submarine, so that must be making them hungry," Mia said. "Tell everyone to get into position to man the buffet lines."

Missy left to spread the word among the waitstaff and Mia hurried to Dee. "Can you count to thirty and then announce the buffet's open?"

Dee gave her a thumbs-up, accompanied by a sexy smile. "You got it, boss."

Mia sacrificed an opportunity to flirt, instead opting to find the errant Tinker the Drinker. As people lined up to heap plates with Cimmanin's requested lineup of six different versions of mac and cheese ranging from traditional to truffle-infused, Mia scoured the crowd but had no luck spotting him. She found John Grazio out on the terrace sneaking a cigarette that he put out the minute he saw Mia. "Whatever you do, don't tell Alice you caught me smoking," he said. "I don't want that added to the list of crap she's busting my hump for."

"What cigarette?" Mia said. She affected a confused expression. "It's the weirdest thing. I could swear I saw your friend Chris here tonight. His hair was blond, though, and he had a hoodie pulled over his head, like he was trying to hide who he was or something."

John made a face. He pulled out another cigarette and lit it. After taking a few drags, he said, "Don't tell anyone, but yeah. Chris is here. I swear to the guy upstairs, Drinker's lost his mind. He thinks the mob is after him so he 'went into hiding.' Can you believe it? I mean, how crazy is that?"

"Super crazy," Mia said, neglecting to share how she told Chris her mobster father and his associates wouldn't be too happy about the extra money he was pocketing from fake upcharges on cell phone cards.

"He really wanted to come tonight because he has the major hots for Brianna. If you want my opinion, the guy should go into hiding at Bellevue. The mental hospital, not your place."

"Are you sure that's the only reason he disappeared?"

"As far as I know." Grazio looked at her with suspicion. "Why else do you think he would?"

Mia suddenly felt nervous. She gave a nonchalant shrug. "I don't know. It's like you said, hiding from the mob seems *molto pazzo*." She crossed her eyes and made circles with her index finger, the universal sign for "cuckoo." "I better get back and make sure the buffet's going okay."

"The security detail can't eat until all the guests

have." John dropped the cigarette and stubbed it out. "The Kollers can spend a million bucks to get Brianna here but their employees get stuck eating leftovers. Cheap sons of a you-know-what."

"You sure acted like you loved them at your bachelor party." Mia regretted the blurt as soon as it left her mouth.

Again, Grazio eyed her with mistrust. "What's the deal with you? Why are you so interested in what me and my friends do?"

"I'm not. I'm just a nosy person in general. Major character flaw but I can't seem to control myself. Anyhoo, I'll make sure to save you and the other security guys big helpings of all the mac and cheeses."

Mia fled. She pulled up short when she saw an unexpected guest emerge from the elevator—Felicity Stewart Forbes. The real estate agent wore a different collection of designer knockoffs and clutched a large wrapped box in her hands. "Felicity, hello," Mia said, faking a smile. "Welcome to the party. Although I don't remember seeing you on the guest list. I thought you and the Koller brothers had a falling-out."

"We patched things up. I was a last-minute addition. Here." Felicity held up her cell and showed Mia her "Approved" Koller status. She couldn't hide a smirk. "See you inside."

Felicity flounced off toward the party. Mia searched for reasons the Kollers would have done an about-face regarding the unctuous woman. The first one that popped into her head was blackmail. But what could a middling Queens real estate agent have on one of the city's biggest developers? Mia's body buzzed with excitement. The answer to that question might reveal a murderer.

Mia was about to track Felicity when the doors on the two passenger elevators opened simultaneously and pop sensation Brianna emerged, flanked by bodyguards and followed by an entourage of assorted professionals and hangers-on. Mia resisted the urge to squeal, "OMG, you're Brianna!!!!!" Instead, she affected her most professional voice and said, "Hello, you must be Brianna. I'm Mia Carina, the event coordinator."

She extended her hand and a bodyguard instantly jumped between her and the singer. "Jeez, Harlan, take a pill," Brianna said. She pushed him aside. "I don't shake, but not because I'm a jerk. It's because I play the piano and can't risk anyone squeezing these mitts too hard."

She held up her hands, which were tiny, like the rest of her. Mia had read that a lot of celebrities were smaller in real life than they appeared on screen and now she saw it for herself. Brianna was about her grandmother Elisabetta's current height, which had been significantly reduced thanks to age and osteoporosis. The singer's white-blond hair sat in an upright stack on top of her head. She wore a gold leather bra, matching sequined short shorts, and gold thigh-high, spiked-heel boots. Despite an outfit that made her look like a dominatrix, Brianna seemed down-to-earth. She gestured with a swoop to everyone surrounding her. "This is Team All About Me. You don't have to talk to any of them."

"Except me," a young woman wearing severe glasses and a black designer suit said. "I'm her publicist,

Denisa, and I have an NDA I need everyone here to sign. That means Nondisclosure Agreement for you civilians." She spoke slowly, as if Mia was half-witted.

"Ignore her and tell me where to go," Brianna said. Sofeea Sloan appeared around the bend in the hallway, on her way to the ladies' room. Brianna let out a shriek. "Sofeea!"

"Brianna!"

The two women embraced.

"You know each other?" Mia said, nonplussed.

"She was my madam," Brianna said.

Mia thought Denisa might faint. "OMG, you didn't hear that, nobody heard that!" the publicist cried out, helplessly waving her unsigned NDAs in the air.

While Brianna and Sofeea caught up and Denisa hyperventilated, Mia paged Kevin Koller, who came at a run to meet the superstar. He introduced himself and after a few minutes of fawning—none of which impressed Brianna, endearing her even more to Mia—he laid out the plan. "It's time for dessert. As soon as it's been put out, I'm gonna announce that I have a special surprise for Cimmanin." Koller pointed to the pop-out cake. "Mia's people'll wheel you in, you jump out and start singing 'Happy Birthday.' Screams, applause, then you do a few songs. Sound good?"

"Sounds like a paycheck." Brianna yanked at her shorts, which were riding up her bottom.

Kevin returned to the party and Brianna trotted over to the pop-out cake. "I'll make sure dessert is set up," Mia said to her. "Do you need help getting into the cake?"

"Nope. Not exactly the first time I jumped out of one of these. Am I right, Sofeea?"

"So right." The two women chuckled and high-fived. Mia vowed to download all of Brianna's albums as soon as she caught a break.

She left the celebrity with her retinue and Sofeea, and headed to the kitchen. Mia almost collided with Guadalupe, who was heading to the event room with a tray of Evans's cookie cups. "Why isn't Evans setting those up?" Mia asked. "They were his creation."

"He won't leave the kitchen."

"Even to see Brianna perform?"

"Nope. Says there are too many white people here. It makes him uncomfortable."

Mia frowned. She didn't buy this was the real reason Evans was hiding from the crowd. But with party duties superseding her sleuthing efforts, Mia didn't have time to confront him. She needed to alert Dee to Brianna's imminent performance.

She left the service area for the penthouse main room, where she negotiated her way through the drunken revelers to the DJ booth. Dee and Ty were bent over an outlet strip. The music was so loud her ears rang. She leaned over the top of the booth toward the DJs. "I'm powering down a turntable," she heard Dee tell Ty. "These offsite venues aren't equipped for us. I don't want to blow a circuit breaker again like that time at Belle View. Not with this crowd. Brad'll kill me."

Mia's chest constricted. She could recall every minute of John Grazio's bachelor party as if she had the condition where you remembered every detail of your life. No circuit breaker had blown that night, so what was Dee talking about? And "Brad"? When she spoke to Dee about hiring him for Cimmanin's birthday party, he implied he'd never worked for the Kollers before. Yet based on what she'd just overheard, he was on a nickname basis with at least one of the developer brothers.

Living in the heart of the Family, Mia had developed an almost animal instinct for trouble. It was as if she could smell it in the air. Call it a survival skill in a world that could be fraught with danger, but she'd learned at a very early age, if these hyperdeveloped instincts were sending the message that something was wrong, something was definitely wrong. And the message they were currently sending was that DJ DJ, aka Dee, aka mystery real name, had lied to her.

He looked up from the outlet strip and noticed Mia. She plastered on a casual expression. "Oh, hey," he said. "I didn't see you there."

"No bigs," she said, trying to play it cool. "I wanted to let you know they'll be wheeling out Brianna in a little bit, right after Kevin tells everyone there's a surprise guest. You've got her music ready to go?"

"Got it," Dee said, with another of his patented sexy smiles and thumbs-up. Mia managed a weak smile and a thumbs-up in return. She sauntered away. Then, as soon as she was out of his eyeline, she broke into a run, on the hunt for John Grazio. She found Koller's head of security being lectured to by Denisa, Brianna's anal-retentive publicist. ". . . And that means zero photo opps of Brianna coming out of that horrible cake," Denisa said, making zeros with her thumbs and index fingers. "Zero with a capital Z.

I want all cell phones confiscated and not returned until Brianna, like Elvis, has left the building."

John, who didn't look thrilled about being ordered around by the Hollywood flack, said, "It's gonna make a lot of people unhappy, especially Bradley and Kevin, but I'll tell my guys to each take a table and round up the phones."

He escaped from the publicist as she was about to launch into another list of demands. Mia grabbed his arm as he passed her. "I need to talk to you." She pulled him onto the terrace, which was empty. Everyone had moved inside, awaiting the introduction of the surprise guest. "You do security checks on everyone who does work for the Koller company, right?"

"Yeah, why?"

"I can't explain yet; it's just a gut feeling. Do you happen to know DJ DJ's real name?"

"Not offhand, but I've probably got it somewhere in my files."

"Please find it for me. As fast as you can."

John, a serious look on his face, nodded and strode off. Mia hurried inside and down the hall. She remembered how cagey Dee was when she had pressed him to share his real name. That, coupled with his lies, led her to think that his birth name might be the clue to whatever chain of events culminated in Angie's and Giorgio's murders.

She reached the pop-out cake. Missy, Jeremy, Elena, and a few other waiters were waiting for their cue to push it onto the dance floor. Kevin Koller was in the middle of his speech setting up the reveal. Pleased with himself, he was making the most of the moment. "So, I said to myself, what's the best gift for this beautiful lady over here?" A light followed him as he strolled over to Cimmanin, mic in hand, like a lounge singer working a room. "How do I give her a twenty-fifth birthday she'll never forget? A shopping spree in Paris? A Mediterranean cruise on a private yacht? A diamond the size of my fist?"

"Yes, yes, and yes!" Cimmanin yelled, and her guests laughed.

"Not tonight, babe. Those can happen anytime—"

"Not in my world," Elena muttered.

"—But what other birthday girl," Kevin continued, "can say she had 'Happy Birthday' sung to her by the biggest pop star in the world—Brianna!"

"Cue cake," Mia told her crew.

As they wheeled out the cake, Mia pulled out her cell phone to call Ravello and Cammie and share her hunch about Dee. A text from John popped up. **"I got a name for you. Achi—"** Before Mia could finish reading the message, a burly security guard yanked the phone out of her hand. "No pictures."

Mia grabbed for the phone, which he held over his head. "Give that back, I need it. I'm the event planner."

"You've got a headset. It doesn't come with a camera. Use that."

"I need to make some private calls and I can't do that with a headset."

"Take it up with Team Brianna."

The guard trudged off with her confiscated phone, and Mia released a few profanities. Screams and applause came from the event room. She peeked in and saw the singer had emerged from the cake. Brianna sang "Happy Birthday" to a beyond-thrilled Cimmanin while Mia's employees wheeled the cake back into the hallway. Mia searched the room for

Ravello or Cammie, but it was too dark to make them out. Brianna finished the song and launched into her most recent hit, accompanied by strobe lighting effects that made looking for anyone in the room even more difficult.

Rather than hunt for her father and Cammie, Mia decided to find John Grazio. If her instincts were right, DJ DJ's true identity would separate facts from theory and connect the secretive man to Belle View. She scurried down the hallway, checking out the various rooms that lined it, but the head of security was nowhere to be found. She reached the far corner of the hallway, where her employees had parked the pop-out cake by the service elevator. Panicked, Mia froze. A man's foot poked out from behind the cake.

Mia summoned up the courage to approach the scene and pushed the cake out of the way. John Grazio lay on the floor, eyes closed. Mia dropped to her knees. *Please be alive, please,* she prayed. *I don't think I can deal with another dead body.* She placed a tentative hand on his chest and was relieved when it moved up and down. Grazio was unconscious, not dead. "Don't worry, I'll get help," she told the prostrate man.

She stood up. But before Mia could make a move, the world went dark.

Chapter Twenty-Three

Mia groaned as she came to. It took her a minute to figure out why she was having trouble breathing— her mouth was covered with gaffer's tape. She went to take it off and discovered her hands were bound, as were her feet. Mia tried to adjust her cramped position but found she could only move a few inches. She was imprisoned inside the small confines of the pop-out cake.

There was a whirring noise and she felt herself descending. Her stomach went up as the elevator flew down. Mia felt like throwing up, then panicked about what might happened if she vomited while her mouth was taped shut. She willed her stomach to settle. The elevator thumped to a stop, tossing her upward. Mia hit her head on the underside of the cake lid and was overwhelmed with dizziness. As she fought to regain her equilibrium, she felt the cake being rolled along. She tried calling out and throwing herself back and forth to get someone's attention, but her movement was limited by the small space and street noise drowned out her muffled cries for help. She could hear music from the party. Considering it was on the building's top floor, Mia wondered if Dee had purposely ramped up the sound to cover any possibility of her being heard and saved—for she was convinced her kidnapper was Dee, an assumption based on more than Mia's failed poker face when she realized he'd lied to her. She couldn't think of another suspect at the party who had a reason to knock out John Grazio.

The cake rolled upward, and she heard a truck door slam. An engine roared to life and the truck took off at a high speed. It hit pothole after pothole, sending the pop-out cake careening back and forth against the walls of the vehicle, jerking Mia with it. She was overcome with pain and humiliation. Ravello's subliminal "eyes in the back of your head" training of her childhood had failed her. Or she'd failed it—and her father.

After about fifteen minutes, the road grew smoother. Judging by the short amount of time and infrequent stops for traffic lights, Mia figured they'd transitioned to a major road and were heading east, not west. The truck veered right and soon the road grew bumpy again. *We must have gotten off the highway and back onto local streets,* Mia thought. The truck rumbled along for what felt like forever. Eventually it made a left onto a street where the potholes were so large, they felt more like craters when the truck hit one. As Mia rattled around, she wondered what the vehicle's final destination was—and hoped "final destination" wasn't literal. The truck suddenly came to a screeching halt, hurling Mia and the cake forward into the wall separating the cargo space from the driver's cab. Mia's head slammed against the cake's inside wall, leaving her dazed. She heard the truck's back door being rolled up. Then someone climbed into the

back of the truck and gave the cake a push. Before
Mia could make any move to get someone's attention, the cake went flying down a ramp, rolling out of
control until it finally came to a stop. There was the
sound of muffled voices, a door slamming, the truck
roaring away—and then silence. Wherever Mia was,
she was now alone.

She leaned back against the cake and took a few
deep breaths as best as she could, hoping they would
relieve some of the pain from her bumps, bruises,
and pounding headache. The breathing helped.
Mia felt slightly better, or at least more alert. She contemplated her situation. Step one would be getting
out of the pop-out cake. She looked at the cake lid
above her and saw that its hinges had been loosened
by the constant jolts in the truck. Steeling herself for
pain, she stood up and banged the lid open with the
top of her head. Knocked off its hinges, it clattered to
the floor. Mia, head throbbing, examined her surroundings. She was in an old warehouse that was
either abandoned or looked that way. The only light
in the vast, empty space came from an incandescent
lightbulb swinging overhead on a wire. Her bound
hands and feet rendered climbing out of the cake
impossible. But the ancient building had a slight rake
to the floor—and the cake was on wheels. Mia faced
the warehouse's battered wooden doors. She bumped
the cake forward with her body, rejoicing when it
moved a few inches. She bumped harder; it moved
farther. She bumped with all her might and the cake
took off down the rake, bursting through the doors
onto an alley outside, where it hit a crater, tumbled
on its side, and broke apart. Mia crawled through the
pop-out cake wreckage, then somehow managed to

pull herself to her feet. After another deep breath, she began hopping toward the street in front of her, still bound by tape.

As Mia hopped along, each hop a reminder of how much her head hurt, she saw she was in an industrial area that seemed devoid of human life. *Eight million people in this town and not one of them is around here right now,* she thought, disgruntled. *And what borough am I in, anyway? Ouch, my head. My legs. My arms. Boy, am I gonna feel this tomorrow.* After half a block of hopping, she saw a welcome sight—an elevated subway stop she recognized as being in Queens. She began hopping up the stairs, taking breaks to rest.

When she reached the platform, her hopes of finding help from an attendant were dashed. The old token booth was closed, replaced by a couple of MetroCard turnstiles. She fell to the ground and crawled under a turnstile, then managed to get back on her feet. Mia leaned against a pillar and did the only thing she could do—wait for a train. Luckily, she saw one heading into the station. It came to a stop, the doors opened, and she hopped on. There was only one person in the subway car, a middle-aged man wearing a jumpsuit with a patch that read INTER-BOROUGH ROOTER AND PLUMBING. He'd fallen asleep, mouth open, head lolling to one side. The train lurched forward. Mia lost her balance. She fell against the man, then tumbled to the floor. The man, startled awake, saw her and screamed. "Mmm!" Mia mouthed through the tape. "Mmmmm!"

The man pulled Mia to her feet, then ripped the tape off her mouth. She yelped in pain. "Ouch, but thank you," she gasped. "Please tell me you have a cell phone."

Then Mia crumpled to the subway floor.

Mia woke up in a darkened hospital room. She had a vague memory of arriving by ambulance and being rolled into the room on a gurney. "Ow," she said, putting a hand on her head, which pounded with pain. She made out the vague outline at the foot of her bed. "Dad?"

"No, he's on his way," said a woman's voice.

Mia squinted and the woman came into view. She was not happy to see that it was reporter Teri Fuoco. "What are you doing here? How did you get past the nurses?"

Teri plopped down on the side of the bed. "I couldn't decide whether to tell them I was your sister or wife. I went with wife because everyone's too politically correct these days to question that."

Mia, infuriated, let loose with a hat trick of bad words in English, Italian, and Greek. "Thanks a lot. Now, get out."

Teri, still parked on the bed's edge, swung her legs back and forth. "You should be nicer to me, since I pretty much saved your life."

"Yeah, right," Mia said with a snort.

"I did. I saw the truck barreling out of Koller's loading dock and my reporter alarm bell went, ding, ding, ding! I alerted the police and tried to follow it but lost it on the Van Wyck. The reporter at the Trib who monitors our police scanner let me know when the police found you and brought you here. The cops caught the truck driver and his henchman, the ones who dumped you in the warehouse. A couple of guys with the last name Bouras."

"The same as the man who owned Belle View," Mia said.

"Yup. His nephews. That's one big family. Big as an Italian's. They arrested the party DJ, too."

"Achi."

"Gesundheit."

"No," Mia said. "Those were the letters on John Grazio's cell phone. They're the first letters of Dee's real name."

"Really? Interesting. Let's see if we can find out what the rest of those letters are."

Teri quickly typed on her phone with her thumbs. Much as Mia didn't want to give the reporter the satisfaction of showing any interest in her, she couldn't contain her curiosity. "What are you doing?"

"Checking with my sources. I'm in with a lot of the cops in the borough. Ah, here we go. Mister Music's real name is Achilles. Achilles *Bouras*."

"Aha!" Mia shot up in bed, then in pain, said, "Ow."

"Need a couple of aspirin, wife?" Teri gestured to the chunky fanny pack around her waist. "I always carry some in my purse."

"That's a fanny pack, not a purse, and shut up. I had a feeling this whole thing could be solved if we found out Dee's real name. He's related to Andre Bouras."

Teri checked her phone. "Not just related. His son."

"And cousin to Giorgio, who he probably killed. Now all we have to figure out is why."

"I like that you keep saying 'we.'"

Teri said it with an impish smile, which irked Mia.

"I mean it as the . . . what do they call it? The royal we. It has zero to do with you. *Nada. Niente.* Whatever zero is in Greek."

"So . . ." Teri adjusted her position, moving closer to Mia. "What do you think about all this?"

Mia gave her a steely stare. "You're not allowed to record me without my permission in the state of New York."

A guilty look flashed across Teri's face and disappeared. "Fine." She held up her phone and made a show of turning off the voice app. "Off the record?"

Mia, energy flagging, leaned back against her pillow. "To be honest, I have no idea what to think right now. Everything is in bits and pieces. It's like one of those word jumbles where right now it's just a bunch of letters. I can't make out the words hiding inside it. You're gonna write what you write, anyway. Just make it the truth."

"You said exactly that before. And again, I'm all about the truth. Even when people don't wanna hear it."

Teri went to put her cell in her fanny pack, but Mia reached out to stop her. "Wait. Can you find out from one of your sources what I got hit over the head with?"

"Sure." Teri thumbed a few words and waited. "A turntable. Courtesy of Tyler, Achilles Bouras's accomplice."

"Another piece of work," Mia said with a yawn. A nurse stepped into the room. "Visiting hours are over, miss," she told Teri. "Your wife needs her sleep."

"Yes, right." Teri hopped off the bed. "Get some rest, honey. You'll need it for that couples cruise I booked us on."

Teri sauntered out of the room, leaving Mia wishing she had the strength to flip off the reporter.

The next morning, a nurse pushed Mia down the front hall of Jamaica Hospital Medical Center as Ravello kept pace with them. "I'm fine," Mia protested. "I don't need to be in a wheelchair."

"Standard hospital procedure, honey," the nurse said. "You come in on a gurney, you go out in a wheelchair. Or a box."

The glass doors opened, and they emerged from the building. Jamie jumped out of his Prius and ran to them. Ravello helped Mia to her feet. "Your concussion was mild but keep an eye out for any changes in your vision or balance," the nurse said.

"Don't worry, we'll be taking good care of her," Ravello said. "*Mille grazie.* Thank you." He shook the nurse's hand.

"Sir, I can't take—" She looked at what Ravello deposited in her hand. "Oh, it's a gift card. That I can take." She and the wheelchair disappeared back into the hospital.

"Nobody wants cash no more," Ravello explained to the others. "Now, *bella mia,* let's get you home."

Jamie pulled open the rear passenger side door. Mia fended off the men as they tussled over who would guide her into the car. "Will you two stop it? I'm not an invalid. I know how to get into a car."

"How do you feel?" Jamie asked, concern etched on his face.

"Like I'm getting over the flu, but much better than yesterday," Mia said, buckling herself in.

Jamie pulled out of the parking lot and headed

toward Astoria. "So," Ravello said as Jamie drove, "Pete Dianopolis did me a favor and let me see Achilles Bouras. We had a little talk."

Mia knew better than to question the euphemism. She also knew Ravello's "little talks" were extremely effective. "I don't believe this whole thing was about getting revenge on behalf of his father. Dee, or whatever name he's using now, is too self-involved. So why did he do it? And why was Ty the one who bonked me on the head? Don't ask me how I know, I just do. What did he have to do with Belle View?"

"Nothing," Ravello said. "Jamie, you wanna take this one?"

Jamie pulled onto the Grand Central Parkway. "Your dad already filled me in. Seems the two DJs had a side gig going. During breaks, they'd take turns lifting cash or valuables from the women's purses. Not enough to call attention to it. They targeted women who were drunk and might not remember what happened to the fifty-dollar bill in their wallet. Tyler thought you were on to them, panicked, and took a turntable to the back of your head, saving Bouras the trouble."

"Because that's not why you were a threat to Achilles Bouras," Ravello said. "Before Andre Bouras lost Belle View at the poker table, his son Achilles was working a secret deal to sell it to Bradley Koller. Once the family lost the place, Achilles came up with a new plan. He'd torch Belle View, making it useless to us. Koller would swoop in with a lowball offer and Achilles would get a flat fee, a piece of which would go to his cousin, Giorgio. The original plan was to set it on fire the night of the bachelor party. But when Angie showed up at Belle View to take a stab at blackmailing me—"

"Ouch re: that play on words, Dad."

"*Mi dispiace.* Sorry. While she was wandering around the place, Angie happened to overhear Achilles Bouras confirming the arson plan with Giorgio. And she had a new mark who could offer up a much bigger payday than your old dad—Achilles. Giorgio was telling the truth when he said he didn't know who Angie was and didn't kill her. That was all on Achilles. Giorgio saw his cousin hiding Angie's body in the cake and used it to frame me and get revenge for 'stealing' Belle View from the Bouras family."

Mia rubbed her head. It was aching, either from her injury, the tale of two murders, or both. "It sounds like Giorgio should be the Bouras family hero. How did he end up dead?"

"When Giorgio was arrested, he didn't turn on his cousin," Jamie said. "Instead, he used what he knew— that Achilles killed Angie—as leverage to squeeze more out of him. Then, after Achilles tried torching Belle View himself, Giorgio raised the price tag for his silence even higher. Which finally doomed him."

"Did anyone talk to Felicity Stewart Forbes? I'd love to know how she suddenly got on the party guest list after getting axed by the Kollers."

"Pete had a sit-down with her," Jamie shared. "She may be a bottom feeder, but she knows the real estate business. It occurred to her that her conduit to the brothers was through Bradley's assistant. She never even spoke to Kevin's assistant—or to Kevin himself. She did some research on a shell company set up for Koller Queens' acquisitions and figured out that the name was a variation of a fraternity motto. Bradley's frat, not Kevin's. The older Koller was going to cut the younger one out of the deal. She confronted Bradley about this, threatened to tell Kevin, and she was on the party guest list and back in the Koller real estate game."

"Pete's pretty excited about all the twists and turns this case took," Ravello said. "He's already got a title for his next Steve Stianopolis mystery: 'Real Estate Dead.' It's a play on words. 'Dead' instead of 'Deal.' Get it? I think it's clever."

"I get it, Dad."

"Oh, I almost forgot. I got your phone back from the Kollers. I charged it, so it's ready to go."

Ravello pulled Mia's cell out of his jacket pocket and handed it to her from the back seat. "Thanks." She typed in her password. As soon as her home screen opened, an alert from the *Triborough Tribune* popped up. Mia clicked it open. The newspaper's home page blazed the headline "Murder and Mayhem Color Koller Party," with a photo showing a handcuffed DJ DJ, aka Dee, Achilles Bouras, being escorted from the Koller Properties building by a phalanx of police officers. Mia skimmed the post, stopping to read one sentence in its entirety: "Ravello Carina, owner and manager of Belle View Banquet Manor, has been cleared of all suspicion in the deaths of Angie Pavlik and Giorgio Bouras." Mia typed three words into the Comments section: "Truth. Thank you." A second later, Teritup31@tribtrib.com liked her comment.

Traffic on the parkway slowed to a crawl, courtesy of the chronic backup from LaGuardia Airport. Mia glanced out the car window. She could see the second floor of Belle View, with the bay behind it. She still had questions about the events that transpired at the catering hall, including the mystery of why Evans was camping out there. But she didn't have the energy to ask them. She leaned against the window and closed her eyes. "I'm going to rest today, then get back to work tomorrow," she said. "I have a wedding to throw."

Chapter Twenty-Four

Once again Mia's head throbbed, but not because of an attempt on her life. The cause of her pain was the hour she'd spent listening to Alice Paluski and John Grazio argue about their wedding, which was only a few days away.

"What do you mean, you don't like vanilla?" John put the rhetorical question to his fiancée in an exasperated tone. "Who doesn't like vanilla? It's vanilla."

"I hate vanilla and always have." Alice crossed her arms in front of her chest and glared at John. She tossed her own rhetorical question at him. "How could you not know this about me?"

"Maybe it's because all you ever talk about is your stupid sister," John shot back. "I don't care if you want our cake flavors to be better than hers. We're having vanilla. I'm putting my foot down on this issue." John stamped his foot and grimaced. He put a hand on the back of his head where he, like Mia, had taken a blow from Ty's turntable. "That went straight up my leg to my head."

Alice began to sniffle. "All I want," she said as

tears slipped down her cheeks, "is for my wedding to be better than perfect. I don't think that's too much to ask."

"Aha!" John pointed a finger at Alice. "You did it again. You said, 'my wedding.' You always do that. I want this for *my* wedding, I want that for *my* wedding. It's *my* wedding too, Alice."

"It's *both* of your weddings, and if I've ever seen a couple who should call one off, it's you two!" Mia slapped a hand over her mouth, but it was too late. The couple gasped in unison. They were finally united on something—anger at her. "I'm super sorry, I never should have said that. Nobody wants you to get married more than me because if we lose one more booking, I think this place'll go under. But I've yet to see a moment of joy from either of you about this wedding or even about each other. Instead of arguing about cake flavors, you might want to take a good, hard look at your relationship before you make a lifetime commitment to each other. Trust me, I know what it's like to realize after a big wedding that you made a terrible mistake. It's painful. It's humiliating. And it makes you scared of ever getting into another relationship, even one with someone who is probably the person you should have been with all along."

Mia could only watch as Alice and John faced the truth about their coupledom, mentally kicking herself for her big mouth. After a minute, Alice said in a quiet voice, "What do we do? We can't cancel the wedding. Our families will kill us. And all of our friends will laugh at us."

"We'll look like idiots," John agreed.

There was silence as the three pondered the next step. Then Mia had a flash of brilliance. "Have an un-wedding."

John and Alice looked perplexed. "A what?" she said.

Mia, inspired, typed on her keyboard. "There," she said, referencing an article she pulled up on the computer. "I remember reading this story about a couple in Manhattan. The guy dumped the girl a week before her wedding. Instead of canceling, she turned it into an 'un-wedding.' A big party where everyone showed their love and support for her. She returned as many gifts as she could and anything people couldn't or wouldn't take back was donated to charity."

Mia had said the magic word: *Manhattan*. She saw the couple mulling over the idea . . . and liking it.

"Alice," John said. "I'm pretty sure I love you. But I don't think I'm ready to get married."

Mia held her breath, praying that Alice's reaction to this news didn't take the conversation in an ugly direction. "To be honest," the vet technician said, "Tinker the Drinker told me you knew that girl who got killed. When I thought you might have offed her and get sent to jail for murder, I was a little relieved. I mean, I was upset and all, but—"

"Hey, it's okay," John assured her. "I felt the same way."

"Now," Alice said to Mia, "you're sure this un-wedding is a thing?"

"A big thing," Mia said. "But no one's done one in Queens yet. You'd be trendsetters."

For the first time since Mia met her, Alice beamed. "Then I'm in."

"Me, too." John took Alice's hands in his. "Alice, will you un-marry me?"

"Yes, John." Alice was teary-eyed. "I'd be honored to be your un-wife."

The couple embraced and Mia, overwhelmed with relief at saving the event, threw her arms around them, too.

John and Alice's un-wedding was a hit, averting the disastrous direction in which their actual wedding was headed. At first, guests gossiped and grumbled about the change. But their attitude changed once they learned their gifts would either be returned or treated as donations to the non-profit arm of the vet clinic where Alice worked.

Two vintage wooden speedboats delivered the couple, their un-bridal party, and their families. Barbara Grazio's bright blue roses inspired envy in several groom's-mother-zillas at the event, and Mia happily handed out Lin's business cards. The tables in the Marina Ballroom were arranged in the giant *X* that Mia originally came up with for Cimmanin's party. The Koller birthday venue proved too small for the setup, but the Belle View rooms were perfect for it. Mia discovered that the manor's part-timer Cody, the ex-Marine, had a secret talent as a DJ. Clad in a faux military uniform, he yelled to the guests, "Ten-hut! This is your commanding officer, Sergeant Sound, and you are under strict orders to par-tay!" He played a current dance hit and the guests filled all four dance areas created by the *X* table layout.

John and Alice had invited the pet bereavement group and the new pets they'd adopted through

Alice's clinic, who proved to be the most popular guests at the event. "We're a perfect match, aren't we, Sigmund?" Vivien cooed to the large calico cat in her arms, who let out a contented *meow* in response. "Thank you, Mia."

"All I did was send a few e-mails." Mia bent down to scratch the head of Willie Two, the energetic chihuahua mix Gerald had fallen in love with. "It looks like I'll be the only one left in the pet bereavement group."

"As long as there are people who adore animals," Vivien said with a warm smile, "the group will go on. And those of us who've found new fur children will be there to support them."

"Fur children, what a crock," a woman walking by muttered loud enough for Mia to hear. The woman was Alice's twin, the infamous Annamaria. Grumpy and bloated from her pregnancy, all she could do was watch glumly while everyone else drank and danced. Mia derived satisfaction from this, since she'd picked up a vibe that Annamaria was used to being the center of attention, and not happy to be upstaged by her "older" sister, no less a bunch of cuddly creatures. Since Mia's natural inclination was to root for the underdog, she was Team Alice all the way.

John Grazio ended the evening with a touching toast to his girlfriend, who looked stunning in her ivory silk princess-style un-bridal gown. As they shared a kiss with the quiet bay and blinking lights of the air traffic control tower behind them, Mia had a feeling that one day Belle View might play host to their real wedding.

Mia stayed at Belle View after all the guests had departed, under the pretext of helping her staff break down the event. Eventually, only three people were left: Mia, Guadalupe, and Evans. "Well, you pulled that one out of your keester," Guadalupe said with a yawn as they finished cleaning the kitchen. "I'm calling it a night."

"Me, too," Mia said. She faced Evans. "What about you?"

Evans shuffled some pots. "I have a few things left to do. You all take off. I'll lock up before I leave."

"Sounds good," Guadalupe said. She grabbed her jacket and started for the door.

"Except that Evans isn't going to leave," Mia said. "He's going to spend the night here. Like he's been doing pretty much every night lately. Right, Evans?"

Guadalupe stopped and turned back. "He's been crashing at Belle View? Why?"

"That's what my dad and I would like to know." Evans opened and shut his mouth a couple of times, but no words came out. "We're not leaving until you tell us what's going on. Are you homeless? It's nothing to be ashamed of, Evans. We can help you."

"Oh man, no. That's not it at all." Evans strode over to the kitchen's computer and turned it on. The computer booted up and he typed an address into the browser's search bar. He motioned for Mia and Guadalupe to come over. They peered over his shoulder. Evans had called up a website for a company called Diverse Media. The home page boasted assets that ranged from national magazines to a cable TV network. "What is this?" Mia asked.

"My family's business." Evans clicked to a page for founder and CEO, a distinguished-looking African-American businessman named Franklin Tucker. "That's my dad. He wanted all of us kids to work for the company, but I'm not interested. I like making food. Especially desserts. I was tired of him bugging me, so I moved out of the town house—"

"Town house," Mia repeated, in shock.

"Yeah, I was way too old to be living there anyway. But I haven't found a place I can afford yet, so I've been crashing here. I should've asked. But then I'd have to tell you who I was. And I liked being known just for me for a change. Not as the rich kid from a famous family."

Mia and Guadalupe digested this unexpected development. "What I'm hearing," Guadalupe said, "is that there's a town house in Manhattan with an empty bedroom."

"Ignore her," Mia said. "Evans, I think I have the answer to your problem. I know an apartment that's available. How do you feel about little old Greek ladies?"

"That depends," he responded, a little wary. "Do I have to marry one? I'm not saying I won't to get a decent rent in this town, but—"

Mia laughed. "No, you won't have to marry her. But she's lonely and may occasionally show up on your doorstep with a dinner invitation. That's a good thing; she's a wonderful cook. Her baklava is to die for."

Evans's face creased with a smile. She'd never seen the sous chef look so happy. "I could use some Greek dessert recipes. I wonder if she has one for a farina cake."

"She does. I've had it. And *loved* it."

Having solved another mystery, Mia gave Evans Andrea Skarpello's phone number, plus permission to spend one last night at Belle View. In exchange, he gave her a ride home on his motorcycle. "See you tomorrow, boss," he said after dropping her off, "and future neighbor."

The next few weeks were refreshingly uneventful. Mia visited Posi several times. He was still disappointed that his "another hot convict" hadn't gone viral but buoyed by the number of requests for dates he'd received. "Do you know someone named Cimmanin?" he asked his sister about one request. "She's single and says she's a friend of yours."

Mia felt sorry for Kevin Koller until she received delivery of a giant floral arrangement. At first, she assumed it was from Lin or Ravello. Then she read the attached card: "Dear Mia, thanks for making my brother look bad. Brad got demoted by our board and I got promoted. I owe you. P.S. I broke up with Cimmanin. Can I get the number of that waitress Elena from your party staff?"

One morning, Mia was shaken awake by Elisabetta. "Hurry and get ready," her grandmother said. "Philip and Finn invited us over for the unveiling of their cleaned-up Virgin Mary, with cake and coffee after. I'll meet you there." Elisabetta had not only embraced the new couple, she'd babysat for the babies and helped Philip plant tomato seedlings. She even put up with Finn trying to impress her with his rudimentary Italian.

Mia followed her grandmother's order, then hurried down the street to Philip and Finn's home. Elisabetta and the Army were huddled together in the front yard. "Everyone ready?" Philip asked. The small crowd chorused "Yes!" and he whipped off the cloth covering the Virgin Mary. The statue, cleaned and polished to perfection, gleamed in the sunlight, and the women oohed and ahhed. "It's magnificent," Andrea said with reverence.

The others murmured agreement, but Mia noticed Elisabetta seemed perturbed. "What's wrong, Nonna?" Mia whispered to her grandmother.

"Now that it's all cleaned up, their statue's way better than mine," Elisabetta muttered. "I gotta up my grotto game."

Mia, amused, shook her head. "You are too much. I'm going to work." She couldn't resist adding a dig to her competitive grandmother. "Congratulate Philip and Finn on having the prettiest Virgin Mary on the block."

Mia biked to Belle View, reveling in the breezes from the warm spring day. The tidy front gardens of the Astoria homes were beginning to bloom, perfuming the air with a variety of flower fragrances. She chained her bicycle to a newly installed rack in front of Belle View, courtesy of Ravello, and was about to go inside when someone called to her.

"Mia, hey! Wait."

Jamie and his Prius pulled up in front of the building. He jumped out of his car. "I've got a present for you." Jamie opened the car's passenger side back door and took out a cage. Inside, a parakeet—yellow with a green head—chirped happily.

Mia gasped. "Is it? It can't be."

"It is. It's Pizzazz."

Jamie handed her the cage. Pizzazz fluttered around the cage and then settled on his perch facing Mia, chattering away with enthusiasm. "He's talking to me," she said, tears streaming down her face. "How did you ever find him?"

"Dad has people in Palm Beach. When I told him that I was doing this for you, he instantly called in some favors from a bunch of mooks down there who owed him. Those guys move pretty fast when the boss says all is forgiven if they do this one little thing."

Mia laughed through her tears. "You sound just like your dad."

"Yeah, well, sometimes that ain't a bad thing," Jamie said in a perfect imitation of his father's heavy Noo Yawk accent. "Oh, and here's a bag of food."

He extricated a bag of bird food from the back seat and handed it to Mia, who took it with her free hand. Pizzazz tweeted his enthusiasm at the sight of the bird chow. "Jamie, you're my hero. I'll never be able to thank you for this."

Jamie blushed. He was about to say something when an attractive woman wearing trendy, flattering eyeglasses stuck her head out of the passenger window. "Hi, I'm Madison. Sorry to interrupt but we need to get going. We've got a brunch reservation in the city."

"Right, yes." Jamie gave Mia a desultory hug. "I'll talk to you."

He jumped back in the car and took off. "Queens *is* the city," Mia said, her heart heavy as she watched Jamie and his girlfriend drive away. She'd married an adulterer. Been tempted to have a fling with a psychopath who wound up being a double murderer. *Maybe someday I'll make a smart choice,* she thought. *Maybe someday I'll find someone like Jamie and let him into my life.*

Pizzazz chirped, and Mia turned her attention to her beloved bird. "You're right. It's all good. I'm not ready for another relationship, except for the feathered or furry kind. Let's get you some breakfast."

Mia carried Pizzazz into the Belle View foyer. There was a dull roar and the paintings on the wall shook. She put a foot on the foyer's large decorative vase to prevent it from skittering out of place. A prop plane was coming in for a landing at LaGuardia. *The 9:10 from Syracuse,* was Mia's first thought. Her second was, *I can't believe I know that.* Then again, she'd fallen in love with Belle View the minute she laid eyes on it. Her future lay within its warm, if slightly shabby, walls.

She carried Pizzazz into her office, placed his cage on her office chair, and fed him his breakfast from the bag of bird feed Jamie had included with his special delivery. Her office phone rang. "Belle View Banquet Manor," she said as soon as she picked up the receiver. "Want to throw your dream party? We'll make you an offer you can't refuse."

RECIPES

EGGPLANT PARMIGIANA

Ingredients

1 large eggplant
1 egg
½ cup liquid egg whites
1 cup Italian-seasoned bread crumbs
½ cup, plus 1 Tbsp. grated Parmesan cheese
4 Tbsp. flour
1 jar, your favorite tomato sauce
1 tsp. oregano, divided
½ tsp. Italian seasoning
¼ cup finely chopped fresh basil
10 oz. shredded part-skim mozzarella
Olive oil cooking spray

Instructions

Preheat the oven to 400 degrees.

Trim the ends off the eggplant, then slice it into ½-inch round slabs.

Beat the egg and egg whites together in a shallow bowl. In another bowl, mix together the bread crumbs, Parmesan cheese (minus the tablespoon), and flour.

Spray a large cookie sheet with the olive oil spray. Dredge the eggplant slices in the egg mix, and then in the bread crumb mixture, and arrange them in a single layer on the cookie sheet. (Depending on the size of your eggplant, you may need more than one cookie sheet.) Spritz the top of the eggplant slices with the olive oil spray and bake at 400 degrees until they're tender and golden brown—around twenty to thirty minutes.

While the eggplant is baking, empty the jar of sauce into a sauce pan. Add the Italian seasoning, ½ teaspoon of oregano, and fresh basil. Cook the sauce over medium heat, stirring and scraping the sides, until the sauce is heated through.

Spoon enough of the sauce into a 9" x 16" baking pan to coat the bottom of it. (I like glass pans for this recipe.) Arrange the cooked eggplant slices in the pan, overlapping them wherever necessary. Cover the eggplant with the remaining sauce, top with the mozzarella, and then sprinkle with the tablespoon of grated Parmesan and the other ½ teaspoon of oregano.

Bake uncovered at 400 degrees until the cheese is melted—about five minutes. Serve with Italian bread and a salad. You can even add a side dish of pasta.

Serves 6–8.

COOKIE CUP SHOT GLASSES

Ingredients

Cookie shot glass pan
3 cups flour
1 tsp. baking powder
1 cup brown sugar
⅓ cup white sugar
½ tsp. salt
2 eggs
1 tsp. vanilla
½ stick butter (melted and cooled)
⅔ cup chocolate chips
1 cup chocolate melting wafers for coating the
    inside (see note)
Liquor or liqueur of your choice, or milk

Instructions

Preheat oven to 350 degrees.

Mix the flour, sugar, salt, and baking powder together in a large bowl and set aside.

In another large bowl, beat the butter, vanilla, and eggs together well.

Slowly add the flour mixture to the butter mixture, stirring each addition to incorporate into the batter.

Gently mix the chocolate chips into the dough. Chill for about 10–15 minutes. This helps make the dough more manageable.

Take about two or three tablespoons of the dough, roll it into a ball about the size of a golf ball, and place the ball into one of the molds in the cookie shot glass pan. Push down the dough with the metal insert, making sure the dough is pretty even all the way around. Leave the metal insert in place and trim the excess dough from the sides of the insert, then remove the insert. Repeat with the rest of the molds. (As an alternative to pushing down into the ball of dough, you can try building a cup by putting a flat disk of dough on the bottom of the cup, building up the sides with more dough, and placing the metal insert into the dough, pressing a bit to seal.)

Bake the cookie cups around 15 minutes. Remove the cookie cups from the oven. While they're warm, you can gently trim any excess dough from around the edges of each cookie—or not. Let the cookies cool. Extract them from the mold and repeat until you've used up all the dough.

Melt the wafers in the microwave, following the melting directions on the package. When the cookie cups have cooled, use a small spatula or a new, clean brush to coat the inside of each cookie with the melted chocolate. *Check for holes while you're doing this!* You may need to add extra chocolate to seal the hole . . . or just eat that cookie. Let the chocolate cool and harden.

When the cookies have cooled, add the liquor or liqueur of your choice.

Serving: makes approximately 18.

Note: Melting wafers are available at craft stores like Michaels. They come in different colors, so you can play with coating the cookie cups with the colors that are the theme of your event. You can even coat the cookie cups with blue or pink for a baby gender reveal party and fill them with milk to hide the color.

Second Note: You can try making cookie cups with other recipes, like sugar cookies or snickerdoodles. Feel free to experiment.

Third Note: If you don't want to invest in a cookie shot glass pan, there are ways around that to create a cookie cup. You can make a rolled cookie and form it like a cup over a muffin tin. Do an Internet search for "cookie cups" or "cookie shot glasses" and you'll find an array of possibilities.

SPINACH PIE (SPANIKOPITA)

Ingredients
  4 eggs
  2 garlic cloves, minced
  ½ tsp. kosher salt
  2 shallots, chopped
  2 bunches green onions, chopped
  10 oz. crumbled feta cheese (I like to use Trader
    Joe's Fat Free Feta)
  16 oz. frozen spinach, thawed and drained*
  8 oz. phyllo dough, thawed (the sheets that are
    approx. 9" x 13" in size)
  ½ cup olive oil

Instructions
Preheat oven to 325 degrees. Grease the bottom and sides of a 9" x 13" baking dish.

In a medium to large bowl, beat the eggs with the salt and garlic. Add the shallots and green onions. Stir well to combine. Add the feta cheese and stir to combine. Do the same with the spinach until all the ingredients except for the olive oil and phyllo dough have been mixed together.

Layer two sheets of phyllo dough on the bottom of the baking dish. Brush the top sheet with olive oil. Repeat until you've layered eight sheets of phyllo dough. Spread the spinach and feta mixture evenly over the phyllo dough base. Cover with two sheets of phyllo dough, then brush the top sheet with olive oil. Repeat until you've used up the sheets of phyllo dough.

Bake uncovered for 1 hour, or until the top of the pie is brownish gold and crisp.

Serves 4 or 8, depending on the size of the pieces.

*To drain the spinach, I line a strainer with paper towel, spoon the spinach into it, and press down with the back of a large spoon. Once the spinach has drained, I transfer it to the egg and feta cheese mixture.

GREEK FARINA CAKE

Ingredients for the Cake
1 cup flour
¼ tsp. salt
1 Tbsp. double-acting baking powder
2 sticks unsalted butter, softened
1 cup sugar
6 eggs
¾ cup regular, uncooked farina

Ingredients for the Syrup
2 cups water
2 cups sugar
1½ tsp. vanilla
1 tsp. orange zest
¼ cup honey

Optional
Whipped cream
Crushed pistachio nuts

Instructions for the Cake
Preheat oven to 350 degrees. In a medium bowl, combine flour, salt, and baking powder. Set aside.

Cream the butter with an electric mixer. Slowly add the sugar, then add the eggs one at a time at slow speed, making sure to beat well after adding each egg. While running the mixer on medium speed, slowly add the flour mixture, and then the farina. Mix well until all the ingredients are thoroughly combined.

Pour batter into an 8" x 8" baking pan and bake for 35–40 minutes, until a toothpick inserted to test it comes out clean.

Instructions for the Syrup

While the cake is baking, combine the water, sugar, vanilla, orange zest, and honey in a heavy saucepan. Bring to a boil and then reduce to a simmer. You can simmer it for the duration of the cake's baking time. If you turn the heat off, make sure to heat up the syrup again before using it to finish the cake.

Instructions for Finishing the Cake

While the cake is hot, poke about a dozen holes in it. Ladle the hot sauce onto the cake, waiting for one ladle of syrup to absorb before adding another. (You can use all the syrup or half of it, saving the other half for future use.) When the cake has cooled completely, cut it into sixteen squares. As an option, you can add a spoonful of whipped cream to each piece, and sprinkle with the pistachio nuts.

Serves 16.

PARTY PLANNING TIP

Planning a large party? Instead of numbering the tables, personalize them. In *Here Comes the Body*, John Grazio does this to comic effect by marking each table with a different *Playboy* centerfold. You can create an equally unique table arrangement without making a risqué choice, of course! I attended a friend's wedding where tables were labeled with the names of cities that were meaningful to the couple, and each table was populated with friends and relatives from those cities. The couple also decorated the tables with evocative centerpieces. My husband and I were seated at "Hollywood," where a recreation of the iconic Hollywood sign rose from the center of the flower arrangement.

Adding a creative twist to your seating arrangement will help create a truly memorable event.

Connect with

Visit us online at
KensingtonBooks.com
to read more from your favorite authors, see books
by series, view reading group guides, and more.

for sneak peeks, chances to win books and prize packs,
and to share your thoughts with other readers.

facebook.com/kensingtonpublishing
twitter.com/kensingtonbooks

Tell us what you think!

To share your thoughts, submit a review,
or sign up for our eNewsletters, please visit:
KensingtonBooks.com/TellUs.

Catering and Capers with
Isis Crawford!